10118

MERCI SUÁREZ
CHANGES GEARS

MERCI SUÁREZ CHANGES GEARS

MEG MEDINA

CANDLEWICK PRESS

Copyright © 2018 by Margaret Medina

First U.S. edition 2018

Library of Congress Catalog Card Number pending
ISBN 978-0-7636-9049-6

18 19 20 21 22 23 LSC 10 9 8 7 6 5 4 3 2 1

Printed in Crawfordsville, IN, U.S.A.

This book was typeset in Berkeley Oldstyle.

Candlewick Press
99 Dover Street
Somerville, Massachusetts 02144

visit us at www.candlewick.com

IN MEMORY OF DIEGO CRUZ SR.

CHAPTER 1

TO THINK, ONLY YESTERDAY I was in chancletas, sipping lemonade and watching my twin cousins run through the sprinkler in the yard. Now, I'm here in Mr. Patchett's class, sweating in my polyester school blazer and waiting for this torture to be over.

We're only halfway through health and PE when he adjusts his tight collar and says, "Time to go."

I stand up and push in my chair, like we're always supposed to, grateful that picture day means that class ends early. At least we won't have to start reading the first chapter in the textbook: "I'm OK, You're OK: On Differences as We Develop."

Gross.

"Coming, Miss Suárez?" he asks me as he flips off the lights.

That's when I realize I'm the only one still waiting for him to tell us to line up. Everyone else has already headed out the door.

This is *sixth* grade, so there won't be one of the PTA moms walking us down to the photographer. Last year, our escort pumped us up by gushing the whole way about how handsome and beautiful we all looked on the first day of school, which was a stretch since a few of us had mouthfuls of braces or big gaps between our front teeth.

But that's over now. Here at Seaward Pines Academy, sixth-graders don't have the same teacher all day, like Miss Miller in the fifth grade. Now we have homerooms and lockers. We switch classes. We can finally try out for sports teams.

And we know how to get ourselves down to picture day just fine — or at least the rest of my class does. I grab my new book bag and hurry out to join the others.

It's a wall of heat out here. It won't be a far walk, but August in Florida is brutal, so it doesn't take long for my glasses to fog up and the curls at my temples to spring into tight coils. I try my best to stick to the shade near the building, but it's hopeless. The slate path that winds to the front of the gym cuts right across the quad, where there's not a single scrawny palm tree to shield us. It makes me wish we had one of those thatch-roof walkways that my grandfather Lolo can build out of fronds.

"How do I look?" someone asks.

I dry my lenses on my shirttail and glance over. We're all in the same uniform, but some of the girls got special hairdos for the occasion, I notice. A few were even flat-ironed; you can tell from the little burns on their necks. Too bad they don't have some of my curls. Not that everyone appreciates them, of course. Last year, a kid named Dillon said I look like a lion, which was fine with me, since I love those big cats. Mami is always nagging me about keeping it out of my eyes, but she doesn't know that hiding behind it is the best part. This morning, she slapped a school-issue headband on me. All it's done so far is give me a headache and make my glasses sit crooked.

"Hey," I say. "It's a broiler out here. I know a shortcut."

The girls stop in a glob and look at me. The path I'm pointing to is clearly marked with a sign.

MAINTENANCE CREWS ONLY.

NO STUDENTS BEYOND THIS POINT.

No one in this crowd is much for breaking rules, but sweat is already beading above their glossed lips, so maybe they'll be sensible. They're looking to one another, but mostly to Edna Santos.

3

"Come on, Edna," I say, deciding to go straight to the top. "It's faster, and we're melting out here."

She frowns at me, considering the options. She may be a teacher's pet, but I've seen Edna bend a rule or two. Making faces outside our classroom if she's on a bathroom pass. Changing an answer for a friend when we're self-checking a quiz. How much worse can this be?

I take a step closer. Is she taller than me now? I pull back my shoulders just in case. She looks older somehow than she did in June, when we were in the same class. Maybe it's the blush on her cheeks or the mascara that's making little raccoon circles under her eyes? I try not to stare and just go for the big guns.

"You want to look sweaty in your picture?" I say.

Cha-ching.

In no time, I'm leading the pack of us along the gravel path. We cross the maintenance parking lot, dodging debris. Back here is where Seaward hides the riding mowers and all the other untidy equipment they need to make the campus look like the brochures. Papi and I parked here last summer when we did some painting as a trade for our book fees. I don't tell anyone that, though, because Mami says it's "a private matter." But mostly, I keep quiet because I'm trying to erase the memory. Seaward's gym is ginormous, so it took us three whole days to paint it. Plus, our school colors are fire-engine red and gray. You know what happens when you stare at bright red too long? You start to see green balls in front of your eyes every time you look away. *Hmpf.* Try doing detail work in *that* blinded condition. For all that, the school should give me and my brother, Roli, a whole library, not just a few measly textbooks. Papi had other ideas, of course. "Do a good job in here," he insisted, "so they know we're serious people." I hate when he says that. Do people think we're clowns? It's like we've always got to prove something.

Anyway, we make it to the gym in half the time. The back door is propped open, the way I knew it would be. The head custodian keeps a milk crate jammed in the door frame so he can read his paper in peace when no one's looking.

"This way," I say, using my take-charge voice. I've been trying to perfect it, since it's never too early to work on your corporate leadership skills, according to the manual Papi got in the mail from the chamber of commerce, along with the what-to-do-in-a-hurricane guidelines.

So far, it's working. I walk us along back rooms and even past the boys' locker room, which smells like bleach and dirty socks. When we reach a set of double doors, I pull them open proudly. I've saved us all from that awful trudge through the heat.

"Ta-da," I say.

Unfortunately, as soon as we step inside, it's obvious that I've landed us all in hostile territory.

The older grades have gathered on this side of the gym for picture day, and the door's loud squeak has made everyone turn in our direction to stare. They don't look happy to have "the little kids" in their midst. My mouth goes dry. They're a lot bigger than we are, for one thing. Ninth-graders at least. I look around for my brother, hoping for some cover, but then I remember that Roli got *his* fancy senior portraits taken in July at a nice air-conditioned studio at the mall. He won't be in here at all today. He'll be helping in the science lab, as usual, and working on all his college applications in between.

So here we are, trapped thanks to me.

"Oh my God, they're so cute," a tall girl says, like we're kittens or something. She even steps forward and pats the top of my head. I look at my shoes, my cheeks burning.

Edna pushes past me as if we're not surrounded. With a flip of her black hair, she takes over, the way she always does. "Follow me," she says.

This is no time to be picky. I stay close behind her as she marches us toward the other side of the gym.

Thankfully, Miss McDaniels, our school secretary, doesn't notice that we came in the wrong door. She's usually a stickler for rules, but she's too busy collecting payment envelopes for the sixth-graders and running crowd control. Still, she *does* notice that we're all snorting and giggling the way you do after surviving an especially scary roller-coaster ride.

"Quiet please, girls," she snaps, without looking up from her clipboard as we reach her. "Ladies to the left. Gentlemen over here. Shirts tucked, please. Have your forms and money ready."

I get in line behind a girl named Lena, who's reading while she waits, and try hard not to look at Miss McDaniels as she checks everyone's selections. Mami only marked the cheapo basic package, and I happen to know (because it said so in gigantic font on the letter we got at home this summer) that picture day at Seaward is one of our biggest school fundraisers. You're supposed to buy a lot, like for your family in Ohio that barely knows you and whatnot. But my family mostly lives on the same block, one house next to the other. We see one another every single day.

Besides, my portraits don't ever turn out so great. It's my left eye that's the trouble. It still strays sometimes, pulling out as if it wants to see something far off, all on its own. When I was little, I wore a pirate patch on my good eye to make the muscles in the bad one get stronger. And when that didn't help, I had a surgery to straighten it. But even now, my eye still gives me trouble when I least want it to.

Like picture day.

If only Miss McDaniels would let me take my own picture instead. The camera in my phone is awesome. Plus, I downloaded PicQT, so it's fun to edit the pictures I take. My favorite thing is turning people into their favorite animal. Puppies, alligators, ducks, bears, you name it — even better than on Snapchat. Now *those* would be good yearbook photos. I glance over at Rachel, who's behind me. With her big eyes and tiny nose, she'd make an awesome owl.

I move up in the line and scope out the photographer's setup. There's a screen background, sheets on the floor, and those big umbrellas to filter the light. She looks sort of grumpy, but who can blame her? It's just point and shoot all day long, no fun. When she dreamed of being a photographer, she couldn't have meant *this*. I mean, if *I* were a photographer, I'd be on safari somewhere, perched on top of a jeep and shooting rhinos for *National Geographic*. Not here in a hot (though expertly painted) gym.

"Next," she says.

Miss McDaniels motions to Edna, who, in no time flat, starts posing easily on the stool like some sort of school-portrait supermodel. I glance over at Edna's order form on the table. Just as I suspected, her envelope says "Gold Package Supreme." I sigh and shift on my feet. It's going to take a while for the photographer to take five poses with different backgrounds. In the end, Edna will get pictures in every size, too, including enough wallet photos to make sure everybody at this school has one. I swear, all that's missing from that package is a billboard. What's even crazier is that it costs a hundred bucks. For that kind of money, I could have half the deposit for a new bike.

"You'll be there tomorrow morning, Merci?"

Miss McDaniels's voice startles me. I turn around to find that she's next to me, watching Edna, too. I can tell she's pleased. Edna is just the kind of portrait customer the administration lives for.

"Yes, miss. I'll be there."

My stomach knots up even as I say it. Sunshine Buddies is having its first meeting tomorrow, and I most definitely do *not* want to go. I was a mandatory member last year when I changed schools. New students are paired with buddies (aka fake friends) from August to December while they get used to things at Seaward. Miss McDaniels, our club sponsor, expects me to "pay it forward" and be a buddy for someone who's new this year. I suppose it's fine if you get a good buddy, but it takes a lot of time, and I want to try out for soccer this year. All this friendliness is going to cut into after-school practice.

Anyway, all day I've been trying to think of a way of getting out of it, and now here she is, cornering me before I've nailed down an excuse.

"Seven forty-five sharp," she says. "And be prompt. We have a lot to cover."

"Yes, miss."

"Next," the photographer calls.

Edna stands up, but just as she's about to surrender the stool, she takes one look at Hannah Kim and stops.

"One minute," she tells the photographer. She whips out a travel-size bottle of hairspray from her backpack and spritzes a tissue. Then she taps down the hairs that always stick up like antennae along Hannah's part. "That's how you get rid of those fly aways," she says.

Hannah holds still, looking grateful.

I sneak out my camera and snap a shot of Hannah as the photographer positions her. With two clicks I stretch her neck and turn her into an adorable giraffe, complete with head knobs. Hannah wrote a report on giraffes last year when we were studying the African plains. They're graceful and gentle—and a little knobby-kneed—just like Hannah.

Smile, I write underneath, and press send to her phone number. A second later, I hear her backpack vibrate.

"Merci Suárez."

I slip my phone out of view just as Miss McDaniels looks up from her clipboard. She keeps a whole collection of the stuff she confiscates, and I don't want my phone to be part of it. My heart races and my cheeks get blotchy as I step forward. Luckily, she's only calling my turn. The boys in our class start making faces and flaring their nostrils to try to make me laugh. Normally, I wouldn't care, especially since no one can make faces better than I can. Last year, we used to have contests at lunch, and I always won. My best face is when I push up my nose with my pinkies at the same time that I pull down on my lower eyelids with my index fingers. I call it the Phantom.

But Jamie, who's behind me, shakes her head at the boys and sighs. "Idiots," she says.

I ignore them as best I can and take my turn.

I sit on the stool exactly the way the photographer says: Ankles crossed. Torso swiveled to the left and leaning forward. Hands in lap. Head tilted like a confused puppy. Who sits like this, ever? I look like a victim of taxidermy.

"Smile," the photographer says, without an ounce of joy in her voice.

Just as I'm trying to decide whether to show teeth, a huge flash goes off and blinds me.

"Wait. I wasn't ready," I say.

She ignores me and reviews her shots. It must be really bad for her to hold up the line this way. Do-overs mean time, and everyone in business knows that time is money.

"Let's try again," she says, adjusting my glasses. "Chin up this time."

Chin? Who is she kidding? I already know that's not the problem. My eye is fluttering, and I can feel the soft pull to the left.

"Look *at the camera,* honey," the photographer says.

I blink hard and fix both my eyes on her lens, which always makes me look angry, but it's the best I can do. She shoots again and again in an explosion of shutter clicks. I must look as awkward as I feel, because I can hear the boys snickering.

When it's over, I jump off the stool and head for the bleachers, where the others are sitting. My head is pounding from this dumb headband. I yank it off and let my hair hang down in my face.

Edna moves down as I take a seat to wait for the dismissal bell.

"Shut it," she tells the boys behind us, smiling at them anyway.

"Thanks," I mumble.

She glances at me and shrugs. "Don't worry about the pictures," she says. "You probably didn't buy many anyway."

The final bell rings, and everyone scatters.

CHAPTER 2

ROLI HAS ONLY HAD HIS license for a few weeks and already we've lost a mailbox and two recycling bins to his skills behind the wheel. Even our cat, Tuerto, has learned to hide when he hears the jingle of car keys. Still, Mami has promised to let Roli drive us to and from school every day so he can practice. But today, as Roli lurches around the puddles in our driveway, I see there's even bigger trouble at home.

A police cruiser is parked in front of Abuela's house.

"Stop the car," Mami orders.

He slams on the brakes, startling the ibises that are digging for worms in the soggy grass. Mami doesn't even shut the door behind her as she hurries out to see what's the matter.

My heart squeezes into a fist. The last time cops came to our block, it was because Doña Rosa from across the street had died. I glance around nervously, but I don't see an ambulance anywhere.

"What's wrong?" I ask Roli.

"Zip it, amoeba. I'm trying to hear." He motions with his chin at Abuela and a policeman, who are talking near our banyan tree. Abuela's face is twisted in worry, although that's not unusual on its own. She's the manager of the Catastrophic Concerns Department in our family, after all, so it's pretty much her resting face. If you want to know all the ways you can be tragically hurt in everyday life, just talk to Abuela. She keeps a long list—and she doesn't mind sharing details.

"Get back from the canal," she yells whenever one of us kids wanders too close to the fence behind our house. "An alligator will close its jaws on you and drag you to the bottom!"

"Put shoes on!" she'll say whenever I'm barefoot. "You'll get worms in your belly the size of spaghetti."

She can't watch anyone climb a ladder without mentioning a neck-breaking fall. Or sharpen the knives without recalling a fulana de tal who sliced off a thumb. And forget poor Lolo. She's after our grandfather nonstop for one thing or another — a fall, heatstroke, even a patatús, whatever that is.

"Is there a problem, officer?" Mami says when she reaches them. Her voice is extra polite, and she tugs nervously on her work scrubs. Roli and I are out of the car by now, watching, too. That's when I notice that Lolo is in the back seat of the cruiser.

Was Abuela right about something bad happening to him after all? The idea sets my heart racing again.

"No, ma'am. We've just had a little confusion during dismissal time for kindergarten at the elementary school — that's all. I thought it best to bring your sons and their grandfather home."

"*That* is my son," Mami says, pointing back at Roli, who stands up a little straighter and waves. "If you mean the twins, they're my nephews."

Good move, Mami, I think. Cute as they are, it's never safe to claim those two until you have the full report. Even the friendly librarians downtown have banned them from storytime unless they come with two escorts — and harnesses.

Still, I don't see how this could involve Lolo — or why he's in the cop car. What could have gone wrong on a walk home from school? It's only five blocks. If you stand at the end of the driveway, you can even see the flagpole. Plus, for as long as I can remember, Lolo has been in charge of walking us home. He did it for Roli and for me. In fact, it used to be my favorite part of the day when I was still at Manatee Elementary. We'd stroll, nice and slow, so I could tell him all that had happened each day, especially the highlights from recess. Then we'd stop to get a snack, even though Mami said it ruined my appetite. I only quit walking home with him in the third grade because that's when everyone in my class started to ride bikes to school. Only babies were walkers after that.

"You think Lolo's taking the rap for something the twins did?" I whisper to Roli. I crane my neck for a better look. It's not that far-fetched. Lolo loves all of us grandkids like crazy. He calls me preciosa—precious one—and Roli and the twins his compadres del alma. Lolo would never let anything happen to the twins. A full day of school would have given my cousins plenty of time to unleash trouble, as everyone around here knows. Maybe he's trying to save them from starting their careers in the state penitentiary early.

"Shh," Roli says, giving me a sharp look. That's what everybody says around here when I ask too many question, like I'm still a little kid.

The cop checks his clipboard and looks up and down

the pebble walkway that connects all three of our houses. "But your nephews live here, with you?"

"Yes . . . well, no," Mami says.

How we live confuses some people, so Mami starts her usual explanation. Our three flat-top houses are exact pink triplets, and they sit side by side here on Sixth Street. The one on the left, with the Sol Painting van parked out front, is ours. The one in the middle, with the flower beds, is where Abuela and Lolo live. The one on the right, with the explosion of toys in the dirt, belongs to Tía Inés and the twins. Roli calls it the Suárez Compound, but Mami hates that name. She says it sounds like we're the kind of people who collect canned food and wait for the end of the world any minute. She's named it Las Casitas instead. The little houses. I just call it home.

I creep closer to the cruiser as Mami talks, being careful not to make any sudden moves the whole way. Cops are community helpers and all that, but a billy club and gun don't ever look very friendly. In fact, they make me feel prickly all over.

He spots me, though, and I freeze, my eyes darting over to Lolo, who *still* hasn't gotten out of the car. Whatever it is, he needs my help.

"Can we have a word in private?" the policeman says to

Mami, motioning her to join him and Abuela in the shade. I lean toward them, trying to listen, but Mami turns and gives me that stone-cold look.

"Merci, this is an adult conversation," she says. "Keep an eye on the twins, please. They've gone inside. I'll be right there."

I feel my cheeks turn the color of my blazer. I'm in the sixth grade, am I not? I'm old enough to babysit the twins, clean Abuela's sewing room, start dinner, and save up for stuff that I want. But suddenly I'm too young to know why my own grandfather has been busted? Go figure.

"I'll see what I can find out," Roli whispers importantly as I walk past.

"Seventeen is *not* adult," I say, but he pretends he can't hear and doesn't respond.

I know I should go check on the twins, but I walk around the cruiser instead. I lean in the open door. Lolo's hands are folded in his lap, and his white hair is sticking up funny, the way it does on a windy day.

"What did they do, Lolo?" I whisper. "You can tell me. Did they pull a fire alarm? Start a food fight? Tie up the teacher?"

Lolo looks at me and shakes his head. "Merci. Such ideas! Those angelitos are innocent," he says. "I swear it."

Love is blind, as they say, but why argue? I study the blinking contraptions that are bolted to the dashboard, my mind racing. "Then why are you sitting in a cop car?"

There's a long pause. "Nada," he says finally. "It was a little misunderstanding."

Nada? Everybody knows the police are like teachers. They don't call your family about misunderstandings or to say what a great job you're doing.

"Lolo," I say.

He pulls off his wire-frame glasses and wipes them on his T-shirt. "Fine. It's these glasses!" he says in disgust. "They're terrible! I've been telling Abuela to schedule me another appointment with the optometrist. Maybe now she'll listen."

"What do glasses have to do with anything?" I say. "You're not making any sense!"

Lolo looks at me sheepishly. "No, I suppose I'm not." He turns his head away from me to stare out the window. "That's the trouble," he mumbles.

I peer over the roof of the squad car. Mami and Abuela are still talking to the officer; Roli is standing nearby, quietly observing like the scientist he is. Abuela, on the other hand, is glaring at our neighbors who've come into their yards to stare. This is her worst nightmare—gossip about us. Lolo's going to be in trouble with her later, for sure. Maybe *that's* why he's not budging from this spot. Last week Abuela made a fuss because Lolo lost his wallet again. He was sure he'd been pickpocketed at the bakery, and even called Tía Inés to warn her about common criminals eating at the luncheonette where she works. "Keep an eye out for thieves," he told her. "The world has changed; trust no one!" Turns out, he wasn't pickpocketed at all. When Abuela found his billfold in the bed of lantana he'd been weeding that afternoon—¡Ay-ay-ay! ¡Qué escándalo! Her volume button got stuck on high, and the whole block could hear her yelling about how he had to pay more attention.

The twins barrel out the back door just then in their play clothes. In a flash, they're pressing their noses against the steamed window of the cruiser to make twin pig snouts. Son la candela, as usual. Tomás is also eyeing the mobile radio system on the dashboard. I stop him just as he yanks open the door to make a grab for the transmitter.

"Quit it," I say, pulling him out by the waist, "and tell me what happened."

He shrugs me off as soon as I put him back on the ground. "We rode in the police car!" he says.

"So I hear. But why?"

Axel butts in with the rest. "Lolo tried to take the other twins home by accident, the ones in Miss Henderson's

21

class. They didn't like it. They yelled loud like we're supposed to."

"No! Go! Yell! Tell!" Tomás shouts at the top of his voice.

I recognize that chant right away. It's what our old teachers taught us to do if ever someone tried to snatch us. We had assemblies about it and everything.

"Shhh," I hiss, but too late. Abuela and Mami have already heard them.

"Merci, I told you to watch the boys. We're busy here," Mami snaps. "Just a few more minutes."

I turn back to Lolo. "Is that true? You took the wrong twins at dismissal?" I know exactly who those kids are, of course. They were in the same preschool as Axel and Tomás and were generally known as "the good ones." They're also Vietnamese. How could he mistake them for ours? I stare at Lolo's glasses, wondering if he's right about the prescription.

Lolo won't meet my eye. He stares out the other window, his cheeks bright red. "All that yelling for a simple mistake," he mutters. "And then the parents were pointing and pulling them from me as if I were a criminal. There's no respect for an anciano anymore. What's this country coming to?"

"They called the cops!" Tomás adds excitedly. "Eric's mom took a movie with her phone!"

The air is thick and hot, and I realize that I'm sweating again in this silly uniform, even with my blazer tied at my waist. Overhead, the afternoon clouds are gathering into their usual black popcorn. Any minute, we'll have our daily rainstorm, which will cool off exactly nothing.

"Why don't you come inside for a snack with us, Lolo?" I say. "Your head is getting shiny with sweat." I lower my voice. "I want to tell you how school went. You're not the only one who had a tough go. It was picture day today."

If anyone can make me feel better, it will be him. Lolo and I always talk after school. We share Danish cookies from the tin he keeps hidden in the toolshed. And when I talk, Lolo isn't like Mami, who says things like *give it a chance* or *look on the bright side* or *learn to ignore small things* and all that basura that makes me feel like it's my fault that my day was a hunk of smelly cheese.

But right now, Lolo doesn't seem that interested in what happened to me today. Instead, he shakes his head. "I'm not very hungry, Merci. You go on, preciosa."

"Merci!" Mami calls again. She tosses me an exasperated look and points at the twins, who are poking a fire-ant mound with a stick, practically begging to get swarmed.

I go off in their direction, and they race away from me so I chase them, pretending everything is OK.

When I get to our screen door, I turn around, hoping Lolo has changed his mind. Maybe he'll say, "Wait, Merci," and ask me to share my pudding at the kitchen table, tell me how he made such a strange mistake, ask about my day the way he's supposed to so that I can breathe easy again.

But no. Maybe talking in the afternoon is something we won't do anymore, like when we stopped walking to school.

A rumble of thunder shakes the ground, and a gust rattles the palm fronds like shells. Inside, Tuerto is up on the counter, meowing for his food. The twins are shrieking with fear and fun, doing God-knows-what. As the first drops of rain start to fall, Roli jogs toward our car to roll up the windows.

And even as Mami and Abuela coax him, Lolo still sits in the hot cruiser, his eyes fixed on something in the distance that I can't see.

CHAPTER 3

SEAWARD PINES ACADEMY, established MCMLVII, has always reminded me of a cemetery, even though it's a fancy private school. It was the first thing I noticed about the place when I started here last year in the fifth grade. Seaward has a big stone entrance and all those perfectly planted begonias like the ones at Our Lady Queen of Peace on Southern Boulevard. And there's always that big vase with fresh flowers in the front office, too, with a smell that gives me the creeps. It's just like the scent of Doña Rosa's funeral, where it was wall-to-wall with stinky carnation wreaths all over the place. Doña Rosa died in her house across the street from us, watching *Wheel of Fortune*, like she did every night. Abuela and I used to go over and watch with her sometimes to keep her company, since her niece lived down in Miami and didn't visit much. Doña Rosa didn't speak enough English to be good at solving the puzzles; mostly, she just liked Vanna White's gowns and the prizes. Anyway, I guess we were busy that week and didn't think to go. It was three whole days before anyone called the police and found her in her chair. To this day, Abuela makes the sign of the cross when we go by the condo, just in case Doña Rosa is still mad that it took us so long to notice. Papi repainted her place for nothing so her niece could sell it, but you never know. "Rosa was always one for grudges," Abuela says.

Roli drives slowly past the entrance gate, waving at his science teacher, who's on duty directing traffic.

"Good morning," she calls out to us.

Roli swivels around to smile in a classic display of distracted driving, which is his downfall every time. Mami dives for the wheel (again), this time to spare the lady's feet from being flattened by our tires. The crutches and orthopedic boots Mami keeps for her rehab patients clatter to the car floor, along with her file folders that were stacked beside me. I don't know why she let him have the wheel this morning. *Practice makes perfect,* Mami always says, but I can see this is going to take a while.

"Can you step on it, please?" I say, pointing at the speedometer. The needle is hovering at seven miles per hour. "I can walk faster than this."

"False," he says, glancing at the dash. "The average human walks at about 3.5 miles per hour."

My phone says it's 7:41 a.m. My message reminder keeps blinking that my meeting with Miss McDaniels is in exactly four minutes. I can't be late; her number-one peeve is tardiness. Not that it stops there. Uniform length, gum chewing, loudness of your voice — you name it, she monitors it better than our headmaster, Dr. Newman. I should know. Last year, when I didn't know any better, Miss McDaniels gave me a detention for wearing my lucky sneakers instead of the regulation loafers.

"Hurry, Roli. I'm going to be late!"

Roli glares at me in the rearview mirror. "Talk to Tía about it. It was her idea that we drop off the twins," he says. "And take that thing off your head, will you please? You look stupid."

"Absolutely not." He doesn't like that I'm wearing my bike helmet in the car with him, but you just can't be too careful.

"Enough, both of you," Mami says. "We're trying to work out other morning arrangements for the twins, but you'll need to be patient until then."

I roll my eyes without letting her see. Since the mess with Lolo yesterday—and all the time it took to get Abuela calmed down—Mami's been a little crabby and impatient, too. This morning I asked her for my consent form for soccer tryouts and she didn't have it, even though I put it right on the refrigerator so she wouldn't miss it.

"I can't think about that right now," she said, shooing me out of the room.

Mami turns to me now and frowns as she changes the subject. "And why didn't you mention your meeting with Miss McDaniels, anyway?" She narrows her eyes in suspicion, probably thinking back to my contraband footwear incident. Since that day, I have been forbidden from causing any more phone calls home unless I am burning alive with a fever or projectile vomiting.

I shrug. "We have some business to discuss," I say vaguely.

"Business."

"Yes."

"About?"

"She gave out our community service assignments yesterday."

"And?"

I slouch in the back seat. We have a strict policy in our family about always telling the truth, so I have no choice but to say it. "And my assignment is the Sunshine Buddies Club."

Roli meets my eye in the rearview mirror and snorts. "Friends of the friendless!" he says.

"That doesn't sound so bad," Mami says. "It was useful for you last year, wasn't it?"

I stare out the window. Mami's blind enthusiasm is one of her more predictable and annoying qualities.

"Not really," I say. The truth is, I hated it, but only Roli knows that. Mami was so excited that I'd been accepted at Seaward, she wouldn't have listened to my complaints. Instead, I would have gotten pep talks.

Like now.

Mami sighs. "You know, Merci, a good attitude goes a long way. Half my patients would never walk again if they didn't think positive." She turns back around. "And this family could really use some upbeat thinking these days."

"Why?" I say. "What's wrong with our thinking?"

She doesn't answer.

Instead, she points to the sign for the drop-off loop. "That way, Roli," she says. "And watch for the younger kids."

I lean back and look out the window as we roll past the lower school. I wonder when Seaward is going to start to feel like home? A lot of kids in my class started school here in kindergarten, like these little kids, but not Roli and me. He came when he started middle school, and I joined him last year because a spot finally opened up in the fifth-grade class when a kid moved away over the summer. Mami almost fainted with joy when the office called to tell us. She is all about getting a good education, no matter what. She wants Roli to apply to the best colleges and for every scholarship. And when I complain about homework—even a little bit—she reminds me how Papi took on extra lawn jobs so she could go to college at night. She went for three extra years while I was a baby so she could become a physical therapist. Because of her job, we were able to buy Las Casitas, even when Papi's paint business wasn't doing so great. That's why I have a new phone and Roli has a laptop. That's why we can help Tía or Abuela and Lolo if they need a little extra money sometimes, too.

Which all means that Mami doesn't think community service is a big deal *at all* if it means I get to attend Seaward. She's the one who agreed to the scholarship without even asking me if I minded. "It's a golden opportunity!" she said, and inked her name without reading the fine print. It turns out Roli and I have to do sixty whole hours of free labor every year, while keeping up a B-plus average. That's twenty hours more than the other kids.

Plus, it makes it hard to do all your homework, which was one of the hardest parts of coming here last year. There was suddenly a lot more work than I'd ever had at my old school, and no matter how much I studied, I wasn't quick enough. I didn't have the answer to the math problem as fast as the kid next to me, or I hadn't read as far as everyone else in the book we were reading in class. "Be patient," Miss Miller told me when I got teary after I got a D on a quiz. "You're settling in." And I did settle in, I guess, because I didn't get kicked out. But this year, with new teachers and changing classes, it's all supposed to get even harder.

Roli doesn't have this problem, of course. He's never seen a B stain his spotless report card in his whole life, not even here at Seaward, where we get worked to death. That kind of genius status means that he gets a cushy job working in the science lab as a teacher's assistant for his community service. He may be a terrible driver, but I can't deny that he's a brain—a very, very big brain— which is why he's been getting invitations to apply to colleges for years. In fact, he's probably smarter than anyone in Seaward's history. Just check out the glass display case outside the front office. The biggest trophy in there is for the science fair project he did in his freshman year. It was about how to make plastic from banana peels instead of petroleum. You can practically smell the future Nobel Prize on him.

Finally, the drop-off area comes into view.

"Brake," Mami warns, but it's too late. I have no choice but to brace for impact.

One of our front tires scrapes the curb before Roli manages a full stop. I toss off my helmet and hop out fast in case he forgets to throw the gear into park like last time.

"Gotta dash!"

Mami looks a little pale as she switches back into the driver's seat. Her patient notes flutter out to the sidewalk. "Pull up your socks!" she calls after me.

But who's got time to worry about saggy socks, even if it *is* a uniform violation? I have to make a run for it if I'm going to get to Miss McDaniels's meeting on time. She can't stand excuses. You're supposed to plan for set-backs, she always tells people, not react to them. Lateness is a symptom of poor planning and all that.

Luckily, I'm up to the challenge. I didn't win every field-day footrace back in elementary school for nothing. I dodge through the sea of red blazers like a running back, my arms pumping, head tucked. It doesn't take long for me to feel drenched in the armpit region thanks to the heat, even at this hour. I can't even remember if I put on deodorant, and now it's too late to worry about it. Tía Inés will have a fit if I come home smelly again, though. She's the one who does the laundry for the whole family and is always complaining about my stinky stuff. This summer she made a big deal of taking me shopping at Walgreens because Roli made repeated complaints about my so-called bromhidrosis. (It means BO, if we're speaking, you know, like ordinary people.) Thanks to him, the very next day, Tía Inés dragged me up and down the drugstore aisles as she filled a plastic basket with sprays and powders for places I didn't even know needed them. Meanwhile, the twins were in the candy aisle sampling their favorites.

"You're not supposed to smell good when you're play-ing outside," I grumbled, but Tía Inés wouldn't listen. She dumped the whole basket of powders, razors, and deodor-ants at the cashier's counter just the same.

"Merci, a young lady takes care of herself," she said, handing over her two-for-one coupons. "Like it or not, it's time."

Time for what, exactly? I wanted to know, but I didn't dare ask.

I round the corner and charge toward the front office. It's exactly seven forty-five when I reach the door nearest the bike racks. I suck in gulps of air to ease the stitch in my side, but I still feel like I'm being knifed. My socks are puddled down around my loafers, and my headband has slipped back on my head. It is very apparent that, no, I did not use the frizz tamer that Tía bought me.

That's when I hear a familiar voice in my ear.

"Move it, please, Merci."

Edna straddles her flashy bike, obviously waiting to park in the spot that I'm blocking. I can't help gawking at her ride in admiration. She's on a hot-pink Electra with brightly colored stencils on the fenders that remind me of one of the modern art paintings we saw on our class trip to the Norton Museum last year. Edna's bike has hand brakes, a silver headlight, and whitewall tires, like those old-fashioned Cadillacs Lolo loves so much. I hate how much I love it. My bike at home is a heap. It's Roli's old ten-speed, which is (unfortunately) just my size now and in working order, thanks (or not) to Lolo, who can fix anything, even our old washing machine from 1996. The handlebars are speckled with rust (ferric oxide, per Roli) and stuffing flies from the seat when I pedal hard. The twins say that it looks like I'm farting cotton.

Edna's eyes trail over me. She takes in everything from my hair all the way down to my scuffed shoes. It's like I'm getting a primer coat of ugly for the day.

"No offense, Merci, but you're a wreck."

I squeeze my eyes shut, trying not to let my eye stray. It's only Edna being Edna. I should be used to it by now. *No offense,* Merci, but you're singing off-key. *No offense,* Merci, but I want to study my spelling words with somebody else. It took me a while to figure Edna out last year, but I finally got wise. *No offense* is what Edna says right before she takes a hatchet to your feelings.

"Give me a break. I just ran across campus," I say between gasps.

But she doesn't seem moved.

Edna swings her leg over her seat and slips her bike past me to get into an empty slot. Jamie is with her, too, and — surprise — she has almost the exact same bike, only hers is pale yellow and the stencils are paisley. It's Edna's mojo again, I suppose, that dark magic that can turn perfectly ordinary people into mirrors. Jamie always gets bewitched. If Edna wears her hair in a high bun, Jamie wears one, too. If Edna gets mad, Jamie tosses in an ugly look as backup. If Edna is going somewhere, Jamie is always invited, even if no one else is. Last year, when Edna got the flu and was absent for a week, I thought there was some hope to break the spell. Jamie sat next to me and Hannah at lunch and played kickball on my team at recess. I thought we were becoming friends. But when Edna came back a few days later, pale and chapped at the nose, it was the same old same old. "Move over, please, Merci," Jamie said. "Edna wants to sit there."

Thank goodness Lolo gave me an azabache to protect me. Mami says mal de ojo is nonsense, that no one can hurt people with just an evil eye. But I believe. The world isn't all logic the way she and Roli think. It's got mystery the way Lolo says. So I wear my protection on a chain next to the gold cross I got for Holy Communion. It may look like an ordinary black rock, but who knows what would have happened to me at Edna's hands without it? Lolo says no evil gets past it.

I decide to ignore her and walk toward the glass doors, but just as I start to open them, Edna reaches for the handle, too, and she and Jamie barge in ahead of me. There's no time to argue, of course. A group of kids—the other Sunshine Buddies, I guess—has already gathered around Miss McDaniels's desk. The office is a beehive all around. Teachers are signing in. Kids wait to get new schedules, and a few parents who've signed up for tour appointments are chatting on the sofas while they wait. Kids apply a whole year in advance to go here, so people are always touring, even on the first week of school.

The flower stench socks me in the nose so hard that I start breathing through my mouth. I wander around to find a spot that's far from the vase.

"Good," Miss McDaniels says over the din. "The Sunshine Buddies for the sixth grade have arrived at last, so we can get started." Her voice is sharp, like high heels clicking on tile floors.

Edna snaps her head in my direction. Jamie turns, too. I swear it's like I can see the thought bubble forming over their heads, clear as day.

"*You're* a Sunshine Buddy this year?" Edna asks.

Miss McDaniels steps in. "Indeed, she is. What better kind of buddy than someone who knows what it's like to be new at our school?"

I may not want to be part of this club, but it's almost worth staying a member just to see the look on Edna's face. If only I could whip out my phone camera right now to capture Edna's mouth hanging open. I'd find a face filter to turn her into a green chameleon with its fleshy pink mouth wide open in shock.

Luckily, Miss McDaniels stays mum about how it's part of my required community service. That's all I'd need— another reason for Edna to think she's better than me. She isn't here on scholarship, of course. *Her* dad is a podiatrist, not a paint contractor like Papi, and she never lets us forget it. "My-dad-the-doctor *this*. My-dad-who-saved-a guy's-toe *that*." I'm pretty sure he mostly clears up athlete's foot and plantar warts. Why is that so great? I mean, Mami helps people learn how to walk again after they've had strokes or terrible accidents. I mentioned that to Edna once, but she wasn't impressed. "No offense," she said, "but she's still not a doctor."

Miss McDaniels hands bright red folders to everyone.

"I trust that you all had a fine first day back yesterday, and that you're ready for a productive school year, especially as part of the Sunshine Buddies program." She glances at me and, if I'm not imagining things, frowns a little. I straighten my skirt, noticing that the seam got turned.

"Inside these folders, you'll find your buddies' schedules, as well as a paragraph with a little bit about the person assigned to you. I'd like you to make your first contact this week, please. You'll need to check in every Friday for the remainder of the semester to give me updates on how things are going. Remember, you are ambassadors for this school. It's your job to make our new students feel welcome and comfortable in their surroundings."

Just then, the phone rings, and Miss McDaniels turns to answer it. "Excuse me."

Everyone opens their folders. I shouldn't even care

because I've already decided that I'm going to ask Miss McDaniels to switch me to some other community service. I'm barely comfortable at this school myself. How can I help anybody else? Still, I can't help being curious. I mean, does Miss McDaniels really know what she's doing with this matching stuff? For starters, Edna is going to be someone's buddy again, which is like pairing a baby mouse with a boa constrictor. I should know. She was my buddy last year.

I still remember our first day. At lunch, she told me stories about her family's cruise to Newport, Rhode Island, and how she slept in a real lighthouse where they told scary ghost stories and everything. "Where do you vacation?" she wanted to know. "North or south?"

I could have told her the truth. We don't vacation. But I'd been watching Roli go to school here for a while, so even as a newbie I knew that wasn't the right answer, not at Seaward. "East," I said, dressing up our day trips to the beach. I told her about our favorite bonfire at Lake Worth, where we go on spring and summer nights after Papi gets off work.

"Oh," she said. "We don't go to that beach."

We ate at the same lunch table for a while. Our cubbies were near each other. We were in the same class all day long. But somehow, we didn't start to share secrets or do sleepovers the way she does with Jamie. Which makes me wonder: maybe this matching business is a sham? It could be sort of like that dating service that introduced Tía Inés to the guy with the pinkie rings and toupee. It might have looked good on paper, but—¡Ay, chihuahua!—what a mess.

Edna and Jamie start reading about their new buddies. I don't want to raise suspicions, so I fish through my papers and read the name inside. It says Michael Clark. Well, now I'm positive that Miss McDaniels doesn't know what she's doing. He's the new kid from Minnesota, a cold place—and I hate the cold. He likes ice fishing. He has no favorite color (suspicious). We only have social studies and PE together. Absolutely nothing about him makes a good match to me, except both our names start with *M*.

A hand snatches my paper. Before I can stop her, Edna is reading my stuff and grinning stupidly.

"Gimme it," I say.

She arches her eyebrow. "Ooooh . . . you have Michael Clark."

"You got paired with a *boy*?" Jamie asks.

"No offense," Edna says, handing back my sheet, "but that's awkward."

I could tell her that I'm probably not going to pal

around at all, but I'm still enjoying her shock over the fact that I've been chosen.

"What's the big deal?" I say. "We play with boys at recess all the time, don't we?"

Edna gives me a look of pity. "This is sixth grade, Merci," she says, as if I don't know. "We don't have recess anymore like in the lower school." *Baby,* she wants to say, and just like that my eyelid starts to feel heavy, and I feel the drift.

Miss McDaniels hangs up the phone and turns back to all of us. "So. Where were we? Are there any questions or concerns?"

No one says anything, but I can feel Edna watching me, like a not-so-friendly dare.

"All right, then; if there's nothing else, you're dismissed." Miss McDaniels checks her watch. "First bell is in exactly three minutes, and I have no plans whatsoever to write tardy slips for any of you. Good day."

Everyone hurries out, but my feet have somehow turned to deadweight. I stare at the walls and baseboards, noticing that they'll need a fresh coat soon, especially that scuffed spot near the copier. Maybe I could do paint for community service on a Saturday when no one is here.

I wait for the others to leave before I inch a little closer to her desk. It takes a second for Miss McDaniels to look up from her paperwork to see me still standing there. She peers at me over her half-moon glasses. "Yes, Merci? Is there a problem?"

I try not to breathe through my nose. The stink of dying flowers is making me queasy. My mind spins with all the ways I could answer her. Roli says you should always build a case carefully, cool and logical, like a Vulcan. So I take a deep breath and start slowly, the way I've been practicing.

"There are so many problems, Miss McDaniels," I say, trying to warm up. "Word problems, social problems, money problems . . ."

She crosses her arms and gives me a stern look. Miss McDaniels doesn't like nonsense. Not one bit. There's never any time for nonsense.

"Merci Suárez, take your fingers off your nose and tell me why you are still standing here."

I have no choice but to knuckle right down on the tough negotiations. I put the folder on her desk. "I'd like another community service assignment, please," I say.

"I see."

"Something that will take less time during soccer season. Maybe some painting or . . ." My eyes slide over to the wicker basket in the corner. Last year, I helped clear out the lost-and-found bin after every quarter. Quick and easy. That's how I scored several unclaimed gel pens and a necklace that I gave Abuela for her birthday, too.

She cocks her head. "Are you aware that it's an honor to be selected as a Sunshine Buddy ambassador?"

"So you'll have no trouble filling my spot," I tell her, smiling. "That's good."

She shakes her head. "It's not everyone who is lucky enough to be picked to represent our school in this way," she says.

I feel my cheeks getting red. Lucky? Is that how I should feel? I think back to Edna on the first day we met. "You're lucky to be here," she'd said, showing me around the cafeteria's salad bar. Matching chairs were arranged around maple-colored tables in the middle. "You could be at a school that has a drug dog and smells like mold." She made a face and giggled.

And it was true: I could have been, which is always what worried Mami and Papi, too, especially after what happened at the middle school that I was zoned for. A boy brought a knife because another kid liked his girlfriend. Luckily, somebody saw it in his locker and told before anybody got hurt, but the story made the evening news.

Still. It would be easier to go to school right down the street, and plenty of the kids from my old elementary school go there and they're just fine. Mold couldn't smell any worse than rotting flowers.

And, most important, no one would tease me about being Sunshine Buddies with a boy.

The warning bell startles me. I don't have much time.

"It's not that I'm not grateful," I begin. "I am. For everything."

Miss McDaniels eyes me and considers things. "I should think so. Let's give this a few days. Check in with me on Friday after you've interacted a bit. We can make any necessary adjustments after that."

She sits down and gets back to work to let me know that the conversation is over. When I don't move, she taps her watch and frowns.

I'm down to a minute and a half by the time I tuck the folder in my backpack and walk outside. Everyone has scattered to the four winds, as Lolo says. I hurry toward language arts class, reading the names in the bricks as I go past the girls' restroom. Our family name is not there, of course. You've got to give a lot of money to be chiseled into something permanent around here.

I try to think of some non-dorky way of officially introducing myself to Michael later. Maybe I'll take a picture of myself and send it to the phone number listed in his folder.

Hi, I'm your fake friend for a couple of weeks.

Hi, I'm here to make sure you don't barf because no one is talking to you.

Hi, did you go to a moldy school in Minnesota?

Unfortunately, I don't get far before I hear giggling right behind me. Someone has stepped out of the girls' bathroom.

"Ooooh, Michael, let's be buddies."

I don't turn around. I already know who it is.

CHAPTER 4

LOLO'S NEW GLASSES ARE ROUND and enormous, but they seem to have cheered him up. He got them this morning with Tía Inés, who's still mad that she had to get time off work again to take him. It was Papi's turn to drive Lolo to an appointment, she claims, which is one of their favorite sibling arguments. I don't get it. If it were up to me, I'd take off every chance I got to hang out with Lolo. But with them, it's always a fight.

Anyway, the thick lenses magnify Lolo's eyes, so they look really big and green from some angles.

"You like them?" he asks.

His voice sounds so peppy that I don't have the heart to say the truth.

"Circles are my favorite shape," I say.

"He insisted on getting the largest pair in the shop," Tía Inés says, as if he isn't sitting right there at the luncheonette counter she's wiping down. "It's the exact same prescription as last time, but he swears that he sees better."

"And I do," Lolo says. "Nothing is going to get past me now. You'll see." He takes another loud slurp of the tropical smoothie he's drinking. The pineapple chunk from the rim of the glass has already been reduced to rind. "Sit down and have a snack, Merci," he says.

I climb up on the stool next to Lolo, who is perched at his usual spot in the corner, acting more or less like himself again, thank goodness.

I biked over to El Caribe as soon as I got home from school. It's peaceful in here today, nothing like Sunday mornings, when the line snakes all the way out the door and people shout out their orders to Tía for takeout coffee, pastelitos, and warm loaves of bread. Everybody knows this is the best bakery between Miami and Tampa, so it gets crazy.

Tía Inés is busy refilling the cups of toothpicks that are decorated with mini Cuban flags. "She can't stay long, viejo," she tells Lolo. "Merci has to help Abuela with the boys today."

We both stare at her.

"Oh, she needs help, does she?" Lolo says. He's still bitter about the new arrangements. Abuela is going to be walking the twins to and from school, too. She bought new kicks at Foot Locker just for the job, white Chucks that I may have to borrow from time to time when she's not looking.

But he's not the only one annoyed.

I should mention here that 1) no one ever *asks* me if I want to babysit the twins, 2) Roli almost always gets out of it thanks to his tutoring job and working on his college applications, and 3) I get paid exactly zero for keeping them from swallowing pennies and running blindly into traffic. How am I supposed to buy a bike when nobody pays me for anything?

"I wish you'd find somebody else, Tía," I say. "There are kids at school who took that Red Cross class and actually want to babysit. I can get you names. Hire them. I won't be able to watch them once soccer season starts, anyway."

She frowns at me. "Who in their right mind would hire a stranger to watch their kids when they have relatives around?"

I sigh. It's no use fighting. When it comes to helping, the motto around here is *family or bust.*

"Can't I at least have a snack before I go?" I say. "I've

had a long day, in case you're interested. And I'll need my strength for the twins."

She sizes me up and slides over a small guava square, still warm, on a plate. "Ten minutes, then out you go."

"Put it on my tab, Inés," Lolo tells her.

"I already have, Lolo," she says. "Along with the three smoothies." She takes the glass from him. "Are you even watching your sugar the way the doctor said last time? Repeat after me: diabetic coma."

Lolo ignores her. Instead, he turns to me. "Bueno, ¿Y qué me dices? What's the news from the sixth-grader?"

"I was starting to wonder if you'd ever ask," I tell him. "Bad news. Edna Santos—remember her?—she's in lots of my classes, *and* I've been drafted into a club that I hate."

"Oh. Me, too. The Old Man Club." He chuckles at his own joke.

"I'm in the Sunshine Buddies," I say, rolling my eyes, "which means I have to pal around with a new kid instead of getting ready for soccer tryouts. And he's a boy, which Edna thinks is hilarious. She's going to bug me about it every day, I just know it."

I take a savage bite of my pastry.

Tía Inés stops what she's doing and wiggles her eyebrows at me. "Well, so what? Is the boy cute at least?"

I give her a steely look. This is almost as bad as dealing

with Edna's teasing. Tía just loves the idea of love and romance. "Cute if you like giants," I say. "You can't miss him. Michael Clark is almost as big as Papi."

"A six-footer?" Lolo says, whistling.

"Ah. Tall, dark, and handsome," Tía says. "I've always been partial to that type."

I glare to let her know I mean business. Then I scroll through my photos until I get to the shot I'm looking for. To kill time as we waited for our rides home, I was turning kids into animals. I snapped a picture of Michael and turned him into a moose in honor of Minnesota, but I chickened out before I could show him. What if he thought I was saying he looked like a moose?

"He's the biggest and the *whitest* boy I've ever seen." I hold up the original shot of Michael as evidence. "There is either no sunshine in Minnesota, or this kid is a vampire."

Lolo squints at the picture. "You're still wearing your azabache, aren't you?"

"Sometimes vampires are nice," Tía says, wiggling her eyebrows again.

I lay my phone on the counter. "The solution is to drop out," I say.

"Of school?" Lolo asks.

"I meant the Sunshine Buddies, but now that I think

about it, why not the whole thing? I already have a career plan, you know."

"Of course! CEO of Sol Painting, Inc.," Lolo says, patting my back.

"Ave María"—Tía Inés closes her eyes—"this again."

I give her a dark look.

Sol Painting is Papi's company, but it's only a matter of time before I'm running the show. It's not like Roli is ever going to step up when Papi retires. He hates painting, for one thing, and his spackling is a disaster. He should definitely stick to easier things, like sewing people's limbs back on or inventing new substances.

"You'll see," I tell Tía. "One day, I'll be rich. If I were you, I'd start being a lot nicer to me if you want me to pay for the twins' college."

"But what if you change your mind?" Lolo asks. "You're young. It happens, you know."

"Oh. *I* know," Tía Inés says, interrupting. "She'll become a waitress here at the bakery." She waves her arms across the expanse of the counter. "Behold your empire. Wiping crumbs from a counter and listening to the same tired jokes from your nonpaying customers."

"People have always liked my jokes," Lolo says.

"Listen, Merci, just be nice to the new kid and ignore Emma."

"Edna," I say.

She rolls her eyes. "Who-evah. And *you*," she tells Lolo, "stop encouraging a dropout. She's finishing school and going to college like her mother. They all are, even the twins — if I don't have to send them to reform school first." She checks the clock and pulls the plate away from me. "Time's up. Off you go."

I slide out of my seat, but Lolo swivels his stool toward me. He puts his big hands, warm and callused, over mine. All at once, I remember that day when he taught me how to tie my shoes, two rabbit ears twisting together, those chapped fingers guiding mine.

"I have a job proposition for you that may get your mind off your troubles. It involves money."

"Then I'm listening."

"Your Papi booked a big job coming up soon, and it's going to pay nicely. Why don't you come along with us, too, and lend a hand?"

"Where's the job?" I ask.

He pushes up his glasses and chuckles a little. "Where is it again, Inés?"

"At the beach clubhouse." Tía is standing by the coffee maker as she reminds him. Her voice is soft but he hears it just the same.

"Exactly. At the beach clubhouse," Lolo repeats. "We're painting the bathrooms."

I scrunch my nose. "All day in the john?" Last time I helped paint trim at the marina on Singer Island, I smelled like bait for days. This could be worse.

Lolo pats himself on the belly. "I can guarantee you twenty dollars, plus a delicious hot dog and soda if you say yes." Lolo used to be in charge of payroll before Mami took over the books. Lucky for me, he still manages the petty cash.

I put on my poker face. Lolo has taught me everything I know about the art of making deals. Rule number one: Never settle for the first offer.

"I don't know. I might have plans. How about making it thirty bucks instead?"

His eyebrows shoot up. "That's robbery, Mercedes Suárez!"

"I'm saving for a new bike." I pick some fluff off the seat of my jeans and hold it up. "For obvious reasons."

He purses his lips as if he's bitten into a lemon. Everybody knows Lolo's a tightwad.

"Come on, Lolo," I coax. "Your only granddaughter needs new wheels. Kids like Edna Santos are rolling around on two-wheeled Cadillacs this year, and what have I got?"

He glances outside at my bike, which I parked right next to the one he's been riding for years. They're practically time machines.

"You're a ruthless negotiator," he says at last. "I like it." He sticks out his hand. "Thirty bucks."

"Then I'm in." We shake on it, and I'm gone.

CHAPTER 5

"HIS EYEBROWS ARE WEIRD," Edna whispers. "Pale but so bushy!"

I pretend I don't hear her—as I have tried to do all week when she brings up some other dumb thing about Michael Clark. So far, we are up to sixteen mentions, which have included comments on his sneakers (some mountain-climbing brand), the color of his eyes (like shark skin), how his voice squeaks (kind of adorable) and blah, blah, blah. I just don't get it. Edna made a big deal of the fact that I have Michael as a buddy, but now *she's* the one who can't seem to take her eyeballs off him. Seriously, you'd think he was a hunk like, oh, say, Jake Rodrigo, the star of all the Iguanador movies. Now *that's* dreamy. A long braid down his back. Dark skin. Muscles. And those green eyes with reptilian pupils, not to mention his aeris zoom that lets him hover and glide through the air. I keep a magazine poster of him in my locker. Edna saw it and rolled her eyes. "He's fake, you know," she said. "Maybe, but he's still better than the real boys around here," I said.

Including Michael Clark.

Besides, who actually cares about the hair above somebody's eyelids, except Edna? I'll bet she noticed his brows only because she plucked hers over the summer. I still can't look at her without feeling pain. Tía tried to convince me to thin mine out at the beginning of the summer. "Just over the bridge of your nose," she said, coming at me with tweezers. When she yanked out the first hair, I was sure my brain came loose, too. No, thank you. I hid in my room all afternoon.

"Look," Edna says again.

All the other girls in our group turn to Michael's table and gape. Wouldn't you know it, mojo strikes again.

I shift in my seat, trying to follow what Ms. Tannenbaum is saying about our first learning packet in social studies. She's a thin lady with unruly hair and hippie clothes, right down to her sandals. She's everybody's favorite teacher. We're starting a big unit on ancient cultures that will last until December. The first and most boring part is about a place called Mesopotamia, so it's taking some work on my part to look interested. Project number one: we'll be making a relief map of the Tigris and Euphrates river basin.

I'm actually a little worried. Not about the map itself. Ms. Tannenbaum is big on projects, which should be fun. But the trouble is that she's even bigger on building group skills. "The world is interconnected. Collaboration is the key skill of the future," she claims. Which means, you don't usually work alone and in peace, the way I like. Instead, she wants you to learn by solving problems with others. So, here's lesson number one, which has nothing to do with rivers. When she says, "Get into groups," you better move fast or you'll be a leftover and get placed in a group where the kids will look at you like you're bringing the plague. Case in point: I was looking for a pen when she gave the word this morning. I stood there feeling like an orphan until Ms. Tannenbaum walked me over to Edna's bunch and said I was joining them, even though the group was already full.

"Have you even said hello to your buddy, Merci?" Edna whispers as Ms. Tannenbaum goes over the scoring rubric. "It's Friday. You should have done it by now, you know. Miss McDaniels said that we have to check in every week, remember? You're going to get in trouble."

"Shh."

"Just trying to help," she says.

"Girls, is there something you want to share?" Ms. Tannenbaum stares at us from the front of the room.

"No, miss." I give Edna a sharp look. How can I possibly pay attention with all her yapping?

Of all my classes, this is the one I most wish I didn't have with Edna. I've been looking forward to having Ms. Tannenbaum since Roli was in her class all those years ago. Her big claim to fame is the Great Tomb Project. Every year, her whole classroom and the surrounding hall are turned into a life-size walk-in tomb. All semester, you work on building it, and then your parents come to see. It gets in the newspaper and everything. But now I don't know how much fun it will be with Miss Boss-of-the-Universe Edna around.

"I encourage you to dig deep. Be daring in your thinking!" Ms. Tannenbaum says.

About maps?

"Be responsive to one another as you plan your projects," she says. "Your group skills will be reflected in the grading."

A groan rises, but she doesn't bat an eye.

I check over her point system. Factual accuracy: 60 points. Originality: 20. Cooperation: 20.

"If there are no more questions, you may begin."

The girls in my group go back to whispering and giggling about Michael as Ms. Tannenbaum starts to roam the room. I glance over at him guiltily. It's true what Edna says. Not about his eyebrows, but about the fact that I haven't exactly said hello yet, even though we were supposed to. But how can I? If I hang around Michael, Edna will probably start in about how awkward it is. Or worse, she might start asking me a million questions about him. Besides, Michael Clark obviously doesn't need me to reach out. The boys in our class already seem to like him just fine. They talk to him as if he's been here his whole life instead of five measly days. He's that always-popular type. Or maybe they're scared of him. A kid that big can probably do some damage.

"Staring at your boyfriend again?" Edna asks.

"Quit it."

"Boyfriend?" Rachel's mouth drops open and her blue eyes get big. It's like she's going to pee her pants. "Are you going out with Michael Clark or something?" Rachel likes to be shocked by everything. *You got a B?* (Big eyes at you.) *You live in Greenacres?* (Hand over mouth.) But nothing thrills her more than love. Last year, when she saw two eighth-graders kissing behind the gym, I was sure she was going to spontaneously combust. She could barely catch her breath to tell us. I saw that same pair of lovebirds kissing behind a tree in the parking lot where Mami sometimes waits for us if we're staying after school. To me, it looked like they were sucking each other's faces off, like in a sci-fi movie. There were sound effects and everything. I wasn't sure either of them would survive. Honestly, it was scary.

"No, he is not my boyfriend," I say.

"Boyfriend?" Hannah sighs and makes a face. "My mom won't even let me go to the mall without her."

Edna gets a devilish look in her eyes. She balls up a sheet of paper and tosses it at Michael's table. She's a lousy shot, of course, so it misses him completely and hits Lena instead.

"Airmail?" Lena asks, opening it. "In invisible ink?"

"Oops," Edna says. "Michael!" she calls. "Merci needs to talk to you today."

"Stop," I say, pinching her.

"Ow!"

He looks up from his work and then over at us. It turns my blood to ice. Thankfully, the boys in his group are in no mood for Edna today. A few of them make ugly faces at us, just like the twins do to me at home. Then they turn away.

"How rude!" Edna calls out, giggling. "I hate you all." It's new this year, that giggle, and it definitely doesn't say *I hate you*. It's more like *look at me, look at me, look at me*. All I know is that it's going to be tough to listen to it all year. Maybe I'll invest in a pair of earplugs, like the ones Lolo uses when Abuela is watching novelas.

"Focus, scholars!" Ms. Tannenbaum calls out.

Edna taps the learning packet icon on her tablet and skims over the directions for the project. "OK, Merci, make a doc for notes. We'll start with supplies. Who's going to buy the clay?"

"Clay?" I ask.

"To make the relief map. Hello?"

Edna thinks so quickly. If she weren't annoying, it might actually be an asset.

"I'll get it," Rachel says.

I open a new file for our group, but I don't write anything under my heading for materials. A clay map is fine, but I have other ideas about how to make a map, too. Ms. Tannenbaum told us she wants us to use unusual supplies. Only yesterday, I helped Abuela straighten out her sewing room. It's like a treasure chest, since she throws nothing out. "Everything has more than one use in this world," she always says about even the smallest fastener or elastic band. How about all those things? We could use the green satin that was left over from a blouse. The coffee cans are filled with buttons of every color, too. The glassy ones that look like fish eyes could make a great river— and nobody else will have those.

"I have another idea," I say.

But no one is listening to me.

"Are you sure he's in sixth grade?" Hannah whispers, still staring at Michael. "Has he been left back or something? He's ginormous."

"Ask Merci," Jamie says. "She's his girlfriend, right, Edna?"

I give her a stony look. "His *Sunshine Buddy,* and I have no idea. Why do we have to use clay?"

"You have Michael Clark as your Sunshine Buddy?" Rachel's voice is practically a scream. The boys look over at us and scowl again.

Edna leans forward, smiling. "I know, weird. Anyway, he can't have been held back. We don't take dummies at Seaward. Duh."

Sure we do, I think.

"I can print out good fonts for the legend and stuff," Jamie says. Her dad owns a print and design shop.

"Perfect," Edna says. "Merci, are you taking notes or

what? We need them in the classwork folder at the end of the hour. Don't get us in trouble."

"Wait. Why am *I* the secretary?" I ask.

Edna squints her eyes in Michael's direction again. "His hair is long," she says suddenly.

Seventeen mentions and counting.

The others look over at him, unsure what to say. I sneak another peek. Michael's white-blond hair hangs over one eye as he works. It's thin hair, straight and shiny.

Just then, Ms. Tannenbaum, who has been circling the room, stops by our group. I look down at her feet. There's a tiny tattoo on her ankle, which Abuela would hate.

"I hear a lot of chatter back here, ladies. I trust it's productive?"

There's an uncomfortable pause. I push up my glasses and put an arm over my blank screen.

"We're all organized," Edna says, saving us. She tucks a strand of hair behind her ear and sits up taller. "We're making a clay map. Our group was just about to split up the readings."

Ms. Tannenbaum nods thoughtfully and tugs on one of her earrings. They're tiny metal mummies, I notice. She smells nice, too. Like laundry detergent and baby powder. "I like a decisive group," she says. "It's a sure sign of strength. But I wonder: Have you percolated properly?"

We stare at her blankly.

"Have you considered all the possibilities for your project or just the first one? Have you let your ideas bubble and froth properly?"

No one says anything at first, but I think I know what she means. It always takes me a while to think of how to do a project. So I take a chance. "I was thinking of maybe a collage-style map instead," I say quietly.

Ms. Tannenbaum's eyebrows shoot up. "Ah," she says.

"We can use fabric scraps and buttons," I continue, making sure I don't meet Edna's eye and lose my nerve. "I can get lots of that stuff for free."

"That's a very interesting concept," Ms. Tannenbaum says, smiling. Her teeth have a little space between them in front. "Recycling materials for another purpose. Very timely. What do the rest of you think?" Her blue eyes dart around hopefully.

Think?

Poor Ms. Tannenbaum. All these years teaching and she still doesn't know that *thinking* is the trouble with groups. Sometimes it's not allowed, especially if somebody like Edna is around.

Still, a tiny balloon of hope fills my chest as I look

around at the others. Ms. Tannenbaum might make them brave. She has a picture of herself on a misty footbridge in Peru. She went to the Canary Islands to learn how they talk in whistles in the mountains. She went to Africa to help protect gorillas. She's basically a courage machine in every way.

"The buttons are swirly, like water," I add.

Ms. Tannenbaum smiles again and waits patiently in the silence that lingers. If it bothers her that we're not speaking, she doesn't show it. Finally, she folds her hands.

"Over the years, I've noticed that developing ideas usually requires some time. Sometimes you have to mull things over for a bit to get what you're really after."

Edna and the others keep staring at her like dead fish.

"Here's a thought. Why don't you get started on the readings this weekend and think about the materials for the map on Monday? It isn't due for a while."

She walks away to the next group, leaving her sweet smell lingering.

"That's just great," Edna whispers, clearly annoyed. "My family has plans this weekend. Can't we just vote now and get it done?"

"But—"

She cuts me off. "It's just a map, Merci. What's the big deal? And it's the only fair way to decide anyway." She looks around at us. "All those in favor of buttons for water, raise your hands."

I lift my hand and look across the table at Hannah, Jamie, and Rachel. Hannah starts to join me, but she ends up waving her palm in a so-so sign and shrugs.

"Clay?"

Sure enough, Edna's mojo has worked like a charm. Rachel's, Jamie's, and Edna's hands shoot up. "Three to one and a half," she says.

"But it's not original." Even as I say it, I can hear the pleading in my voice, and I hate myself for it.

"Cooperation," Jamie says pointedly.

"No offense, but buttons are *not* that original," Edna says. "They're on, like, everything!" She points at my blouse. "See?"

For a second I think of backing down. Edna has all As, all the time, after all. But then I think of Papi. He's not school-smart, but nobody has better ideas about how to paint things. So I use a sales skill that Abuela has perfected. She claims it's why she has never lost an argument with any of her clients over what she should sew for them. Give your idea calmly, she says, and find somebody else to say it's brilliant. Lolo is usually the one for that job.

"It's how we're *using* them that's different, Edna," I say. "How about buttons just for the water?" I look to Hannah, since Lolo isn't around. She likes pizzazz. She wears shimmery clips in her hair every day. "Some bling is always good, right?" I say.

Hannah looks to Edna. "It sounds kind of nice," she says softly. "What's the harm in compromising?"

Edna sighs and rolls her eyes. "Fine. Merci can bring the dumb buttons." She gathers her things and drags her desk back to its place, grumbling about how I'm a pain. I hurry up and finish our group notes before the bell.

The midday sun feels bright enough to melt my eyes when I step outside after class. I walk along to math, trying to feel better. I kick a piece of balled-up loose-leaf paper as if it's a soccer ball, working on swiveling my feet around the front as I go.

It's not a big deal, I tell myself. *And I won, sort of, didn't I?* But somehow it still feels as though I did something wrong with the girls in my group. Maybe I *am* a pain. Or maybe buttons are stupid. Or maybe I'm stupid. If I had gone along, it would have been easier, and Edna wouldn't be mad. And who really cares about a dumb map, anyway?

The lower-school kids have just had lunch, and now they're outside playing in the small field, just the way we used to in fifth grade. Miss Miller is sitting on the bench reading her book, the way she always did when we were in her class. I pause for a second to watch her new kids, wishing that I could take a few pitches in kickball instead of having to figure out equations for the next hour or remember my locker combination or even get to class before the bell rings. Last year took some getting used to, but I always fit in at recess—more than Edna, who was a total klutz. I would kick that red ball far into the outfield: hard, and on-target. It's all that practice I get, I suppose. Papi lets me sub on his fútbol team in the last quarter sometimes. You'd think grown men might go easy on me, but the only break they give me is not tackling, which Papi made absolutely off-limits. Anyway, those kicks are why I'm always picked first for a team in gym and why I never have to wait and wait, pretending it doesn't bother me not to hear my name called.

But then all that changed last spring when some of the girls just stopped standing up when we picked teams. Instead, they wandered off and watched from the stands, whispering behind their hands while I rounded the bases, arms pumping.

"You have to grow up, Merci," Edna told me when I sat next to her in class one afternoon, still sweaty from the game.

I take the long way around to class, hoping I might be able to peek in at Roli in the science lab, which is on the way. He hates when I do that—especially if I make a funny face at him against the windows. But sometimes I just want to see him, even if I don't tell him so.

He's not there, so I walk by *Sierpiński Sonnet,* a kind of spooky sculpture made of white resin. To me it looks like a big piece of cauliflower with the top hacked off. But last summer, Roli showed me a secret—and why he loves it almost as much as he adores the science lab. We were taking a break from painting the gym. He brought me and Papi here and told me to climb on his shoulders so I could look at the sculpture from above. That's where you could see that the canopy formed triangles, lots and lots of triangles, one inside the other. Everything was a pattern. "They're fractals," he said, holding me as I stood on his shoulders like a cheerleader. "Triangles that repeat in smaller and smaller versions, forever."

I stare at the lopped-off branches for a while, realizing that I'm still too short to see the magic from down here. But then I notice someone on the other side through the spaces. The face is so pale that it's camouflaged almost perfectly.

Standing on the other side is Michael Clark, all by himself.

"That girl Edna said you need to ask me something," he says. "What is it?"

My mouth goes dry. For a second, I'm not even sure he's talking to me, so I turn around to be sure he doesn't mean someone else.

"Oh. Nothing really," I say. I hope no one is watching us. I don't want to hear Edna teasing me about him being my boyfriend anymore.

"Oh." His bushy brows knit together. (Curses on Edna for making me notice them!)

I'm sure my eye is pulling, so I push up my glasses and blurt it out. "It's just that I'm your Sunshine Buddy. They assigned me to you in the office."

He cocks his head. "My what?"

"Sunshine Buddy. It's sort of a temporary friend that the school gives you, if you're new."

"Oh," he says, blushing.

"It's kind of dumb," I say.

I blink hard and shrug. I could tell him I want nothing to do with it, but that might hurt his feelings. And I can't exactly say that I'm working off my scholarship debt, either. Or that I'd rather play soccer than be his pal.

"It's not *that* bad," I say.

Then the warning bell rings. Dr. Newman, who's out roaming the halls, starts to wave people to class.

"I know you don't need a buddy," I tell him. "Everybody

likes you, obviously." My face feels like it's on fire as I say it, and my tongue feels twice as thick. "The boys, I mean."

Then, because Dr. Newman is heading our way, I hurry off to class.

That afternoon, Miss McDaniels looks up at me from behind the vase of flowers. It's the end of the day, and most of the kids have gone home already. The only one left in the office besides her is a lady waiting to see Dr. Newman. Miss McDaniels stops clipping a few browned flowers when I come in.

"At last," she says, turning to me. "I was starting to wonder." She puts the scissors away in her desk drawer and opens a file on her computer's desktop marked "Sunshine Buddies." Even from here, I can see an open space in the column next to my name. I guess I'm the very last one to submit a progress report this week.

"And how is it going with your buddy?" she asks.

"Michael Clark is doing just fine," I say carefully. "He's already friends with the boys. Maybe he'd like a boy as his buddy," I say, trying to give her the hint.

But no. She just looks at me over her glasses. "You've made initial contact? You've been friendly and welcoming?"

I pull out my form and hand it to her quickly. It took

some creative thinking to fill it out. I look over my shoulder, like someone might be listening to me about to lie.

"Well . . . we stopped at the Sierpiński today," I tell her.

"Ah. Very good." She types in a note and closes the file. "I'm sure more things will come."

I stand there in silence, my eyes glued to the new flat-screen monitors that are bolted near her desk. It's a security system like something out of a NASA control room. I watch as random kids and parents walk in and out of view, unaware, they're being watched.

Miss McDaniels glances over her shoulder and then frowns a little. "Is there something more?" she asks.

I wonder if I'm wasting valuable time. That's another thing Miss McDaniels doesn't like. Every minute of her workday seems precious. But she did say we'd "revisit" this arrangement, didn't she?

"It's just . . . well, are you sure Michael Clark even wants a buddy?" I ask. "He seems kind of happy already. No sense messing with success, is there?"

She looks at me until my eye starts to quiver. "Everyone new to Seaward Pines Academy gets a buddy. It's policy — not to mention good manners."

With that, she stands up and turns to the lady who's still waiting on the cushy sofa for our head of school. "Dr. Newman will see you now, ma'am. Follow me."

I watch them go through the fancy wooden doors. What a kid wants is not part of the formula, as usual, not here and not anywhere.

I look up at the camera that's mounted near the ceiling and stick out my tongue. Then I turn and let myself out.

CHAPTER 6

I DON'T KNOW HOW IT HAPPENS.

One minute, Lolo and I are pedaling home from El Caribe on the shady side of the street, and the next minute he's gone.

At first I don't even notice that he's disappeared because I'm caught up in my latest story.

" . . . and then she said, 'OK, Merci can bring her dumb buttons,' like she was the queen doing me a favor. Can you believe it? She said I was a pain."

As usual, we've taken the long way home so we can catch up without anybody listening to our conversation or telling us what chore we have on our list that day. But when he doesn't say anything, I look over my shoulder.

That's when I see him sprawled on the street.

"Lolo!" I toss down my bike and race back to him. "What happened? Are you all right?"

He looks just as stunned as I am as he tries to untangle himself from his bike. In all the years we've been riding, he's never fallen. In fact, Lolo's the one who taught all of us to ride—including Papi and Tía Inés when they were little. He showed me how to balance with no hands, fix a slipped chain, and lube the gears to keep things smooth.

A trickle of blood drips from his eyebrow where his new glasses have dug in. They're crooked now, and the lenses are all scraped. Pebbles are stuck against his bloody palm, too.

"It's nothing, nothing." He winces and gets to his knees. "I hit a sandy patch, that's all. The tires are getting old on this thing."

I look around for the skid, but there's none. There's no sand anywhere, either. In fact, there's just the same little buckles in the sidewalk that we've been riding over every Sunday for as long as I can remember.

I help him get to his feet, remembering sheepishly that he did look a little wobbly this morning as we pushed out of the driveway. I should have paid more attention, but Lolo never has so much as a cold. Plus, he's always been a sports nut, just like me. Baseball, swimming, biking—he does it all.

All the pastries we bought at El Caribe are strewn on the ground.

"Let's pick these things up before the ants start feasting," Lolo says. "We might be able to salvage some if we hurry."

Lolo and I always go to El Caribe on Sunday mornings to get bread and desserts for later. It's the one chore I don't mind because it's our private time together. We leave the house when the sky is still pink, and we get there at seven a.m., when Tía Inés is pulling out the first loaves from the oven. We buy them for our Sunday dinner, which is the one time every week that we all eat together. It's not technically dinner, though. It's almuerzo cena, which I think should be called *lunner* or *dinch,* because we eat at around three o'clock—and just have a snack before bed.

It's not Sunday dinner without the bread and desserts, though. There is no way we can show up empty-handed without Abuela yelling.

I dust the end of one of the loaves. Luckily, the second loaf stayed in its paper wrapper and is just fine.

Lolo picks up the box of cookies and peeks inside. "A few are broken, but it's not a total catastrophe. We'll stick the bad ones on the bottom before Abuela can see."

"We should clean that cut up, though," I tell him. Blood has made a long drip along his cheek. I unhook the water bottle from my bike's frame and aim the nozzle at him. "Ready?"

He pockets his mangled glasses and scrunches his face. "Fire."

I squirt him until we're both laughing. Then we walk back down the street to get my bike. Lolo's shirt is soaked, so I point at the corner bus stop. "Why don't we rest on that bench while you dry off?" I say. "I'll check your tires."

Lolo sits down while I get to work. I go over absolutely everything, but the bike looks perfect — for a relic. "The tires look OK to me," I tell him. "You've got plenty of tread."

"Mmmmm," he says, ignoring me. He rummages inside the box of cookies and takes out a broken one. "I bet a little sugar will give me a lift. Want one?"

I join him on the bench, and together we watch the early traffic go by for a little while as we eat. Hardly anybody is out at this hour, so it still feels quiet, with just the sound of our munching on the broken treats.

"Do you think Edna is right about me? Am I a pain? You can tell me the truth." I hate the way the words sound aloud. All I can think of are the times when the twins are being impossible. *You're such pains,* I tell them. But something about how Edna talks to me always makes me feel like I'm not as good as she is, like there's something wrong with me.

Lolo wipes the crumbs from his lips. "A pain! That's ridiculous," he says. "When it comes to people, sometimes it's a matter of taste, like these cookies. We like some more than others. That's not bad. It's just human."

I give that some thought and sigh. "I thought sixth grade would be different, Lolo. I really wanted it to be fun, better than fifth grade, anyway. But there are all these classes to keep track of now. Miss Miller told us that switching classes would be fun, that it meant that we'd meet more people. I think she lied. I see Edna all the time, and she's no nicer than last year."

He nods, thinking. "Well, it's early yet, preciosa. Let's see what happens."

We sit there for a long time until the Sunday-schedule bus comes into view. "We should go, or he'll stop to pick us up," I say.

I straddle my seat, but Lolo doesn't get back on his bike. Instead, he stands alongside it and grabs the handlebars.

"Why don't *you* ride for now, preciosa?" he says. "I'm going to walk mine the rest of the way and enjoy the scenery."

I give him a doubtful look. "The scenery of strip malls? Are you sure you're OK?"

"I tell you, I'm fine. I can't help it if my bones aren't made of rubber like yours. Now let's go. I promised the twins we'd color."

So I pedal backward and practice riding no-hands, and I make big figure eights like a circus clown to keep slow pace with him as we go.

When we finally get to our carport, he leans his bike against the house and puts his big palm on my head.

"Óyeme. Do not tell Abuela that I fell," he whispers. "Not a word of this at dinner, you understand? Not to anyone."

"Why not?" I'm thinking of our family rule about no secrets.

"You know how Abuela worries," he says. "We won't hear the end of it. And what if she decides that we can't ride our bikes on Sunday anymore?"

The thought of not riding with Lolo suddenly makes me sad. And it's true. Abuela can make us crazy with her fears.

So I pretend to lock my lips and toss the key.

"Thank you, Merci. I can always count on you."

He pats my cheek and goes inside. I watch him through the window as he opens the pastry boxes on the counter. I wonder for a minute about his fall and not telling Abuela. It doesn't feel right. But then Lolo looks up and smiles at me, the same as always, and the thought vanishes. He waves and then turns back to arranging the prettiest cookies on top.

CHAPTER 7

ROLI PIPES UP FIRST, naturally, and I wish I were closer so I could kick him hard under the table.

"Whoa! That's some shiner." The bump near Lolo's eye has become a purple bruise by dinnertime. It makes him look like a raccoon. "Did you go a few rounds in a boxing ring?"

"Come close and I'll show you," Lolo says from the head of the table. He air-jabs a couple of times, which sets the twins off like crazed luchadores. They shake their fists and growl until Tía Inés hushes them.

"Boys! We're at the table!"

Abuela just clicks her tongue as she sits down next to me. "El viejo opened one of the kitchen cabinets and hit himself in the face this morning," she says. "I want you to check the hinges later, Enrique."

"I'll take a look after we eat," Papi says. "The hinge is probably too tight."

"No te molestes," Lolo tells him calmly. "I already fixed it." He points at the chicken chunks. "Send those this way, por favor, Inés."

My eye starts to tug. It's one thing to keep a secret. But Lolo is telling a lie, and it makes it feel as though mice are running around in my stomach.

"The cabinet, huh?" Tía Inés hands over the platter and arches her brow the way she does when she's interrogating the twins. There's a quiet I don't like, and a long look between her and Papi, but in the end, she lets it go.

Mami touches my shoulder, and it makes me jump. "Merci?" She holds out the basket of sliced bread, waiting. "Don't you want some? It's your favorite."

I stare at the loaves we spilled onto the street, searching for even the tiniest speck of dirt we might have missed. But it all looks fine.

"Thanks," I say, and then, my hands a little jittery, I pass it down.

Papi's phone rings as Mami and Tía are clearing the table. I'm in Abuela's sewing room, picking out green and blue buttons for Ms. Tannenbaum's map.

"Hombre, ¿qué me dices?" he says. I can hear him loud and clear in the next room. Already I know it's Simón, who paints for him occasionally and who lives in Davie. They always say hello to each other like that. So I walk into the living room to listen. Papi's face brightens, so I'm hoping it's good news.

Sure enough.

There's an open field for a fútbol game if we don't mind the drive. And best of all, they'll be playing against Papi's arch nemesis, Manny Cruz.

"We'll be there by six," Papi says, hanging up. He looks at me and wiggles his eyebrows.

"Yes!" I say.

I follow him to the kitchen. "I've got the new moves down, Papi," I tell him. "You'll see." All summer, he helped me work on how I pivot and stall. Now I can clamp a ball in my instep and turn so fast that no one will be able to keep up.

Mami isn't quite as excited about what we have planned.

"But it's a school night, Enrique, and it will take an

hour to get there," Mami says as she does the dishes at Abuela's sink. "Merci should be doing her schoolwork, not out playing with a bunch of grown men." She turns to me. "Don't you have a map you're working on?"

I hold up the bag of buttons. "I just had to bring supplies. We're building it in class. And I'm done with all the rest of my homework," I say.

"I haven't checked it," she says.

"Mami, I'm in the sixth grade," I tell her. "You don't have to check everything anymore."

She looks at Papi, who shrugs and smiles at her. "The guys always take it easy when I put her in," he says—to which I make a face. I happen to be able to dribble past some of his friends with no problem, especially the ones who smoke. If anything, I'm easy on *them*.

"Come on, Mami," I say. "I need the practice for try-outs for the school team this year."

Mami gives me a long look and sighs before she goes back to scrubbing the grease off a pot.

Papi slips behind her and kisses her cheek. "You could pack up the cooler with some drinks and come watch," he adds. "Your man is about to exact revenge on the enemy, you know."

Mami looks up at the sky. "Can't we let this grudge go?" She turns around and puts her sudsy hands on his shoulders. "Maybe we could watch TV together as a family instead?"

Alarm bells sound in my head. At dinner, Roli and Mami were talking about a "fascinating" documentary on HeLa cells that help cure cancer. Who wants to watch something so boring?

"Never," Papi says. "In some villages, blood has run like rivers for lesser offenses."

So, here's the history.

Manny Cruz owns Cruz & Company Plumbing over on Federal Highway. He and Papi went to high school together back in the day, but after that, Manny went to a trade school and found his calling in clogged drainage. Now he's got shops in Dade, Broward, and Palm Beach counties. The bad blood isn't because Manny is a big shot. In fact, Papi gives him props for that. No. It's because Manny poached two of Papi's best employees a few years ago by offering to pay them more. To this day, there's nothing more satisfying to Papi than stomping Manny's team in a friendly game of fútbol.

Tía Inés walks into the kitchen with the last of the drinking glasses.

"Did I hear you talking to Simón on the phone?" She dumps everything into the soapy water and turns to Papi.

He gives her a knowing look. Whenever Simón shows

up at the house to work as part of Papi's crew, Tía wanders into the yard, hair combed and smelling nice, to say ¿hola, qué tal? She comes to soccer games when he's playing, too, even though she's fuzzy on the rules of the game.

"What?" she says. "It's a simple question."

"We've got our clásico with our arch rivals in Davie tonight," Papi says.

"Way down there?" Tía says, disappointed. "I can't go. The twins need to get to bed early."

"Exactly," Mami says, raising an eyebrow at Papi. "It's a school night."

Tía glances at the platters of leftovers on the counter. "Let me send some food at least. We have plenty here."

"We're playing *soccer*, Inés, not picnicking with our sweethearts," Papi says.

Tía puts her hands on her hips. "I'm being kind, Enrique. Simón has no family here, remember?"

It's true. Simón shares an apartment with housemates he met on a job. His parents and younger brothers are all in El Salvador, and he misses them. Maybe that's why he always likes to say that if he had a little sister, it would be me.

"Family, no, but maybe he has some admirers?" Papi teases.

She turns bright red and pulls open the drawer where Abuela keeps the foil and plastic containers. "Don't start."

"Wait two minutes, Papi," I say. "I just have to get my shin guards."

"I'll have her home by ten," Papi tells Mami, following me to the back door.

"In one piece, please, señor," she says.

What I love about driving to soccer games with Papi is that it puts him in a good mood. I can tell because he whistles just like Lolo does when he's in the garden. He doesn't look tired or grouse about fussy customers or talk on the phone to remind someone politely to pay him for a job he's done. His face relaxes and he seems fun. Plus, we both like Davie. It feels like the countryside down here even though we're still in crowded South Florida. There are horses and cows. People sell produce at roadside stands. Occasionally, you hear a peacock screech for no good reason. Papi says that it reminds him of the few memories he has of when he was little in Cuba.

Our van creaks as we drive along the small roads. I lean my head out the window as he turns down the last dirt lane. Up ahead, a dozen or so men have gathered. I recognize a lot of them because they work shifts for Papi when he can hire them. Sometimes he gives them work when he can't afford it. "They needed the cash," he tells Mami when she's paying the bills and worries that there's not enough in the bank to cover them. He'll say they have kids or rent due or something else. Papi always tries to help them with other problems, too, like where to sign up for an English class if they need it, or how to get a license so they can drive to their jobs. Stuff like that.

Manny's guys are also gathering. They're slipping on cleats and passing along the bug spray. The mosquitoes are ruthless once we start to sweat. They'll swarm over our heads and buzz in our ears.

Simón spots Papi and walks over to his window. "Pérez called to say he can't make it. We've got no keeper tonight, hermano."

Papi groans. He hates tending the net. He'd rather be a striker, moving fast up and down the field, heart pounding.

"We'll rotate, then," Papi says. "Go see who's willing."

"Hi, Simón," I say, leaning over Papi.

"Merci!"

I hand him the bag that's loaded with food.

"What's this?" he asks.

"Tía sent you some dinner," I say, shrugging.

Simón's eyes dart to Papi before he peeks inside. He

barely hides a smile as he takes a long, deep whiff. "I'll have to text her to thank her," he says. Then he gives Papi a shy look. "Let me put this in the car, and then I'll be back."

"Why don't you let me play keeper?" I say as we watch Simón jog off. "I don't mind."

Papi stops me before I can go on. "Forget it, your mother would kill us both." He reaches under his seat in search of his banged-up cleats.

"She wouldn't have to know."

I say it softly, testing the sound of my idea on the air. For a second, I'm not even sure I've dared to say it out loud.

Papi stops what he's doing and looks over at me, surprised.

"What did you say?"

I don't repeat it.

But he heard me. "You'd want me to lie to your mother?"

"Not a *lie*," I say. "Just . . ."

The air is sticky in the van now that we're not moving. He looks at me for a long time, thinking. It's weird. Papi, who is strong about everything, suddenly seems unsure.

"Listen," he says finally, "that's not the way we should

do things. What would your mother think if she heard you? We shouldn't hide things, Mercedes. You know that, right? We tell each other the truth in this family. Right?"

He only uses my whole name when he's being serious. The mice in my stomach are back. It's not that easy, I want to say. I think of Lolo trying to keep our Sunday bike rides safe. Sometimes you have no choice but to keep things hidden. Like now.

"Yes," I say.

I slide out of the van and grab my lucky ball from the back and warm up while Papi says hello to his friends, slapping their backs and asking about their families. I toss the ball high in the air and capture it in my feet. Then I start on my pancake skills. *Fwack, fwack, fwack, fwack!* I juggle from one foot to the other. Then I pop the ball high up, swivel, and end with my ankle flat to the ground. The ball bounces against it and I keep dribbling.

A few of our guys applaud and whistle as they watch.

"So, who's tending the onion bag first?" Papi says. Somebody's hand goes up.

In a few minutes, he seems to forget all about our conversation.

"Suárez, hermano." Manny steps forward with a hand outstretched. He's a short man with a pinkie ring, muscled arms, and a big smile. He's wearing pricey cleats, I notice:

the Nike Hypervenom Phantom IIs. His teammates have already pulled on red scrimmage pinnies. *Cruz Plumbing* is stenciled on the back. "Ready to lose?"

The guys around us hoot. Papi closes his bear paw on Manny and gives him a firm handshake. "We'll see what you're made of," he says.

Manny motions with his chin. "Your girl is playing tonight?"

"Merci will be in later," Papi says. "I didn't want to demoralize you too early in the game."

Manny throws back his head and laughs.

I blow a bubble with my chewing gum and give him a cold stare as everyone takes positions.

It's a tough game.

For most of it, I sit on a cooler along the sidelines and snap as many action shots as I can, especially when Papi makes a sweet goal, faking around one of Manny's center-backs and launching a bullet into the net.

"Goooooooooooooooool," I shout from the sidelines.

But Manny's guys know what they're doing, especially his forwards, and they can cover a lot of ground fast. They score two goals in a row as revenge.

I've been chewing my nails to nubs all night when Papi finally trots over.

"You ready, Merci?" Papi asks. He's out of breath and smeared with dirt.

"Ready."

Papi whistles to a guy named José, and I'm in as a fullback.

There are no fancy feet anymore, just straight-up speed and endurance, which is what I have on these guys. One of Manny's strikers sprints near me, but he dodges before I can take the ball, and he shoots. For a second, I think it's the third goal, but luckily Simón stops it at the box and clears the ball.

I'm ready the next time the guy dribbles my way. This time, I'm quick with the pressure, determined to steal and start a counterattack. I speed toward him, then slow down just in time to confuse him on my approach. Arms wide, I angle myself to keep him from getting past, and it works. I snatch the ball with my heel, pivot, and pop it forward. Then I start up the field.

I cross-pass to Papi, who's closer to the goal, but as he moves to the corner, he's covered quickly. So he sends it back again. I trap the ball with my stomach, then knee. In a flash, I see that I've got the perfect shot.

It all happens in seconds, but somehow time slows down and everything disappears around me, even the yelling. I see it clearly. There's space to the left of the keeper, calling my name. So I fake to the right, where I see Manny coming to help cover the goal. Papi's on the move, too, his eyes on me in case he has to assist.

At the last second, I turn my hips and shoot hard with my left instep.

The ball sails into the net, but before I can throw my arms up, I see Papi and Manny crash like two Mack trucks. They fall with heavy grunts in the grass.

We all run over.

"I'm fine. I'm fine," Manny says, but it's hard to believe him. He looks woozy as he gets to his knees. His lip is split wide open, and it's dripping blood to his cheek and shirt. Papi is still on the ground holding his cheek. There's a tiny cut, but a bump is already swelling.

"You OK, Papi?" I ask.

"Gooooooooooooool," he says, winking up at me.

I flash him my biggest smile.

"I'll get the first-aid kit," I say.

It's way past ten when we finally climb back into the van and drive back down the dirt path. Papi's got a huge bump on his chin from where he ran into Manny. My legs are wobbly, and the front seat smells of bug spray and our sweat as we bump along the deep rut in the road, but I feel so good and tired here with Papi. I don't even care that Mami is probably going to be mad that we're back so late. What could we do? We had to ice Manny's face and get him patched up before we went home. Manny's lip gushed so much that I got queasy just looking at it. Papi's the one who cleaned it out and gave him ice, told him he might need a stitch.

"You were nice to help him up, even though he's your enemy," I tell Papi. The first-aid kit is still open in my lap; I've been trying to fit the packets of gauze and rolls of tape back in place before shutting it in the glove compartment again. The bumps and sway in the van are making it tough.

Papi takes a swig of water. "Anybody would do the same. Anyway, Cruz and I aren't really enemies, Merci. We're in business, each of us trying to get by, that's all."

I give him a look. "He stole your guys."

He shrugs. "Nobody forced them to go work for him. They wanted jobs where they could earn the most money. Who can blame them?" He drains his water bottle and crushes it in his hand before tossing it to the back. "Cruz has never been my favorite person, I'll give you that. But an enemy? There's no sense in having those if we can help it."

I finish jamming the supplies in the box and close the metal box back inside. Then I grab my phone off the floorboard.

"What are you doing?" Papi asks when the flash on my camera goes off a couple of seconds later.

"Hang on." I check the shot. Sweat drips along the side of Papi's face. His beard is stubbly. But his eyes look bright and shiny. With a few taps, I make the colors pop with a filter and adjust the lighting, too.

"Not bad, right?" I hold it out to show him. "You look sort of fierce, Papi."

"Fierce, huh?" he says, chuckling. He reaches over and squeezes my head in his palm, the way he used to when I was little.

Then we turn onto the highway for home.

CHAPTER 8

BY THE TIME I PRIED open my eyes, Roli was already pulling into Seaward. Mami had no sympathy as she shook me awake this morning. Papi and I got home after midnight, and boy was she mad, even when we told her about my perfect goal shot, arced just right. "The goal you need to be thinking about is doing well in school, Merci," she snapped.

I can't worry about that too much, though. My bigger problem is figuring out some way to be a Sunshine Buddy this week until Miss McDaniels cuts me loose. She sent us all friendly e-mail reminders to turn in our weekly reports on time.

Roli was absolutely no help in figuring out a plan, either. "You're my older brother. You have absolutely no ideas for me?"

"Bring the kid by the science lab," he offered as we walked from the drop-off loop. "We're launching a fascinating study of the energy usage here at Seaward."

Roli. He means well. But what can you really expect from someone who asks for chemistry kits and brain models for Christmas?

No, I am not going to torture Michael Clark with Roli's science lab, but I need *something* to prove to Miss McDaniels that I did try and that it's just not the right job for me. But by the time I get to social studies, I still have no ideas. Leave it to Edna to make me feel worse.

"I took Alexa for ice cream after school last week, and she's going to eat lunch with us today. Oh, and I might sign us up to do the food drive, too," she says while we glue the buttons on our map.

Jamie looks up and pouts. "I thought you and I were doing the food drive."

"Can you hurry, please?" I tell Edna. "The bell is going to ring soon and we have to hand this in." She's glued down maybe four buttons while the rest of us have worked at full speed. I have Elmer's glue crusted under my nails.

"What's your problem?" Edna says. "Don't like your Sunshine Buddy?"

I'll admit that it bugs me to see Edna is being a better buddy than I am. But it's hard to even get near Michael without causing a scene — even at lunch. It's like our class broke into two pieces and we floated apart, the girls one way and the boys another. The girls sit at a long lunch table near the windows and the boys have a big round table of their own across the room.

Our group finishes the map just as the bell rings.

"I have to meet Alexa," Edna says, and she runs off without helping to clean up a single thing.

By the time I get to the lunchroom, my stomach is making embarrassing noises. I'm just hoping Mami remembered to add enough jelly to my sandwich, despite her war on sugar, which Abuela calls downright anti-Cuban. She says Mami reads too much for her own good, especially food labels. Mami flat-out refuses to pay for the lunch plan, which she says isn't healthy enough — *and* too expensive. So I am usually stuck with a brown bag and her healthy sandwiches instead of sinking my teeth into the meal of the day made by the school chef.

As soon as I step into the lunchroom, I can smell the

tortilla soup in the air. Today's dessert? Key lime pie, my favorite. The girls look up from their trays and smile as I take a seat. My stomach lets out another astonishing gurgle. "Heeeey," I say to mask it.

Luckily Edna doesn't take a breath from her blabbing. You can learn a lot if you listen. That's how we all know, for instance, that Mr. Patchett is dating Ms. Lowe, who teaches fourth grade. (She saw them kiss in Mr. Patchett's car, news that nearly made Rachel faint.) Today's big story is especially interesting. It's about the junior soccer team. No one at the table is trying out. I can't believe my ears.

"I hate to sweat," Edna says.

"But it's a crucial bodily function," I say. "I'm pretty sure it was in the health textbook — the part about why we should use deodorant."

"Gross," she says.

"Very," Jamie adds.

Alexa says that she's not going to try out either, but only because she already plays on a travel league that takes her all the way to Orlando and Tallahassee for tournaments. Hannah's mom only lets her play one sport a year, and she's playing basketball in the winter.

"Are you trying out?" Alexa asks.

I think of the consent form that's still under the frog

magnet on our refrigerator. Mami keeps forgetting to sign it, even though I remind her every day.

"Absolutely."

"Sixth-graders hardly ever make it," Edna says. "No offense."

I take a bite of my sandwich, thinking about the game against Manny's team last night. Simón told me I feint and cross over almost like a FIFA pro.

I glance across the room at the boys' table now. Even sitting down, Michael Clark is taller than almost everybody around him. They make them moose-size in Minnesota, that's for sure. I wonder if he's going to be on a team this year? If we were sitting at the same table, I'd just ask, no big deal. But now it takes a special trip.

"Who wants my dessert?" Edna asks, pushing her pie away. No one makes a move.

I stare at the beautiful wedge of key lime pie and my mouth waters.

"I'll take it," I say. "No sense wasting it."

"Don't be greedy." She blocks my hand. "Maybe my buddy wants it?"

She looks sweetly at Alexa, who says, "Oh no, that's fine. You can have it, Merci."

Edna pushes it toward me. Suddenly I feel funny

digging in as she watches. If it weren't for the graham cracker crust, I might not.

But this is key lime pie we're talking about, so I do. It's delicious.

"So. The new Iguanador movie opens downtown this weekend," Edna says. "My dad said I could go see it on Saturday night. Who wants to come?"

Iguanador Nation Rises! I've been dying to see that movie since the trailers came on TV. Dinosaurs and humans in a genetic splice become robots and take over the world. And of course, Jake Rodrigo, our hero, will save everyone from doom. I don't know if it's the pie or the thought of two hours of his face on the screen that makes me feel light-headed. My cheeks suddenly feel hot. All I can do to calm down is take another bite of pie.

Rachel wrinkles her nose. "But I don't like robot movies. They're boring."

"Boring?" I say, wiping my mouth. "Come *on.*"

"If we don't like it, we can leave and walk around," Edna says.

"If we *don't like it?*" I ask. Are these people nuts?

"What time is the matinee?" Hannah asks. "I have my piano lesson in the afternoon."

"*Not* a matinee," Edna says. She leans in and wiggles

her eyebrows. "We're in middle school now. We should go at night. We can be there until the ten o'clock curfew."

The table goes quiet. The theater downtown is one of those really big ones that looks like a street in Paris. The building has fake balconies and street lamps, and the ushers dress in black berets and striped shirts. It's across the street from a fancy restaurant that Mami likes. Last year, when Roli won the state science fair, we had a special dinner there. I ate twelve raviolis.

"Forget it. My mother will never let me go at night," Hannah says.

"Why not? What's the big deal?" Edna asks.

Nobody answers right away. I'm thinking back to the tequila bar that always draws a crowd down there and the older kids who walk around. Would Mami and Papi even let me go? I don't know. And yet, this is the sixth grade. When are we allowed to be on our own?

Hannah blushes. "She's psycho, I guess."

"Guys. Why don't we go bowling?" Rachel says.

Edna makes a puss. "Because, no offense, we aren't nine-year-olds, Rachel."

That ends that.

"I don't know . . ." Hannah says.

"If we *all* go, we'll be in a big group — she can't say no then," Edna continues.

"You don't know my mom. She'll want a whole army," Hannah says.

Edna gives that some thought. Then she turns to Jamie and grabs her by the hand. "Come with me."

We sit watching as they walk across the lunchroom. Edna has her shoulders pushed back and her nose high as she walks over. Jamie looks back at us a couple of times. She's picking nervously at a pimple on her neck as they stop at the boys' table.

Rachel covers her mouth. "Oh my *God!*"

"What's she doing?" Hannah asks.

"Who knows?" I say. But one thing is for sure. Edna is doing all the talking, and the boys are doing all the listening. Even Michael is hanging on her words. From way over here, I hear her giggle as she tucks her hair behind her ears and shifts her hips.

Mojo to a new level.

They come back to the table a few minutes later. Jamie looks like she wants to vomit, but Edna's eyes are bright with victory.

"We have our army," she says to Hannah.

"Huh?"

"The boys are coming, too." She looks around at all of us, as if she hasn't lost her marbles.

"The boys?" I don't even know what else to say. Wasn't

she just teasing me about Michael? Didn't she stop playing with the boys? Why are they suddenly coming along with us? In public?

"Don't be a baby, Merci. It's a seven p.m. show on Saturday. Just go home and ask."

"CityPlace by yourself at night? I don't think so, Merci," Mami says. "Those bars fill up with a rowdy bunch, especially on the weekend."

Mami shoos Tuerto off the kitchen table, where she's finishing up records for the patients she saw this week. I'm sitting across from her with a pot of dry beans, sifting for little rocks. It's the most pointless job ever. I have never found a single tooth-busting pebble.

"But we're not going to a bar," I say, swirling my fingers inside the pot. "We're going to the movies."

Papi turns around from the onion he's chopping and points at me with the blade. "You're not going. There was a shooting over there not too long ago. It was on the news, remember? Some kids were fighting."

"You can drop me off right at the entrance," I say.

"When's dinner?" Roli is at the kitchen door. He's been watching a show about face transplants in our room. It's how he relaxes, but geez. Even though he was wearing headphones, I had to leave because it was making me queasy.

"Half an hour," Papi tells him. "Did you drag out the trash? You forgot your grandparents' last time."

Roli salutes and opens the fridge.

"Everyone is going," I say. "It's going to be a big group. And besides, I'm supposed to be doing things with my Sunshine Buddy, which is kind of hard. This is perfect. He's going to be there."

Papi turns around slowly. "He?" His eyes bore into Mami.

She sighs and closes her laptop and looks at him. "Merci was chosen to be a buddy for a new student," she explains. "Michael Clark."

He frowns and turns back to the onions, and chops a little harder.

"What is the big deal about this happening at night? The only thing different is that there's no sunshine outside."

"So see it in the daytime, and we have no problem," Papi says.

"But that's not the plan. Everyone is going *at night*. Why can't I go?"

"Because I don't like it, that's why, and that's enough of a reason."

"Enrique," Mami says.

"Kids get out of hand, Ana. She's eleven. She has no

business wandering down there. Certainly not with boys."

The way he says *with boys* makes my face go hot. It's like the day when he put up the curtain to divide the room for Roli and me. He'd seen my training bra in a pile of dirty clothes on my bedroom floor and said it wasn't proper.

"Mami," I say. "The girls will call me a baby. And what am I supposed to tell Miss McDaniels when she asks me what I've done with my buddy?"

"You tell her you've done nothing because you're eleven," Papi says. "She can come see me if she has questions. ¿Qué se han creído?"

"Enrique," Mami says again. "What's the real harm if all the other girls are going? It's a big group."

There's a crack in the parent wall, so I decide to strike with lightning speed. "Please," I say. "I'm not in elementary school anymore, you know."

"Why don't we compromise?" Mami says finally. "What if Roli goes along, too? He's seventeen. He can have a passenger with him in the car until eleven p.m."

"Wait, what?" My brother bangs his head as he jerks up from inside the refrigerator. A cheese stick hangs from his lips. "You mean like a chaperone?"

"Not exactly. You can drive Merci," Mami says. "Sit

away from them in the theater and see the movie, too. You'll be around just in case."

Roli closes the refrigerator door and crosses his arms, appalled. "So you mean a spy chaperone for little kids. No, thank you. I have better things to do than see a movie with a bunch of sixth-graders."

"Like what?" I ask. "Bragging on your college applications?"

He gives me a death glare.

Papi shakes his head. "This is a bad idea, Ana. What if trouble breaks out down there?" His voice trails as he casts a long look at Roli. I've heard them talk to him before he takes the car. What to do if he's stopped by police, where not to be, how your hands never go into your pockets. It seems crazy since Roli is clearly of the pocket protector variety, even if he does like to listen to his music loud.

"You sound like Abuela," I say.

Papi gives me an ugly look. "Don't be a smart mouth."

Mami is quiet for a second. "We can't keep them in a bubble, mi amor," she finally says. "There's no way to protect them from absolutely everything, all the time."

Papi taps the knife on the cutting board, thinking. Finally, he gives a small nod. "Fine, but only if Roli goes, too."

My brother looks like he wants to strangle me, but fair is fair.

"After all the times I have been dragged to science fairs for you? Come on, Roli. It's *Iguanador Nation Rises*," I tell him. "You've been wanting to see it, too, and you know it." I punch him a little harder than I intend. "I'll buy your popcorn."

"There's a spot." I point at what feels like the very last parking space in the whole lot. It's Saturday—and Labor Day weekend—and CityPlace is more crowded than I've ever seen it in the daytime.

While Roli tries (and tries and tries) to pull in and straighten our car, I catch my reflection in the side mirror and check out Tía's handiwork. It's me, all right, but the girl looking back is different somehow. Tía lit up when Mami told her where I was heading. "Don't move," she said, and came back a few minutes later with a caddy filled with beauty products.

She rubbed Gotas de Brillo on the ends of my hair so it smells nice. Then she helped me pick the right shorts and high-tops. For once I didn't mind. I don't know anything about how to put outfits together or how to wear my hair, the way a lot of girls do, so it's a good thing that Tía has my back. "You're gorgeous," she told me when she finished. And for a quick second, I believed her.

Roli finally gives up maneuvering and cuts the engine. The parking job is a disaster. We're on a sharp angle, and we're crowding the car next to us, so I suck in my breath to shimmy out my door.

He grabs a Marlins cap from the dashboard and pulls it on low. He's wearing old shorts and a ratty T-shirt and flip-flops.

We walk down the steps to the street level and then he turns to me. "Listen up," he says, "I'm walking down to Bilal's house." That's another one of the senior science lab tutors. "Meet back here at ten."

I stand there, unsure. "Wait. You told Mami and Papi that you were going to see *Iguanador.* You're supposed to stay."

He glares at me. It's the same face I make when I'm stuck watching the twins. "I know what I said, but I'm *not* spending Saturday night with your little friends, Merci."

His words sting. First of all, I'm not so little. But what really makes me mad is that he definitely doesn't want to be seen with me.

"What if Mami calls and asks to talk to you?"

"Say I'm in the bathroom and text me."

"Roli," I say.

"Bilal lives a couple of blocks down Hibiscus," he says. "Text me if you need something. I can be here in two minutes."

Before I can argue any more, he disappears into the crowd.

CityPlace is alive with people crisscrossing the streets and waiting in lines outside the shops and restaurants. The air feels steamy with all these bodies around. A few cops are talking under one of the streetlights, too, their eyes scanning the loud group of kids that's near the corner. I think I even recognize the one who brought Lolo home.

I start walking, feeling a little nervous to be here by myself. Maybe it's because this place looks different at night, sparklier. But it might also be that I'm feeling a little guilty, too, now that Roli's gone. Another secret to keep. What's worse is that Papi was gathering his soccer gear when Roli and I left. Turns out that our team is playing Manny in a rematch tonight, and Manny is bringing his superstar son. I'm going to miss it.

"Have fun," Papi said, but his voice didn't sound like he meant it. He looked like I picked my friends over him, which maybe I did.

Up ahead by the entrance, I finally spot Hannah, which makes me feel better. She's all blinged up the way she likes in metallic high-tops. She's not looking too happy, though. There's a woman standing next to her, scoping out the scene like she's a member of the Secret Service. Sure enough, it's her mom.

"Hi, Hannah," I say.

"Oh good." She turns to the lady. "You can go now, Mom."

"Nice to meet you," her mother says, ignoring Hannah. "I'm Mrs. Kim."

"I'm Merci."

She looks me over, and I guess I pass her danger radar, because she turns to Hannah. "I'll be reading over there," she says, pointing to a café. "I have you on navigation locator in case—"

"*Mother.*" Hannah's teeth are practically grinding.

Her mom presses her lips to a line. "All right, all right. Just wait for the others before you go inside. And stay together." She walks across the street and takes a seat at one of the metal tables on the patio.

Hannah turns her back and rolls her eyes. "She's such a warden."

It doesn't take too long before everyone starts gathering. Rachel joins us first and says I look nice. Then a couple of the boys show up: Chase, who likes to play outfield so he can daydream, and David, who's wearing his T-shirt from the Wizarding World of Harry Potter at

Universal. He and Chase went this summer. I've been dying to go, but with our whole family, it's too expensive even with our Florida resident pass, so I ask him about it. At least we can talk about that for a while.

A little later, a van pulls up and Michael Clark hops out. Rachel is struck dumb midsentence. He's wearing tan shorts and a dark blue shirt. I peek in the car and notice that the woman behind the wheel is basically a duplicate of him with long hair and glasses.

"You have your phone?" she asks. When Michael raises it in her direction, she waves at us and pulls away into the long line of cars.

"So, was that your mom?" It's a dopey question, but an awkward quiet hangs over us now, and we need something to talk about.

"Yep,'" he says.

"Duh. It's not his dad," Rachel says, elbowing me.

Michael looks around. "So, is this where everybody comes to the movies?" he asks.

"Sort of," I say. Meaning, *I have no idea.* Mami still rents movies for us at the supermarket since it's cheap and our internet is slow.

Standing this close I realize that I only reach to Michael's shoulder. From here, I can also see that the

Florida sun is already working its magic on him. He's not the color of glue anymore, at least. There are bunches of freckles on his nose. If they connect, it might look like he has some pigment in him.

While we wait for the others, we all start talking about Iguanador and whether this one will be scary or just *meh*. David says the special effects are supposed to be better than the last one.

"Check this out." I show them my latest bitmoji—wearing an Iguanador uniform and weapons. Even my cartoon hair is wild, and I added a patch on my eye to look especially menacing. They all want one.

"How do I make it?" Michael asks, so I show him where to click on the app.

After a few minutes, it almost feels like last year at our old lunch table, only with no one telling us to hold down our voices or clear our trays.

I like it.

Finally, a familiar black SUV with tinted windows pulls up. The license plate says *FUT-ZEES*.

The door opens, and Edna and Jamie slide off the cream-colored leather seats. They have their hair in the same messy buns. Edna is carrying a purse and wearing lip gloss. Jamie's blue eyes are rimmed with eyeliner, and

I notice she's wearing makeup to cover her pimples. Her T-shirt says *#OBVIOUSLY*.

Dr. Santos leans over the steering wheel. A whiff of aftershave hits me. "Hello everyone!"

But Edna doesn't even seem to hear. She slams the door and comes skipping in our direction. Her face is bright and happy.

"Let's get the back row," she says.

And I don't know how it happens, but as soon as she says it, we all stop talking and follow her into the theater.

OK, it's true that 3-D glasses are stupid, and Abuela would say I am destined for pink eye, but somehow it became fun to look like idiots together. Edna and Jamie kept asking me to take ridiculous photos of all of us in our wraparounds. We might have gotten a little loud, because one of the dressed-up ushers came over and pointed his flashlight in our direction during the trailers. "Restez tranquille, s'il vous plaît. In other words, chill out and be quiet or you're out." He jerked his thumb at the exit sign.

Anyway, the movie turns out to be even better than the last one. My favorite character was Lupa, the pterodactyl mutant, killed in the last five minutes by Jake Rodrigo with a saber to her cold, mechanical heart. And I wasn't alone.

"She was sick," Michael tells me as we dump our trash on the way out. "The claws at the end of her wings were like the bats back in Minnesota. There was a cave near my house. One got in my room once."

"I saw you duck down when she came flying at us," I say.

We start to laugh, but as soon as I say it, Edna pipes in.

"I was right next to Michael. He wasn't scared," she says.

The Milk Duds and popcorn churn in my stomach. "I didn't mean like really *scared*," I say. "You know . . . like fun scared . . ."

Jamie comes over and wedges herself near Edna.

"Well, duh, Michael is too big to be scared." Her voice is so gooey that I'm sure I'm going to be sick.

Michael turns the color of watermelon.

Edna checks her phone and drops me from her jaws without a second thought. "Let's get ice cream," she says. "We have time."

The line is endless, but we don't mind. Edna springs for all the ice cream with a fifty-dollar bill she pulls from her purse. All night, she laughs the loudest and tells her stories while we listen. She makes the night crazy and funny as we eat our cones, trying not to get brain freezes. She makes Michael have a taste of her raspberry-chocolate-macadamia scoop.

When her dad picks her up, she and Jamie hang out the side windows, waving and yelling good-bye. The rest of us stand on the sidewalk, laughing. But when the car disappears, there's a strange quiet that's left behind. We look at one another, and suddenly our mouths feel sticky from sugar and empty.

Bye. Gotta go. There's my mom. Later.

It doesn't take long before we've scattered.

I tell Roli all about the movie on the drive home, just in case Mami and Papi ask.

"Notwithstanding the bad science, it sounds pretty good," he says.

"What do you mean?"

"Genetic mutation of that type is impossible, Merci," he says.

"For now," I say. It takes me a few streetlights to get him to admit that there are plenty of things that science called crazy before they were done.

We pull into our driveway around ten thirty, my lips still tasting of chocolate-almond. Papi's van isn't back, so the game has probably run long, or else, without me, they've stopped for a cold beer on the way home. The

lights are on in our living room, so I know Mami is waiting up. But as we start up the path, it's Lolo and Abuela
that I spot first. They're sitting on their porch glider in
the dark, and they're staring up at the sky. The only light
is from the citronella candles they're burning to ward off
the bugs.

"Um . . . hi," I say, glancing up.

"Buenas," says Abuela.

"What are you guys doing out here?" Roli asks. He's
too polite to mention that they're outside in their paja-
mas, usually a big no-no. Abuela is always reminding us
about what's decent. No undershirts or pajama pants in
public. No chancletas in church. No curlers outside the
yard. Never, ever go inside a fast-food restaurant barefoot
or in a bathing suit.

She purses her lips. "El viejo was pacing all evening. I
think it was all the therapy exercise your mother did with
him. It got him all worked up. I was afraid he was going
to wear a hole in the floor and fall through. Who can sleep
with that?"

"Exercise usually calms people, though." Roli sticks
his hands in his pockets and shrugs.

"Is something bothering you, Lolo?" I sit down next
to him.

Abuela waves my question off with her hand before

he can say anything. "Niña, olvídate. Don't worry yourself about this. We came out here to look at the beautiful stars, like young romantics." She pats Lolo's hand. "Right?"

The bruise on his eye is still there, although it's starting to fade. I put my ear on his chest and listen like I used to do when I was little.

"You went to the movies?" His voice echoes in there, along with his heartbeat and the rhythm of air in his lungs.

"Yes. It was crazy and scary, but good."

"So, you had fun with your friends?" Abuela asks. I lean my head back and look up at the dark blue all around. My mind wanders to Hannah, Edna, and the others, even over to Michael, flinching when that beast came soaring.

"Yes," I say.

"That's good. You're a young lady now, going out to places on your own."

I yawn; all the fun of the night is dying down, and my eyes are growing heavy. All around us the toads are croaking to one another in their strange night song.

"Look. Mars." Roli points it out and then starts in with mumbo jumbo about summer triangles and degrees of brightness.

Lolo listens for a while. Then he sighs and gives my shoulder a squeeze. "You went to the movies tonight?" he asks again.

I stay very still, listening to the echo of his odd question.

Abuela's voice is low in the dark. "Shhh," she says. "Of course she did, viejo."

And then, with a careful quiet wedged between us, Lolo and I stare up at the stars.

CHAPTER 9

"PUT THIS ON MICHAEL'S DESK," Jamie whispers.

She holds out a triangle made of folded loose-leaf paper. The corners are tucked in tight like a paper football we might have flicked through straw goalposts last year. But this one is different. The initials *MC* are written on the outside in glitter markers.

"What is it?" I ask.

She glances at Edna and then presses it into my hand. "A note, silly. Go."

It's Tuesday, and we're all in school mode again, like Cinderella and the mice coachmen all gone back to their ordinary form. I'm returning the pop quizzes for Ms. Tannenbaum, whose back is turned to us as she hangs up our finished maps. Our group got an A, so it's going up on the bulletin board, which is newly decorated with fake fall leaves to remind us we're in September. There's another map made entirely from seeds, and one made from cut straws of different sizes and colors, too. Those, and ours, are the best ones.

"Finish up, please, Merci," Ms. Tannenbaum says. "We have a lot of exciting material to cover today."

I turn back to the stack of papers. The next one belongs to Lena, who got a C even though her group's map is probably the best. It's the one made of seeds. I guess I'm not the only one who struggles with tests sometimes. Luckily, she sits on the same side of the room as Michael. I return Lena's quiz and walk by his desk. When I get close enough, I drop the note like a bomb. Michael looks up at me, but he doesn't make a move for it.

"It's not from me," I say, and hurry back to Ms. Tannenbaum's desk with the no-name and absentees' papers.

I can't help it. I think about that note all morning long, even as they march us down to the auditorium for an assembly.

What was in the note, exactly? Maybe it's an invitation to a party that I don't know about.

I keep thinking back to last year, when Carlee Frackas had a birthday party. Carlee was Edna's friend, but she skipped sixth grade and went straight to seventh, and now she doesn't hang out with Edna at all. I was invited to her party because Edna was my Sunshine Buddy and she put in a good word for me. It was a big deal, Edna told me, and I should be thrilled. Carlee's dad owned Frackas Yachts in Jupiter, in case I didn't know. She lived near the beach — in a mansion, practically — and she had a pool with a slide in her yard.

But what Edna was most excited about was that it was a boy-girl party, the first one she was going to. I thought that was weird. My own birthday parties have always been boy-girl. They've been young-old, too. That's because my whole family is always invited, from the tiniest screaming cousin who lives in Tampa to Abuela's sister, Concha, who is almost ninety. Mami's brothers come from up Hialeah to spend the day. Even Doña Rosa, when she was alive, used to drag her walker across the street for cake.

Carlee's party was different. The adults said hello at the door, but after that, it seemed to be just kids. We swam in the pool and took turns going down the slide in a long train we made by holding on to one another's slippery shoulders. We ate pizza and drank as much soda as we wanted. After, we lay around with fizzy stomachs playing video games on a gigantic TV screen in something Carlee called her media room. I couldn't believe a house that big was only for three people. I got lost when I went to find the bathroom. One of the ladies who work for Mr. and Mrs. Frackas had to help me. Her name was Inés, just like Tía, but she was quiet and serious, which isn't like Tía at all. "This way, miss," she said in a thick accent, handing me a fresh towel and leading me down the long hall. I was in bare feet and dripping the whole way. I half expected her to scold me the way Tía would have done. But no. This Inés led me as if I were an important guest.

Anyway, Dr. Newman is onstage looking cheerful, the way he's supposed to since he's trying to get us pumped up about the gift-wrap sale this year. I look at the catalog of prizes. Not bad. A top seller can win a giant stuffed ram, our school mascot. Not that I have a chance. Mami will probably buy just one roll to be nice, but that's all. We get our wrapping paper at the Dollar Store. She says it's only going to be ripped to shreds anyway.

I notice the huge fund-raising thermometer behind Dr. Newman. It's for the first PTA meeting next week where they'll start asking for money. The mercury is at $5,000, but the goal is $250,000, which is in big red numbers on top. YOUR DONATIONS MAKE THE EXTRAS POSSIBLE, a sign next to it says. There's a collage of pictures: the crew team with

123

their new equipment, the kiln in the art room, and even one of those high-tech security cameras that are all over campus now. It also has the words SUNSHINE SCHOLARS.

"This year, our goal is to have all of you involved in the gift-wrap sale," Dr. Newman tells us. "Remember, no effort is too small. What matters is your commitment to the Seaward Pines tradition. Go Rams!"

Uh-huh.

You can just take one look at Dr. Newman's expensive suit to know he doesn't really mean it. Not that Lolo didn't try to test the idea. "The man said we could give as little as a dollar to the annual giving campaign," Lolo argued last year. "And I'm already giving him the two most priceless things in my life: Roli and Merci!" Abuela wouldn't hear of it, of course. She called him a tacaño and made him get the checkbook anyway. Lolo never did tell me the amount they donated, but it couldn't have been *that* much. I looked in the program at the year-end awards assembly. *Suárez Family* was listed in the very last bunch of names. Frackas, on the other hand, was in big letters and had its own category, since they donated the new chairs in the auditorium. Santos and a few others were in the front, too.

Mr. Dixon gives our row a warning look. The girls are whispering.

"Edna says she likes Michael. Does he like her back?"

We all hear it thanks to the clear-as-a-bell acoustics in here.

"Quiet, please, girls." I flinch as a little piece of spit flies out of Mr. Dixon's mouth and lands on my arm.

Jamie scowls and turns to face front again.

I delivered a love note?

I don't know why, but the thought makes me mad. The idea of Edna and Michael liking each other is gross. *Like* liking comes with giggling and walking people to class. And more. Will he ask her to the dance in the spring? Meet her at the movies alone? Kiss her like those eighth-graders I saw?

When the bell rings, we wait for Dr. Newman to dismiss each class by row. When it's our turn, the boys file out in front of us. Michael walks by quickly, without a word or even a glance at the girls. It's like he can't get away fast enough. It's David who slows down when he gets to Edna. He waits for Mr. Dixon to look away.

"Michael says maybe." Then he runs off after the other boys.

Next to me, Rachel's eyes have become saucers. "He maybe likes her," she whispers, tugging on the ends of her hair.

Jamie and Edna, meanwhile, break into grins. I don't get why they're smiling, though.

"*Maybe likes?* Well, that's dumb."

I don't even realize I've said it aloud until the girls ahead of me swivel their heads in my direction.

Edna's dark brown eyes get beady. "What's that supposed to mean, Merci?" In all the time I've known her, I've never made Edna blush. But here she is, her cheeks flaming.

I swallow hard and feel my eye start to pull away from me. "I'm sorry. It's just that *maybe* seems like a silly answer. You either like someone or you don't. Doesn't he know?"

No one says anything for a minute, but I notice that Hannah gives me a worried look and then sighs, like she's waiting for a big *ka-boom.*

And sure enough.

"What do *you* know anyway?" Edna snaps. "No offense, but you're not exactly up on these things. Look at you, Merci. You're like a little kid with that stupid crush on *Fake* Rodrigo." She rolls her eyes. "I swear, sometimes I think you still play with dolls." She says that last part in a really loud voice. Every word seems amplified.

Now it's *my* face that feels like it's on fire.

"I don't play with dolls," I say just as loudly. "I never did." My words are sharpened to angry spears now. "I know this, though. When my mother says *maybe,* she usually means *probably not.*"

Edna flinches. And I won't lie: It feels good, just this once, to know that my words have pinched her hard for a change.

"Who cares what your mother says?" she says.

"Nobody at all," Jamie adds.

"Guys, we have to move," Hannah says. "Let's go."

Mr. Dixon snaps his fingers to signal us. "You're holding up the line. Come along, ladies."

Edna and I glare at each other. Then, without another word, we file out of the auditorium like we're supposed to.

CHAPTER 10

FOR MOST OF LAST YEAR, Roli was in scientific competition with Ahana Patel, whose dad is a physicist at NASA. They took turns edging each other out for the number-one spot in the junior class. Every time he talked about her, Roli rolled his eyes and seemed to spit tacks. She challenged his answers during class discussion, he said. She used "questionable reasoning" (his words) in her research paper. She was annoying and obsessed with being valedictorian one day.

So imagine my surprise when junior prom time rolled around and Mami told me Roli's date was none other than Ahana Patel.

"But they hate each other!" I said.

"The heart is a mystery," she said.

Ahana wore a dress with bell sleeves, and Roli rented a tuxedo at the mall. Tía made the corsage herself from flowers in our garden, and we took pictures of the whole thing in the yard. Roli and Ahana made a gorgeous couple, according to everyone who saw them, but even now I can't imagine what they said to each other while they danced. Maybe they challenged each other to repeat long chemical formulas? Ahana moved to Merritt Island at the end of the year when her father got a big promotion at the John F. Kennedy Space Center. Roli was moody for a month.

Anyway, if somebody's going to know about romance that makes no sense whatsoever, it will be him. We're in our room, and he's punching numbers into a graphing calculator with a clicking sound that's driving me nuts. I keep my eyes on my language arts book and call to him from my bed.

"I need a definition, Roli," I say.

"Google it."

"It's not in there."

"Liar." *Click, click, click.*

"I'm serious." When he doesn't look up, I lower my voice. "Please."

He sighs and puts down his pencil.

"If I answer you, will you finish your homework in the kitchen? I can't concentrate with you here."

"Well, it's not easy reading with all the noise you're making on that thing either, you know."

He crosses his arms. "What's the word?"

"Maybe like." I say the phrase carefully, like I'm announcing a spelling bee word. "As in, a boy says he 'maybe likes' you."

He looks at me, astonished. "Somebody said that to *you*?"

My face flames. "Don't be ridiculous. They said it to someone I know. Edna Santos, to be precise." I roll my eyes.

"Ah." He turns back to his work. "Is this why you've been a pain in the neck all afternoon?"

"I'm *not* a pain in the neck," I shoot back.

He raises his hands in surrender. "OK, fine. You're a pain somewhere else."

"So answer me already. What does that mean: maybe like?"

"You realize that I'm a logophile, Merci, not a love doctor."

I toss down my book in frustration. "So, you have no hypothesis even? I'd say that's grade-F work as a brother."

He blinks, and I feel sort of bad about what I've said.

He turns his chair to face me again and sits back, thinking.

"Look, Merci," he says. "I'm not trying to mess with you. It's just that absolutely nothing about liking a person—or even disliking someone—is firmly logical all the way through."

"Why not?"

He shrugs. "It has a whole layer of illusion and contradictions that are placed there on purpose. It's like encryption on a computer that scrambles things and hides the valuable data. You have to know the code to be able to read what's really there." He smiles hopefully. "Do you understand now?"

"Not at all," I say.

He rubs his eyes and sighs like when he's trying to break down a physics formula for somebody he tutors. "What I mean is, it's a puzzle." He tosses me his Rubik's Cube and smiles. He can make each face a solid color in less than four minutes.

I lie back on my bed, disgusted. I've tried to do the Rubik's for years, but I always give up.

This feels even harder.

CHAPTER 11

THE TWINS, STILL IN THEIR Batman pj's, are hunched over my old game of Operation on Saturday morning.

"What are you guys doing up so early, anyway?" Looking around, I can see they've been busy here for a while, even though it's only six thirty a.m. The patio already looks like a toy chest detonated.

"Playing with Roli, dodo bird," Tomás says a little too loudly. He's inching his electronic tweezers near the clown's leg on the game board.

"Yeah. Playing for a long time," Axel adds, even louder. He holds up a plastic piece to prove it. "I got the wishbone."

"What did I tell you? It's the clavicle," Roli corrects. "You have to use the right words or it doesn't count. We agreed." He's lying on his back with his knees bent and his eyes closed. He's stuck babysitting today while I go on the big paint job with Papi and Lolo.

"They're five years old, you know." I nudge him with my toe.

"Why don't you babysit them instead of me?" he says.

"Because I always do it."

"Well, I'm supposed to be working on scholarship applications. Plus today I have a chance to tutor a kid in chem for some good cash. He called me, desperate."

I hold up my hand. "Not a chance. You make enough money tutoring after school. It's my turn to earn some cash. Besides, I want to squeeze in some soccer practice afterward. Tryouts are next week, remember?"

The clown's nose lights up with a clanging siren. "Agh!" Tomás shouts.

"Gimme," Axel says, grabbing. "I want to get the Adam's apple."

"Larynx," Roli says. "Laaaa-rinks."

Oh, boy. Advanced Placement Biology II is going to be a killer for all of us.

Just then, the kitchen light snaps on inside, and Tía Inés steps out through the sliding door. It's usually her day off, but there's no one to work the lunch shift. Boy, does she look like she needs some shut-eye. I think the problem might be the head full of rolos. I don't know how she sleeps in those hard curlers. I don't say so, of course. *In a closed mouth, no fly will enter,* as Lolo always says.

"A family of insomniacs," Tía Inés says, yawning. She surveys the mess of toys littered all over the patio, poking some game pieces with her painted toes.

"Buenos días, familia." Lolo steps out his back door and waves to us. He's showered and already dressed in his Bermuda shorts and a T-shirt that matches mine. We ordered the new company uniform last month. It was all my idea. "Advertising matters," I told Papi, and I designed the whole thing. The front says *SOL PAINTING* with a logo of a sun rising over the ocean. On the back: *REASONABLE RATES, HABLAMOS ESPAÑOL,* and then our phone number. We've got hats to match.

Tía starts to loosen her rollers. "Oye, Lolo," she calls to him across the yard. "I think I'm out of milk for the twins' cereal. Do you have any?"

He peeks back inside his kitchen window for Abuela. "Your handsome grandsons need milk." Then he turns and heads my way. "Are you ready, Merci?"

"Almost." I hold out my hand and smile. "But are

you forgetting our financial arrangement? Thirty bucks, please."

He shakes his head and digs in his pocket. "I still say it's robbery," he says as hands me the crisp bills.

Abuela walks outside shaking two cans of evaporated milk like a pair of maracas. She comes over to Tía's screened porch and hands them over.

"Canned? Is this all you have?" Tía asks.

Abuela gives her a withering look. "¡Por Dios! Yes, it's all I have, and there's nothing wrong with it. You were raised on leche evaporada!"

"But the twins only drink fresh milk. You know they're picky about food."

"The twins aren't on social security, Inés."

Axel pipes up. "I'm hungry. I want Coco-Chews."

"Me, too!" Tomás springs to his feet. "¡Tengo hambre! Coco-Chews! Coco-Chews!" In a flash, they start circling their arms like wheel rods on a steam train. "Coco-choo-choo-choo-coco-choo-choo-choo!" Their train plows over the game board as they barrel inside.

"Nada de Coco-chews," Abuela calls after them. "That's not food! Your teeth will rot and a dentist will have to pull them all out! You'll have to eat soup your whole life!"

"I think there are interim steps, Abuela," Roli says. "Fillings, for example."

She narrows her eyes at him.

Tía turns to Roli, exasperated. "Get my purse and drive to Publix for me, would you? They open at seven."

"Me?" he says. He's still in his pajama pants. "I'm not dressed."

"So find some shorts. Besides, I can't go like *this*." She motions at her head and shoos him off. Then she spots Papi across the yard. He's loading the last of the buckets into the back of the van. "Is Simón helping today?" she asks me.

Oh, boy.

"It's just me and Lolo this time," I say.

Tía looks disappointed as I turn back to Lolo. "We've got to go. Papi doesn't like employees to be late, you know."

"¡Un momento!" Abuela runs her fingers down the shoulders of Lolo's T-shirt to smooth it out before we go.

"Keep an eye on him, Merci. No standing in the sun too long." She frowns a little and taps gently over what's left of the bruise on his face. I stare at my shoes, in case my eye goes berserk. "His head burns, and this heat is no good for a man his age," she adds. "And no ladders. He could break a hip and have a limp for the rest of his days."

Wow. That's a long list of potential damages, even for the Catastrophic Concerns Department.

"Déjame en paz," Lolo says, kissing her cheek gently. Then he pulls out his Sol Painting cap from his back pocket and puts it on. "Mira. One problem solved."

"Don't worry, Abuela," I say. "We'll be inside most of the day." But even as we walk away, I can still feel her doubtful eyes following me.

"Ready, crew?" Papi says when we reach him.

"Reporting for trim duty," I say. Papi claims he can't put me on payroll because 1) Mami wants me to think about school first and not my painting empire, and 2) all those pesky child labor laws could land him in jail. Still, I can do prep work, like taping and such. And of course, we all know that I'm management-in-training, so I use the time to soak up as much as I can. Today, for instance, I've decided to focus on quality control. Last time, Lolo forgot to clean the brushes, and Papi had to throw them out and get new ones. I'd hate to have to write Lolo up, but it could happen with the way he's been forgetting things lately. Hopefully it won't come to that.

"I can sit back here," Lolo says as he starts to climb inside the rear doors. Papi's van has only two seats in front. The rest is a big open space for our equipment. That means that if there are more than two people, somebody sits on a paint bucket.

"¡Qué va!" Papi says. "You come up front with me, Pops. Merci can sit there."

"Watch out for the seat springs up there," I tell Lolo. "They're tough on the fondillo when they poke through."

Sweat is already trickling down my neck as I settle in among the buckets and drop cloths. Our soccer things are still in here, too. Papi cranks the engine a bunch of times, trying to get it to turn over.

"Hurry, Papi. I need a breeze."

"Patience." He turns the ignition key.

I wipe the sweat from my neck as we wait for the engine to catch. Papi's van is basically an oven on wheels. He keeps adding refrigerant for the air conditioner, but it's busted, along with the door locks, so we always ride with the windows down no matter how hot it is outside. Nighttime driving isn't so bad, but in the day? Yikes.

After a few tries, he finally gets the engine started and we head down the driveway, the chassis squeaking and groaning. Suddenly, Lolo shouts.

"¡Cuidado, chico!"

Papi slams on the brakes. Our ladders clatter overhead, and the bucket slides out from under me. I land on my back with a thump. When I scramble up and look out the window, I see Roli smiling at us sheepishly. His playlist is blasting in Tía's car.

Papi hangs out the window. "Turn that music down, and pay attention like a serious guy, Roli! You're going to hurt somebody! If I see that again, you'll be walking everywhere. Got it?"

Roli nods.

"And see if your mother needs anything before you go," Papi tells him.

Then, with the van creaking under us once again, we pull onto the road.

CHAPTER 12

THE LAKE WORTH CASINO DOESN'T have slot machines or people playing blackjack, the way you'd think from its name. Papi says it did have gambling once, but that was in the 1930s, a long time before anybody in our family was even in this country. Now it's just a nice building with green-and-white awnings that the mayor calls a sign of "our city's commitment to destination tourism." Sometimes couples get married in the ballroom that overlooks the water, but most times people just picnic on the patch of grass outside, or else they fork over forty bucks for a chair and an umbrella in the sand.

I'm glad I'm here today, even though it's a weekend, and by rights I would be getting double time if I were on payroll. The main thing, of course, is that I'm making money for my new wheels. If we finish early, maybe we can go to the bike shop downtown and window-shop. Lolo can help me pick a good bike, plus Papi's usually a good negotiator. He's not afraid to ask for a discount if there's a small scratch or if it's a discontinued model. I'd love to see Edna's face if I rolled in on some sweet cruiser. We live 12.1 miles away from school, according to Roli, but so what? I'll bet that with a little training, I could make it. It might take over an hour, but it would be worth the sweat and cramped muscles just to show her my new wheels.

I spend the morning covering the edges of the baseboards with blue tape, and then I spread the drop cloths to protect the sinks, and put up signs that say WET PAINT all around the women's bathroom. Then I get busy sanding off the chipped paint on the door—*cha-cha-cha-cha*—trying to smooth it down. Papi and Lolo are working on the other end of the hall in the men's room; I can hear their voices echo over the music as I swirl circles with the sandpaper block. It's Lolo's old radio, the one that's covered in paint speckles from all our jobs. Lolo loves music; in fact, he met Abuela at a dance. Now they only dance on New Year's Eve, when we all stay up late and eat our twelve grapes, one for each month of the new year. Abuela smiles; Lolo closes his eyes and presses his head against hers. It's like they're somewhere else, gliding and spinning.

When the door finally feels smooth to the touch, I toss aside my sandpaper block and head off to go find Papi and Lolo. They'll forget to take breaks if I don't remind them.

The double doors to the ballroom are open as I pass by, so I stop for a second to look. One entire side of the room has windows facing the ocean. The huge chandeliers catch the sunshine and make twinkly patterns on the floor. There's a dusty wedding favor made of two plastic wedding rings in one of the shadows, so I pick it up. The dirty ribbon reads *Justin and Leanna* in gold letters. It suddenly reminds me of Tía Inés's wedding to Marco, even though their party was in our backyard. I was five back then, so I only remember bits and pieces. The baker at El Caribe brought in a huge sheet cake on his shoulder. It had a little plastic bride and groom. Abuela ordered champagne and bocaditos of every kind. But what I remember most is how much I wanted to hold Roli's velvet pillow with the rings instead of tossing out flower petals. No matter how much I begged, though, he wouldn't switch.

Anyway, Tía Inés and Marco aren't married anymore. I once asked Tía why they got divorced, but she just said, "He stopped loving me." I wonder if he *maybe loved* her and that was the trouble.

Roli might be right about love being a puzzle.

It's all so confusing. Mami loves Papi, that's plain and boring. I love Jake Rodrigo—secretly, but still true. And I love Lolo and everybody else in our family, of course, and that's not complicated either. But then there's Roli and Ahana. Tía and Marco—and her crush on Simón, too. Michael and Edna in "maybe like," which is a mess. Is *that* love? Oh, gross. I don't know.

I fish in my pocket for my phone and snap a picture of the ocean. Sometimes I take pictures of ordinary things, like the clouds that are gathered far out over the water right now. If you look carefully, you can see the long curtain of gray where it's already raining. If we're lucky, maybe there will be lightning later while we're still here, and I can get some good shots of the bolts hitting the water. Lolo once told me it was Papá Dios getting angry about the stupid things people do, like hurting one another, but Roli says that's not true. "It's humid air colliding and pushing energy upward into the clouds," he insists.

What a killjoy. Lolo's idea is much better.

"Excuse me. Are you lost?" A woman with a brass name tag stands at the open doors.

"No, miss. I'm with the paint crew. I was just taking a picture."

She looks at me like I'm up to no good. This happens

sometimes on our jobs. Some customers watch us, as if we might take things when they're not looking. Maybe I don't look serious enough? I put away my phone and slide past her to find Papi.

He's still working on the inside of the men's room when I finally reach him. I look around. Urinals are very weird.

"Fast work," Papi says when he sees me. His shirt is soaked all the way through in this heat. He's keeping the windows and doors open to let out the fumes or he'll get dizzy. But not even the ocean breeze is a match for the heat today.

"It's ten thirty," I say. "Officially, you're required to give employees a break, sir."

Papi pours the teal paint into the tray and wipes his sweaty chin on his shoulder. "It's already taken care of."

"What do you mean?" I look around. "Where's Lolo?"

Papi dips his roller. "He went out to rest on the veranda a while ago. You know how he likes to look at the ocean."

"And no one told me it was break time? That's playing favorites. You're not allowed to do that, you know."

Papi rolls a few strokes, squinting as he gets up near the top. "Easy, boss." He dips the roller again. "He needed to rest. A good boss makes adjustments when he has to. Lolo is slowing down, you know."

I think back to how Lolo fell. "I guess he is."

Papi glances at me like he wants to say something, but he keeps rolling instead. "Tell you what. I'll be here for twenty more minutes, tops," he says. "Then we can all take a break and get something to eat while it dries. Go tell Lolo."

I step outside through the sliders he points to, but Lolo isn't sitting in any of the chairs there. So I climb down the metal staircase to check the shady spots on the ground floor. It's a perfect place for relaxing.

"Lolo?" I call out.

But he's not here either.

I walk the length of the building calling for him. I even go around to the front where you rent beach gear, because I know that sometimes he likes to stand around and talk to random people.

But he's not anywhere.

A prickly feeling starts in my stomach, but I push it down as I walk to the back of the building again. Shielding my eyes from the glare, I scan the beach. It's crowded even though it's hot out here. Kids are plugged into their music on the sand, and boys in board shorts work their skimboards. There are a bunch of little ones playing in the surf, too. They're screeching and running away from each wave that rolls in, just like the twins do when they're here.

I climb back upstairs, my shirt soaked to my skin and my hair puffed out to new proportions. "Lolo's not there," I tell Papi.

"What do you mean he's not there?" He frowns and puts down his roller. Then he walks out through the ballroom, careful not to get any paint from his shoes on the hardwood floor. "I'll check the men's room downstairs. Go see if he's by the water."

There's something in Papi's voice that seems to shift the ground underneath me. I take the stairs again and cuff my jeans up when I get to the sand to feel a little cooler at least.

I can't help but think back to when Roli and I were little. Lolo and Abuela would bring us here in their car all the time. Lolo sang along to the radio as he drove. Abuela always packed our food in a million plastic containers. Back then, Lolo could swim out to where the water gets darker and the waves don't break. He'd let me cling to his back.

I jog out to the water's edge, hoping to see him. But he's not wading at the shore or swimming either.

Just as I turn to go, I spot something washed up in the surf. It's a shoe, half-buried in the sand.

Lolo's yellow socks are still stuffed inside, covered in pebbles and seaweed from the waves. There's no sign of his other shoe anywhere. From the looks of things, it must have been dragged off in the tide.

I take two shaky steps into the water and call out his name.

"Lolo!"

A few people dodging the waves turn to look at me. Beyond them, a catamaran and some parasailing boats bob in the distance, anchored and bright like candies. Swimmers wearing snorkel masks jump from the deck to swim below.

Keep an eye on him. I hear Abuela's words in my head. It wasn't long ago that she would stand at the shore as we headed in, calling those same words about me. "Keep an eye on la niña," she'd tell Lolo, her voice fading in the crash of waves as we went into the deep.

My eye starts to pull uncomfortably, and I rub my fist against it hard. Where can he be?

The last time Abuela and Lolo brought us here by themselves was a long time ago. I was in second grade, and Lolo went to use the restroom. He didn't come back, and Abuela got frantic and sent Roli to look. "All these umbrellas look the same," Lolo complained when Roli finally found him far away near the parking lot and walked him back. After that, there were no more swimming piggyback rides, no more trips without Tía or Mami joining us, too, now that I think about it.

I turn around to look at the lifeguards to reassure myself. They're talking among themselves. If anyone had gotten in trouble in a riptide they would have seen it. We would have heard the whistles and the sirens.

So I tuck Lolo's shoe and socks under my arm and hurry across the hot sand toward the pier, where I'm not usually allowed to go by myself. I'm out of breath and soaked in sweat when I reach the top step. Gulls screech and hover overhead as I jog closer to see if he's one of the people gathered at the far end.

Finally, I spot his yellow cap. He's with a group of men who are fishing. A surge of relief washes over me, and I break into a run.

"Lolo!" I shout.

But he ignores me. Instead, he leans over the edge with the others, watching as an angler works his line. People yell instructions as the fisherman's rod bends like a C.

"Loosen the drag," a man says. "You don't know how tired he is."

Lolo's face looks bright with excitement. He still doesn't turn, even when I touch his back. I notice that his knotty toes are all red. The sand must have felt like lava; didn't he notice? And he's gotten too much sun on his ears, too. They're the deep color of raw meat, and blisters are already bubbling. We'll hear complaints from Abuela later for sure.

My heart finally starts to slow down as I reach out for his elbow again. "Hey." My voice sounds hard in a way that surprises me. "Lolo!"

"It's a barracuda," he whispers. "Mírala."

I look over the side to where he's pointing. A long silver fish glistens like metal on the line. The men cheer as it's pulled slowly over the wooden railing, writhing for breath. It looks so fierce with those big eyes and its under-bite of spiny teeth, but I can't help feeling bad as everyone circles to watch it flap and die. The sight of it struggling makes me want to cry.

I nudge Lolo hard, and finally blurt out my complaint. "Why didn't you tell Papi where you were going?" I say. "We've been looking for you. And you left your stuff too close to the water."

I'm talking to him the way I do to the twins sometimes—bossy, fed up—but Lolo doesn't seem to notice. In fact, he looks confused for a second, as if I'm no one he knows. It makes me even madder.

"This is all that's left of your things," I tell him, holding up his shoe. "The rest was sucked away. What are we going to tell Abuela?"

Another lie? I want to add.

Lolo looks down at his feet and wiggles his toes, chuckling. The sound of his familiar laugh finally lets me take a breath.

"Here." I pull out his wet socks and slip them on his feet. "It's better than nothing. At least your feet won't burn any more on the sand. We can rinse the gull poop off and buy you rubber flip-flops when we go get lunch."

"Gracias, Inés," he says. "You're a good daughter."

I straighten up and look carefully into his face. "I'm Merci, Lolo," I tell him. "Tía Inés is at home."

"Merci," he whispers.

We start back up the pier. Waves crash against the pilings and spray us as we walk along. He seems a little unsteady, so I link my arm in his elbow, thinking back to the fall on his bike.

Papi is still back at the casino. Out on the veranda, he shields his eyes as he looks for us. I guide Lolo to a bench to rest and send a text.

At the pier. See us?

I watch as he digs in his pocket for his phone and checks the message. Then he looks in our direction and spots me waving. A few seconds later, my phone vibrates.

Wait there.

I sit down next to Lolo. Suddenly I'm feeling drained and sweaty.

"You scared me, Lolo," I say. Tears fill my eyes, so I don't say anything else.

He pats my hand, but he doesn't seem to notice I'm upset.

"You'll never believe it," he says. "Fico caught a barracuda in the river! You should have seen it."

I blink, a heaviness filling my chest.

Fico? The river?

The only Fico I've ever heard of was Lolo's older brother. None of us ever met him. He's the one who drowned when they were boys back in Cuba.

I just watch the gulls dive for the surf, screeching. This time, I don't bother to correct him at all.

CHAPTER 13

THERE IS NOTHING WORSE THAN a tattler, so I keep my mouth shut.

But the strange thing is that Papi does, too.

He didn't ask me for details when he got to the pier at all. He stood staring at us for a second in total silence, red in the face and sweaty, maybe feeling as wiped out as I was. I guess he could see for himself what happened to Lolo's shoes and how he had wandered off.

He bought Lolo rubber shoes at the beach shop, and we ate our hot dogs without talking. Later, he sat Lolo in a chair right outside the bathroom and let me roll some walls to finish up quickly.

Now it's almost ten o'clock at night, and Papi is in the

kitchen with Mami and Tía Inés. They're whispering, but it's a fight. I can tell. The murmurs are fast, and when the volume rises, they're followed by long silences. It's about Lolo, I'm almost positive. Or maybe it's more about how Papi and I didn't watch Lolo—which was Abuela's main thread when she saw his blistered ears this afternoon. Or maybe it's just Tía and Papi arguing again about Lolo the way they always do, with Mami trying to keep peace in the middle: whose turn it is to take him to the store to get new shoes, who can't take off work again for an appointment.

But I don't know for sure because every time they hear me leave my room, they all get quiet. Their eyes follow me when I go to the kitchen to see if my soccer permission slip is signed yet. They don't start talking again until I'm gone.

Children don't need to hear life's ugliness. There's plenty of time for that. I've heard Abuela say that before. She hates when books and movies that Roli and I watch are sad or bloody. But that's so dumb. Plenty of sad things happen to kids all the time. Your dog dies. Your parents split up. Your best friend dumps you for someone better. Someone sends you a mean snap message.

I could go on.

"What's happening?" I ask Roli. He's propped up in bed watching a video about brains on his laptop. "What are they arguing about? Do you know?"

He won't look away from the screen. "Stop trying to eavesdrop and go to bed, Merci. You need 9.25 hours of sleep for proper brain function, you know."

"Is something wrong with Lolo? Tell me, Roli."

"I told you, I'm watching something."

All my anger bubbles up.

"I can't wait until next year when you're gone at college," I tell him, even though that's a lie. "I'll have this room to myself. And I will not leave a single, dumb science thing anywhere."

Then I pull the curtain closed between our beds.

As Roli pulls into school on Monday, I know Mami sees the LED marquee. That's where Dr. Newman posts his annoying inspirational quote every week and where we get reminders of the important things happening, like concerts and field trips.

MIDDLE-GRADE SOCCER TRYOUTS, MONDAY THROUGH WEDNESDAY,
IMMEDIATELY AFTER SCHOOL,
LOWER FIELDS. SIXTH GRADE TODAY.

I stare at the sign. My cleats and shin guards are in my bag. All I'm missing is my permission slip.

Roli gets out of the car, and Mami slides over. I climb out, too, but I stand near the window.

"What is it, Merci?" she asks. "Did you forget your lunch?"

I unzip my backpack and pull out the consent form. "You forgot to sign this again," I say. "Tryouts are today."

She looks at me for a long time in a way that makes my heart start to pound like it always does when I'm scared. She takes a deep breath and looks straight ahead for a minute. Then she turns back to me.

"The truth is, I didn't forget, Merci," she says.

I shift my backpack. "Then why didn't you sign it?"

She looks around at the other moms and dads who are dropping off their kids and lowers her voice. "I know how much you enjoy soccer, Merci. I really do. But you're going to have to stick to playing with your dad's team for now. There's just too much else going on. We need you home after school. Abuela can't manage the twins by herself every day."

My mouth drops open. "I can't try out? But I practiced all summer, Mami. I'm good at this."

"I know you are, mi vida," she says. Her eyes look like they're filling up. "You're excellent at it."

"Then let me play! Tía can find someone else to baby-sit," I say. "Why can't Roli do it?"

"How would you get home? Roli tutors after school, and then he'd have to drive back to get you every day," she says. "He's already so busy working on all of his college applications this fall."

"But it's not fair that it always has to be me!"

"It's not. But a lot of things aren't fair, Merci," she begins.

Just then, the volunteer in the parking loop signals to us and starts to walk over. Mami beams her a smile as though she and I aren't arguing.

"I'm so sorry," the aide says, "but we have to keep the car line moving. Would you be kind enough to pull out?"

"Oh, yes, of course," Mami says. "I'm so sorry."

She shifts the car into drive and looks at me guiltily. "We'll have to talk about this later, Merci."

"But there is no later. Tryouts are today," I say. Tears are brimming, and I can feel my chin quivering. I shove the paper at her again. "Please, Mami, sign it."

She takes the paper from me, but drops it on the passenger seat, unsigned.

"The answer is no this time, Merci. I'm sorry; I know you're disappointed. But I promise, you can try out next year."

I stand there staring, long after the car pulls away.

Rage bubbles up from my stomach. I suddenly hate

the twins for being born, and Tía Inés for not using baby-sitters. I hate Lolo for wandering off the way he did. I hate Abuela for being too tired all the time and Roli for applying to college. I hate Mami. And Seaward Pines. And soccer.

Everything. I hate everything, I think as I run inside the girls' bathroom to hide.

CHAPTER 14

THE WHOLE WEEK feels like misery.

Having PE last hour is usually a blessing, especially on Fridays, but this week it's been hard. The soccer fields have been set up with orange cones and extra nets for the tryouts, so I've had a reminder every single day that I'm not going to be on the team.

To make matters worse, out of nowhere, the boys were royal pests at lunch every day. They kept trying to mess with our food and pretend it wasn't them. They swiped Rachel's apple and Edna's dessert earlier in the week. I thought they weren't going to bug me since I've been in a bad mood, but today when I finished my sandwich and got up to get milk, I came back to find that the rest of my food had vanished.

"Where's my lunch?" I asked. Only the empty paper bag was left.

"Vultures took it," Edna said, pointing at the boys' table. She and Jamie burst into giggles.

When I looked over, sure enough, my fruit snacks were making the rounds at the boys' table. So I marched over. I didn't care who saw me talking to the boys today.

"Give them back."

"Give what back?" Chase asked, grinning. He'd stuck two of my favorite grape-flavored gummies to his front teeth.

"Very funny."

"Wait, OK," David said. "Here you go." He pretended to make himself puke.

Even Michael was laughing, which really confused me. Were these the same people who saw *Iguanador* with us?

"Very mature," I said, borrowing from Roli.

I went back to my table empty-handed and fuming. Hannah split her chocolate-chip cookie with me to make me feel better. "Here," she said. "They're being dumb."

"Not just dumb," I said. "Mean."

I'm the first one out on the field for PE. That's the advantage to wearing your gym shorts under your skirt. Last year, we didn't have to change into PE uniforms. We just had to wear sneakers to play. But this year we have to change, and if we don't, we get a zero. I want no part of figuring out how to get undressed in front of girls who like to open the stall curtains on people for fun. That's how everyone found out last week that Rachel wears a polka-dot bra. And that a girl named Susan doesn't wear one at all, even though Edna told her—"no offense"— that she should because she's kind of big. Susan looked like she was going to cry, and I don't blame her. I wouldn't want anyone to talk about my chest. God. I keep mine pressed close to my body with a sports top for now. But who knows when that will change? There's nothing you can do about it, anyway, and no way to stop people from noticing. Who can you complain to about people making fun of your boobs or underwear? Mr. Patchett?

Our equipment is set up at the baseball field for our class. To me, it's practically an invitation to test it out before the others get here. Maybe I can blow off my bad mood from lunchtime before I go home and things get even worse. I root inside the mesh bag for a ball. Technically, we're not supposed to touch anything until class starts and we're "properly supervised." But these aren't power tools, for Pete's sake; they're baseballs. Brand-new, good-smelling baseballs. What could happen?

I grab a bat and look out over the field, aiming my sights. It's a sea of green, a kind of baseball Emerald City, with not a bald patch in the grass far as you can see. Back in elementary school, our field was scorched, and you had to watch out for pieces of glass that were sometimes crushed in the dirt. But grass is a precious thing around here. Mr. Baptiste, the head groundskeeper, makes his crew set the sprinklers if it doesn't rain, and he orders the soil tested regularly in the science lab to make sure it has the right Ph. I know because Roli is the one who tests it.

Lolo loves to come out here when he visits our school. Mami and Papi may be gaga over Roli's academics, but Lolo thinks this field is the best. Last year, on Grands Day, he came to Seaward with me. He brought his old bat and a jersey from Cuba and told us how he used to be a batboy before he came here in 1980. He told us every detail. The way the stands looked in the stadium. The uniforms. Everything in exact detail so we could practically see it. He never forgets the long ago, which is so weird about him lately. How can he remember all that from almost forty years ago, but forget stuff that happened ten minutes earlier? Even forget my name?

"No offense, Mr. Suárez, but aren't batboys supposed to be kids?" Edna had asked.

"Here yes, they are boys and girls. But back in Cuba, carga bates can be adults, even today. So you see, Señorita Santos, I'm really Bat Man!"

Even Miss McDaniels, who organized the event, liked him. In fact, she asked me about him this morning, because Grands Day is next week, and it's the last year we get to have it. Seventh and eighth graders are too old for grandparents, apparently.

"Will that charming Mr. Suárez be joining us this year?" she asked.

"Absolutely," I said. Then I hurried off. I didn't want her to ask me anything about my Sunshine Buddy. I don't dare tell her that the only new contact I've had with Michael is texting him the reading assignment he missed when he went to the orthodontist. Hmpf. I wonder if giving him a good kick in the shins for eating my food would count as an activity?

I toss up a pitch and load my weight on my back leg the way Lolo taught me. As usual, I get right under the ball with a satisfying smack that sends it far into the outfield. It arcs high and hits near the top of the fence. Another couple of feet and it would have been a homer for sure. Maybe if Lolo stops acting so weird I can try out for a spot on the softball team in the spring.

"The crowd roars," a voice says.

I turn around and find Michael Clark watching me from behind the chain-link fence at home plate. He shakes the hair out of his eyes and grins.

I give him a cold look since I'm still mad about lunch. Plus, Edna might be around and ready to pounce. When she found out that I texted him the assignment, she got all huffy.

"You texted him?" Rachel had demanded, wide-eyed. "You have his *number*?"

"All Sunshine Buddies have each other's numbers. Who cares?" Edna had said, but you could tell that she cared for sure. She shot death rays at me from across the table the rest of lunch. I practically needed an Iguanador Nation force shield to protect me.

I glance around the field. A few boys have come out of the gym doors and are walking our way. Good. Let *them* talk to him.

"I don't speak to food thieves," I say.

"It wasn't me," he says. "I was just a witness."

Michael comes around the fence and scoops up a couple of balls from the bag near my feet. He can hold two in each enormous hand, I notice, just like Lolo. He trots to the mound and faces me. "I have a good arm, you know. Fastball, curve ball — you call it," he says.

I stand there, blinking.

"Scared?" he asks.

"Oh, please."

"Come on then. Five bucks if you can hit it, which you won't." He shakes the hair from his eyes again.

I give him a pitying look. What can a new kid really know about my skills? This will be like taking candy from a baby. Which, now that I think of it, he deserves.

"But I *am* going to hit it," I say. "I'm going to smack it right out of here. And then you're not allowed to touch my food again—or let anyone else touch it, either. Ever."

"Uh-huh. Call it." He waits for me to answer.

Five bucks will inch me closer to my new bike, won't it? Instinctively, I crouch in my best batting position and lift my bat over my right shoulder.

"Send what you want," I tell him. "And then prepare to fork over the dough, Michael Clark. No crying about it, either. You can't say you weren't warned."

"Ha."

By now, kids in our class have gathered on the bleachers, including Edna, who has her eyes trained on us like a hawk. She's sporting her new sneakers that have cheetah-print rubber tips. From the expression on her face, I'd say she might want to claw me to death like a big cat. All week long, she's been giggling and saying Michael's name too loud to get his attention. She's been sending him snaps every chance she gets. I wish he'd just *like* like her already and get it all over with.

"You're not supposed to touch that stuff yet, Merci," she calls out.

But just this once, on this field, I don't want Edna to be in charge.

"Hurry," I tell him.

I hear a whistle blow. Mr. Patchett is jogging toward us. He waves his muscled arms. He is not one for breaking rules, as it violates his army training. I grip my bat and set my feet.

"Come on. Pitch."

Michael pivots slowly, gazes out in the direction of the trees for a few seconds, and then *wham,* he releases the throw.

I focus my eyes on the ball's seam, the way Lolo always says, and I make contact. ¡Ave María! My arms tingle with an electric jolt. Michael wasn't kidding. His throw is hard enough to make my teeth vibrate.

Unfortunately, the ball doesn't arc.

Instead, it ricochets off my bat like a bullet. ¡Fuácata!— the line drive clips Michael squarely in the face. He drops to the mound like he's been shot.

I can't repeat the word I shout, but I toss my bat and race over to him. He's a huge, motionless heap on his back. His top lip is split, and blood dribbles down his pale neck.

Kids shout *ooooh* as they run at us and close in a circle all around. Mr. Patchett blows his whistle again and again, peeling bodies back as he tries to reach us.

"Back! Stand back!"

"Merci hit Michael in the face with a baseball," Edna says, turning on me the second Mr. Patchett gets there. She looks at me angrily. "Jerk!"

Mr. Patchett unhooks his walkie-talkie. "Miss McDaniels, we need Nurse Harris ASAP to Field B. Head injury. Over." Then he starts digging in the first-aid kit he always wears as a fanny pack.

"Who authorized you to begin without a teacher present?" He pulls out gauze and other supplies.

"I didn't begin. We were just . . ."

"*Who?*" he demands again.

"No one, sir."

He pulls on rubber gloves and leans over Michael. "Son, can you tell me your name?"

"It's Michael," Edna says.

"The question is not for you, Miss Santos," Mr. Patchett snaps. "Stand back, please, and be quiet." Then he turns to Michael again. "Name?"

"Uuuuuuggh," he mumbles.

All I can think of is Abuela's warnings about head injuries. Is Michael brain-damaged? Will he ever speak again?

"Sit up slowly, Michael, and let me check your teeth. Move your jaw like this." He demonstrates opening and closing his mouth.

Michael looks dazed as he lumbers to his elbows. How can a lip balloon so fast? It looks like the throat sac on one of those big frogs they show on Animal Planet. He spits a glob of bloody saliva into the orange dirt, making me queasy.

"I'm so sorry! It was an accident," I say.

Mr. Patchett tosses me a stern look as he steadies Michael and checks his pupils with a penlight. He carefully lifts Michael's lips to see what I've done. Thank God, I still see front teeth.

"Nice going, Merci," Edna says.

"Terrific buddy," Jamie adds.

"It was an *accident*," I say again. "We made a bet. If I hit the ball, he'd leave my lunch alone and —"

"Everyone, up in the stands right now." Mr. Patchett growls. "Edna Santos, take attendance." He hands over his clipboard, and then starts to help Michael to his feet, just as Nurse Harris pulls up in a golf cart. She hops out and grimaces when she sees Michael's bloody gym shirt.

"Merci almost killed Michael Clark because he took her stupid fruit snacks," Edna tells her.

"Shut up," I say.

"Silence," Mr. Patchett says. "Bleachers!"

He helps Nurse Harris load Michael into the golf cart and presses an ice pack to his face. My neck feels hot, and it's not from the sun that's baking down on it, either. I walk to the stands and sit alone in the front row, miserable, as everyone stares.

"He might have a concussion," Edna says loudly as they pull away. "You can only have a few of those in your whole entire life, you know. Then you stay loopy."

After Michael is gone, Mr. Patchett takes a deep breath and launches into a long lecture on following rules. It's a full-on sermon, and everyone is giving me dirty looks for bringing this upon us.

Finally, when there are only twenty minutes left, he makes us number off one-two and we break up into teams for an abbreviated game, thanks to what he calls "unfortunate events."

"Not you, Suárez," he tells me as I start to head to the outfield. "Report to Miss McDaniels. She needs to interview you for the accident report." He stands there like an enforcer, his arms crossed and his stance wide. "And she'll need to call your parents about your detention."

"What?" I'm thinking of Mami's rule about how I'm not supposed to cause any calls home from school. I'm not vomiting. I'm not feverish. Those are her two requirements to make it OK to bother her at work.

I try pleading. "But I didn't mean it, Mr. Patchett."

"Rules are rules, soldier," he says. "You broke them and now you pay. Go on."

CHAPTER 15

Dear Michael Clark,
I am sorry I hurt you with my line drive. You
should have listened. I did warn you, remember?

Dear Michael Clark,
I am glad that you still have teeth. It is a hard
life without them, according to my Abuela

Dear Michael,
I'm sorry I smacked you down with that drive.
I'm willing to let you slide on the five bucks you
owe me because you are new and how would you
know that I'm great at

It takes several tries to get Miss McDaniels to approve the sincere letter of apology that is required if I want my detention to be one day instead of two. I gave up trying to explain that it was an accident. It's almost four thirty p.m. on Friday, her quitting time, and she's in no mood to stay a second longer. She drums her polished nails on the desk as I sign my name. I finally just caved and wrote down the highlights from her lecture about the Importance of School Safety Rules.

Dear Michael,

I am sincerely sorry that my reckless behavior did not reflect the values of Seaward Pines Academy, where we respect rules always. School rules are made with the students' best interests in mind. As a Sunshine Buddy, I should have known better, especially since betting that includes monetary exchange violates school ethics.

Sincerely,
Mercedes Suárez

"This will do," Miss McDaniels says as she reviews all the edits. She folds the note and slides it into a fancy Seward Pines Academy envelope before handing it back to me. "You will give this to Michael Clark upon his return to school on Monday. I don't expect to see you in here for breaking safety rules again. I can excuse a first offense for a new student like Michael. He wouldn't know the rules. But you should have known better. It is beneath the standards of Sunshine Buddies. If anything like this happens again, I'm afraid you'll be removed from the organization."

My chance to ditch this dumb club is here, but it's all wrong. Leaving isn't the same thing as being kicked out.

"Yes, miss. It won't happen again."

She gathers her things and flips off the light. "Have a pleasant evening, Merci."

I walk across campus toward the drop-off circle. Mami will think my detention is another badge of shame, like last year when I said I didn't want to be in the spelling bee. It was because I'm always a wreck when I do anything onstage in front of people. It makes my eye go crazy, too. She said, "Merci, how will it look to your teachers, that you don't even want to try?"

It's not her car that's waiting, though. Instead, it's Papi's van, looking especially shabby in the loop. When I open the door, it squeaks so loud that Miss McDaniels turns toward the sound from across the parking lot. I've never been so grateful for the fact that nobody else is still around.

"Where's Mami?" I ask.

"Staff meeting at the rehab center. She'll be home late."

I don't ask who's watching the twins. It's supposed to be me, of course. Abuela is probably struggling, or else Roli is helping.

Papi is chewing on a toothpick. His beard is stubbly at this hour, and he's sweaty. I can tell he's tired, and he's wearing his grouchy work face. I think of last year when I asked Papi what he liked about being a painter. It was Career Day at school. Some parents came in to talk, but if yours couldn't make it, you had to ask your parents about their work and report back. Just my luck, that day somebody had stiffed him $250 for making a dent in a garage door while he was on a job. The guy said Papi had done it when he parked the van, but Papi knew it was already there when he arrived. Papi tries never to argue with his customers, but it's not always easy. I don't think he liked very much about being a painter that day.

He gives me a solemn look as I buckle in, and then he drives extra slow—even worse than Roli. It's like we're in the homecoming parade.

"Why are we going so slow?" I say.

"Are you in a rush?" He makes a hand signal for the turn, which he takes inch by squeaking inch, Roli-style.

I shrug, glancing at the few remaining cars in the parking lot, all shiny with tinted windows and decals of smiling stick families on the back windows. A few moms are waiting for tryouts to finish and talking on their phones.

"It's embarrassing," I say. "Not to mention hot."

"Oh. Embarrassing. You mean our van?"

I nod. For a second I think he gets it, but then I see it's a snare.

"Terrible stuff, embarrassment. I know just how you feel, though," he says. "After all, I feel embarrassed getting a phone call from my daughter's school that she hurt somebody."

"I didn't hurt the kid on purpose. It was an accident."

"I believe you. But not everybody will, and you're calling attention to yourself in a bad way." The little vein in his temple is throbbing. "You have to think about that, Merci, because Dr. Newman can ask you to leave if he decides you're too much trouble."

I stare at him.

"Here's the deal," he says. "You have to show everyone here every day that they did the right thing accepting you. You have to act like a serious girl."

"Other people do dumb stuff here all the time," I point out. "Why do I have to prove anything?"

Papi sighs.

"I know you and Roli are smart enough to be here — more than smart enough. But we don't pay for tuition like most of the other families. So the value you add to the school has to come from *you,* because it's not coming from our wallets."

"That's not fair," I say.

"Maybe not. But I still think it's worth it. Your education will open doors later, Merci, believe me. I just don't want you to blow it."

My eyes fill up, and I don't answer. Instead, I stare out the window in misery, wishing Roli were driving me home. Sometimes Mami points to houses on the way. The streets are narrow and lined with Spanish-style houses, where purple vines climb up trellises to end at balconies. There are play forts in the yards. "Mira," she'll say, under her breath like she's in church.

There have been days when I've wanted to live here, to ride a fancy bike to a friend's house and swim in their pool. I picture Edna and Jamie pedaling to each other's houses. They're not babysitting. They're not writing apologies.

But somehow all these houses seem so ugly to me right now, even worse than Las Casitas and our patchy weeds strewn with the twins' toys in the yard. I slip off my headband and close my eyes as the Intracoastal comes into view. It's too bright to look at today. Leaning my head out the window, I let the wind hum in my ears and drown out this day, even though I know it's tangling my curls into knots.

CHAPTER 16

"¿QUÉ TE PASA?" TÍA INÉS looks down at me from Abuela's ottoman. "You've been moping all day."

"No, I haven't," I snap. Thinking about going to school tomorrow is making me cranky. Michael, the note, the whole ugly thing.

"Moping?" Abuela glances over at me irritably. I can tell she's still mad about Lolo's ears. When we got home last Saturday, she made a big fuss and made me clip a leaf off the aloe vera plant in her front window so she could smear the gel on his blisters. All week she's grumbled, too. Even at Sunday dinner today, she still acted like everything was bothering her. I hope she gets over it by Grands

Day next Wednesday, or it's going to be miserable having her at school.

"What this girl needs are some quehaceres around here. Chores might teach her more responsibility." She looks at me hard, reminding me all over again that I didn't watch Lolo last week like I promised.

"Ay, Mamá," Tía says. "Leave the kid alone already."

More chores? Impossible! It took me an hour to organize Abuela's sewing supplies this morning. (Mami said it was a fair exchange for the trouble I caused at school, which I still think was *not* my fault.) Plus, I biked alone to get our Sunday bread because Lolo said he was feeling too tired, and *then* I watched the twins while Tía worked the Sunday madhouse at El Caribe. Now, here I am after dinner stuck holding a box of straight pins while Tía Inés gets a new pair of jeans fitted.

Abuela walks around her, frowning. I don't know if it's because she's mad at me or because, despite a gap at the waist, the pants pull kind of tight across Tía's behind.

"What kind of women do they sew these pants for?" she mutters. "Has no one thought of hips?" She pinches the gap. "And I'm going to replace this zipper, too, Inés. It's sewn in crooked; didn't you notice? There are more curves in it than a river."

177

Tía Inés looks down, surprised. "So that's why they were marked down."

Abuela shakes her head. "Have I taught you nothing in all these years? You have to be careful when you buy off a clearance rack." She looks up at me. "Get me the marking chalk and the good scissors, por favor, Merci."

I walk back toward the closet, past Tuerto, who is napping on a shelf, curled inside a basket of fabric scraps. I scratch his cheeks while I check my phone to see if Michael has finally replied. He hasn't. I sent him a text on Friday night to see if he was OK, but he hasn't answered all weekend. I don't know what that means. Is he mad or is he brain-damaged? Either way, it's bad.

I take a deep breath and walk to the back of the closet, pushing past La Boba, the headless dress-form mannequin that Abuela keeps in here. She's creepy. It's the black fabric that makes up her lady's torso and the straight pins sticking out of her headless neck. The wheels on her metal base make a strange screeching sound when you move her, too, no matter how many times Lolo oils them. It sounds like she's screaming. Naturally, the twins love this thing. When Abuela isn't looking, they like to toss a sheet over La Boba and push her around the room, pretending she's a spirit that's haunting us. I stare at her for a minute as I work up the courage to reach for the chalk and scissors that are in the bin behind her. She's powerless, I tell myself. What can she really do to me? After all, she's got no head to think her own ideas, no hands to defend herself, and no legs to move where she wants. She's just stuck there letting people twist her any way they want, letting them dress her the way they like, telling her what to do. Maybe we're not that different. I give her a squeaky spin and get angry all over again about what happened with Michael.

I grab chalk and the shears marked *NO TOCAR POR FAVOR* on the handles for the benefit of the twins, who like to play barbershop on each other. I bring them back to Abuela.

"Not too loose, Mamá," Tía says. "They'll stretch out."

Abuela arches her brow. "Who's the expert here, Inés? Turn."

Tía is wearing heels for the fitting. They're her dance shoes for when she takes the free dance class at the Tango Palace downtown. She clears her throat. "Before I forget, Mamá," she says, "I made another doctor appointment for Lolo."

Abuela marks a V at the back seam of Tía's pants. "Appointment for what? Dr. Gupta just saw him in March." She looks up and puts her hand on her heart. "Does that burn look like it's going to give him skin cancer?"

"Can we be reasonable?" Tía's eyes drift over to me and

she pauses. "It's that . . . Enrique, Ana, and I discussed it. We want to stay on top of things, that's all."

My ears perk up. Stay on top of what things? Is this what they were talking about in our kitchen last week?

Abuela's mouth is tight as she pins the waist. "Well, I hope you enjoyed your private conversation." She stabs a few more pins through the denim. "If you'd bother to ask me, I'd tell you that all these appointments are pointless. What do these doctors do? Nothing, except make you sicker with worry."

The air around us all suddenly feels prickly, but I don't want to miss anything. I pretend to study all the family pictures Abuela keeps tacked up crooked on the walls. She's taken pictures of our first day of school since Roli was six. Abuela is a terrible photographer, though. Almost every shot is out of focus or missing someone's head.

"Mamá . . ." Tía says, sighing.

But Abuela's on a roll, and her voice is getting louder. "And why doesn't anybody make house calls anymore? How are two ancianos supposed to get to all these appointments? Those silly shuttles that never come on time? And I don't even want to start to tell you about the cost. They charge you the eye on your face, and then they use it to pay for their fancy lobbies with waterfalls and fish tanks.

¡Qué bobería! They should come to their patients and forget all that nonsense! I tell you, there's no respect for how people our age—"

"Roli can drive you if Enrique or I can't," Tía says, exasperated. "It's just a mile."

Abuela's mouth drops open and she clutches her chest. "*Roli?* Do you even love us?" she asks. "I would be safer to ask Lolo to take me on his bike handlebars."

OK, that might be true. For once, though, I'm grateful Roli isn't here for this.

"Lolo needs to go to the doctor." Tía's voice is suddenly a heavy stick. I can almost hear what she doesn't say. *And that's final.*

Abuela glares at her. I wonder if there will ever be a day when I boss Mami or Papi the way Tía is doing to Abuela. I can't even imagine. It makes the world feel upside down.

"Well, we're busy this week," Abuela says, seething. "We have an event at Merci's school. It's the day for grandparents. And we've been looking forward to it."

Tía cocks her head. "That's next Wednesday, isn't it, Merci? I saw the flyer on your fridge."

I nod, stuck in the middle. Abuela doesn't like being bossed, but at the same time, Tía is just trying to help.

I don't know whose side to go on, so I just stand there, tongue-tied.

"We have four other days to choose from," Tía says. "Pick one."

Abuela ignores her. "Step out of the pants, Inés," she says.

Tía sighs and slips out of the jeans carefully so she doesn't get scratched.

"Call the boys for me, Merci," she tells me quietly. "It's getting late, and they have school tomorrow."

I put down the pins and hurry out, only too glad to get away from this conversation.

When I get to the kitchen, I find a mess. Three plates with sandwich crusts and half-drunk glasses of orange juice are still on the table. The jar of mayonnaise and the sliced ham are room temperature, too. If Roli could see this, we'd get a lesson in botulism.

Lolo is right outside the window, though, pulling up the last of the summer flowers that are scorched and waterlogged. The twins are with him, too. Soaked head to toe, they're filling a bucket with a hose. Paint rollers and brushes lie at their feet.

I dump the dishes in the sink and run the water to soak them. Then I crank open the window and call out, "And what are you two doing?"

"Painting the house," Axel says, dipping his brush into the bucket of water. "Can't you see?"

Tomás rolls as high as his skinny arms can reach and leaves a long dark streak of water on the stucco. "It's invisible paint."

"So you can't see it," Axel says.

"Unless you're magic," Tomás says.

"And you're not magic," Axel adds.

"Your mom says to finish," I tell them. "It's getting late, and you have school."

Tomás gives me a loud raspberry as a reply.

Lolo looks up at him. "We talked about this, Tomás. Is that a way to be a caballero?" he scolds.

I rinse off the dishes and put them in the drain board. Then I wipe the crumbs to the floor, and collect the mayo and ham to put them back in the fridge.

But when I pull open the refrigerator door, I find something odd. An enormous pair of round eyeglasses is sitting in the deli meat drawer.

Lolo's.

A voice inside me tells me to close the drawer and pretend I haven't seen them. But then I think of Abuela, and what she'll say if she finds them before Lolo does.

I reach for the glasses.

The frames are so large and the glass so thick. They're

silly, even ugly—especially scratched as they are. I take mine off and try them on, marveling as the room loses its shape and tilts on its ear. It's weird how we need such different things to see. I take them off and pocket them before heading outside.

"Have you been looking for something, by any chance?" I blink my eyes a bunch of times to give Lolo a clue.

"¿Quién, yo?"

"Sí, tú."

I pull Lolo's glasses from my pocket and hand them over.

A frown clouds his face, but it passes quickly. He chuckles and puts them on, wiping off the foggy lenses. "I thought things were looking fuzzy."

He doesn't ask me where they were or why they're so cold.

I don't dare ask why they were in the refrigerator. The question sours in my mouth as he turns back to yanking the rest of the tattered plants. It's like there's a crossing guard holding a big stop sign in front of me.

Instead, I swat at mosquitos buzzing near my legs and notice several welts on Lolo's neck and arms where the bugs have been feasting. "You're all bitten up. Abuela's going to fuss." I move his fingers to his neck so he can feel the welts. "See? There's spray inside. You want me to get it?"

"I'll go." His eyes flit to Axel and Tomás. "Start cleaning up, men," he calls to them.

I wait until the screen door slams behind him before I walk over to the twins. They're completely involved in their game, their eyes serious as they move their brushes up and down in their make-believe job. I used to love to play this way. Roli and me on a spaceship made of sofa pillows, on a cardboard raft crossing the Amazon. Now, I don't know why, but the sight of the twins playing makes me angry. It's silly and childish. It's all just pretend.

"It's just water, you know."

They ignore me and keep working, but I can't stop myself from wanting to ruin their game. An idea flashes through my head, and even though I know it's not true, I want it to be.

"It's not nice to take Lolo's stuff and hide it," I say, louder. "Especially not his glasses. He can't see well without them."

Tomás is the first to turn. He looks at me blankly. "I didn't hide Lolo's glasses," he says.

"I didn't, too," Axel says.

I barely hear them for the buzz in my ears and the satisfaction at bothering them. They're the reason I'm not playing soccer, so it's hard not to be upset with them. And who's to say that they didn't take Lolo's glasses? It's not so far-fetched. They've fibbed plenty of times about things they've broken, haven't they? Tía Inés's vase. The porcelain girl with the water buckets Abuela kept. Roli's model space shuttle. Who can believe them?

I give them my warden look, growing tall. "You hid them in the refrigerator, and it's a mean trick." The accusation slips easily from my mouth.

"Lolo! Merci is bothering us!" Tomás shouts at the top of his voice and then turns back to me. "Go away." He flicks his paintbrush in my direction like it's a magic wand he's using against an ogre. Dirty water splashes my face, and before I can really think, I grab it out of his hand roughly and give him a shake.

"Quit it, liar!"

He balls his fists and hits my thighs, crying. A second later, Axel is in a snotty heap, too.

"¿Pero, qué pasó?" Lolo comes out of the house, buttoning his shirt.

Tía Inés comes out the door right behind him. "Quiet down. Any minute the neighbors are going to call the cops!"

"It's nothing," I mutter.

"It's Merci's fault!" Axel shouts. "She's mean!"

Tomás sucks his thumb and gives me dagger looks in agreement.

"Ya, ya, ya," Lolo tells them, pulling them into his arms. "Let's all calm down. No one is mean. What happened?"

For a second, I don't know what to say. I started it, of course. I know that's true and that it's wrong. But when I glance at Lolo, I see his crooked glasses and that he's buttoned his shirt all wrong, the way the twins sometimes do. The sight of him makes my temper flash all over again.

"I said it's nothing," I insist. "They're tired and cranky, that's all! They're being their usual bratty selves." My eyelid twitches and starts lowering.

"Liar!" Axel says.

"Merci, don't call them brats," Tía Inés says. "You're a lot older than they are. Too old to upset them like this."

"Then find someone else to watch them," I say. "I'm not your servant!"

"Mercedes."

Papi's voice makes me jump. It rumbles under me like thunder across the yard. He's stepped out of our house in his undershirt to see what's happening. Mami is right behind him.

"What's all this about?" she says.

"I hate watching them," I shout. "I hate watching everybody!"

And then, because hot tears have sprung to my eyes, I give the twins' water bucket a hard kick and march across the yard for home.

CHAPTER 17

THE UPSIDE OF BEING GROUNDED for a week is hard to find, except maybe that you start to appreciate any kind of fun, even if it's in the form of a homework project.

"Guess what? You've left Seaward Pines today," Ms. Tannenbaum tells us.

Oh, if only . . . The girls who made the soccer team had their names announced this morning. I had to put my head down.

"Today, you're all in scribe school instead!"

We've started a unit on hieroglyphics. She holds out an old floppy hat and walks around the room, telling us to pick a name. "This will be your new pen pal for tonight's assignment. You'll have to write this person a note using the writing of ancient Egyptians." She points to the stack of curly "papyrus," markers, and colored pencils near her desk and hands us a copy of the codes to use like a Rosetta stone.

I glance at Michael's open backpack again while Ms. Tannenbaum circles the room. I've been trying to give him my official sincere apology letter all day, but there hasn't been a time when he's been alone. People are all over him like he's a celebrity, thanks in part to the two stitches in his lip. At his locker. In the lunchroom. In the hall. His lip isn't a balloon anymore, but you can see the scab and bruises, even from across the room. Naturally, everyone has been making a fuss over him, especially Edna. What I wouldn't give to have hit a line drive at her instead. Her first question to him was, "So, are your parents going to sue Merci Suárez?" Then she mooned over his purplish chin. "My dad's a doctor. He could look at that, you know."

"I busted his lip, Edna," I told her. "Not his toenails."

"Ha." Hannah covered her mouth when Edna turned to glare.

Anyway, I'm glad he's not brain-damaged. I don't think he's mad at me either. I overheard him tell Edna that his mom took his phone away for the whole weekend because Miss McDaniels told her that he had been breaking school rules when he got hurt. I hope that's why he didn't answer my message.

I look at my pen pal assignment: Lena, who sits in the front row and cracks her knuckles. I don't really know her because this is our only class together. Plus, at lunch, she usually reads by herself outside. She got a spiky haircut over the weekend, though, with the ends dyed blue. She looks a little like a hedgehog.

I slide the envelope with my apology under my arm to hide it and walk to the front of the room. Edna glances up as I brush past her to get my papyrus. I search in the plastic marker bin, grab a couple, then take the long way back to my seat, dropping my note in the outer pouch of Michael's bag.

Lena is the only one who seems to notice. When she catches my eye, though, she looks away.

"What are you doing?" Roli asks me. It's hot in our room. Mami sometimes turns off the air-conditioning when the electricity bill has been too high or when the calendar says it's supposed to be fall, regardless of what the temperature is. Which means the room where I'm serving my sentence is hot and sticky. Plus, a mosquito the size of a small bat has found its way around the screen, too.

"Writing a letter, like most incarcerated people."

I wipe the sweat off my neck. I'm in shorts and a tank top, and my markers are spread all around me on the desk. For once, I claimed the space before Roli could hog it. I pushed back his stack of papers, his brain model, and the glass-encased fossils so I could work.

He picks up one of scrolls and scans it. So far, I am on the third page of my hieroglyphics message. "Writing a letter or a book?" he says.

"The pictures take up a lot of room," I say.

He tosses himself on his bed and sighs as he stares up at the ceiling. "Mami says to talk to you."

"About what?"

He pauses. "School and stuff."

"Well, don't." I color in the wings on the owl that stands for *M.*

He stays quiet for a while, but then he props himself up on his elbows. "Remember when I was the embalmer in Ms. Tannenbaum's class?"

"Is this the start of a 'talk'?" I say.

"But do you remember?"

I look up. He was new to Seaward that year. Abuela

sewed white towels together so he could wrap himself around his middle. She braided a long strip to tie around his head, too. He was bare-chested and wore sandals; he carried Papi's chisel and hammer. He rimmed his eyes with Tía's eyeliner. When he told the audience about preparing for the afterlife, we all believed him.

"Remember that kid who played the dead guy?" I ask. "Scary."

"James Tucker. He could lie still as an iguana. I think he fell asleep."

"And then there was your brain hook thing." I shudder. It was only Abuela's crocheting needle, but when Roli described extracting brains through nostrils, it seemed too real. One of the student teachers got faint, in fact. Mami had to help her to a chair.

"OK, *that* might have been a mistake." He nudges me with his smelly foot.

I put the finishing touch on my letter to Lena and hand the pages over to him. "What do you think? Can you read it?"

I start to give him the code sheet, but Roli puts up his hand to stop me. He loves puzzles, for one thing. Plus, his memory is a steel trap. I watch as his lips move over the hieroglyphs.

He hands it back. "Maybe reconsider the part where you say her haircut makes her forehead look smaller."

The next day in social studies, Ms. Tannenbaum hands out the notes we've written to our mystery pen pals. They're tied in scrolls and labeled with the name of the person they're for.

"You are to read the letter addressed to you and write the translation underneath," she says. "Your quiz grade will consist of two things: the effort you made in constructing the letter to your classmate, and your accuracy in decoding the message you have received. I will be walking by with my grade book in twenty minutes."

David puts his head on his desk. "Nobody said it had to be long," he groans. "Did anybody say that?"

"You may begin," Ms. Tannenbaum says.

I check out Lena from the corner of my eye as she starts working. Then I untie my scroll. It's a really short note, so I immediately think it's from David. But there's a five-dollar bill and a pouch of fruit snacks taped to the bottom. I freeze and pull the snacks and money into my lap as I start to decode. I'm not as fast as Roli, but I unravel the meaning quickly even though the same symbol is used for both *E* and *I*, which makes it tricky.

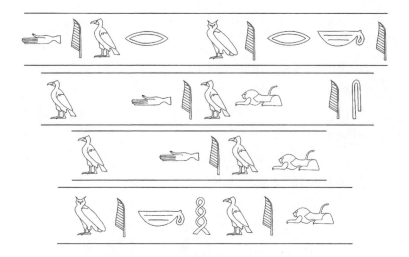

Dear Merci,
A deal is a deal.
Michael

Well, it's not like he's going to get points for being a conversationalist. But wow. Five bucks. I look across the room. Michael catches my eye. He grins, but then his scabbed lip cracks, and he winces and looks away.

"Who is yours from?" Jamie whispers, poking me with her pencil from behind.

I pretend to get back to work.

"I don't know," I say.

That night, Mami sends me over to play dominoes with Lolo. "Grands Day is next week," she says. "No hard feelings allowed. Go make up with Lolo and Abuela."

We're in their kitchen while Abuela finishes making dinner. This is typical of how we say sorry around here. Food and dominoes. Breaded steaks are my favorite, so I'm eating here tonight by myself. No Roli. No twins. And Lolo gets to play his favorite game. It's the perfect peace offering.

Lolo slides a double-five tile on the table and attaches it to the chain.

"Hey, cheater," I say. "You put the wrong one down. You need a four to play."

He looks more closely and pulls back his tile. "A four . . . you're right."

He pushes up his glasses and studies his options. "And how was school, preciosa? You haven't told me a thing. Nothing special to report?"

I shrug. All week, I've been doing my best to forget about the soccer team. If only I didn't have to do Lolo's job and help take care of the twins, Mami would have signed my permission form. I would have been wearing a soccer jersey at school, too, and getting fist bumps all day for making the team.

I take a deep breath and dig in my pocket.

"Look." I show him Michael's note and explain about the money. Lolo can't decode the message, so finally I just read it aloud.

"What do you think of that?" I ask.

"I think he's a man of his word. That's always a good sign."

But Abuela stops mashing the meat with a mallet and turns to me. She arches her brow. "Quizá ese huevo quiere sal," she says.

Maybe that egg wants salt?

"What does *that* mean?" I ask.

"Sió," Lolo tells her. "Merci's too young for romance."

"Romance?" I say. "Yuck."

He scans his tiles for a move. "Paso," he says, even though I can see a tile with four dots at the corner of his stack. He shouldn't skip.

Abuela's eyes linger on me as we play. "Too young? Time passes for all of us, viejo," she says quietly. Then she dips the first piece of meat into the breadcrumbs and drops it, spattering, into the oil.

CHAPTER 18

LOLO DOESN'T WANT TO GO.

He's dressed in his tan pants with the pointy creases and a button shirt. His hair is neatly combed. But something is wrong. He's pacing along the porch in his slippers.

"Leopoldo Suárez," Abuela says, "get your shoes on. We're going to be late for Grands Day. The children are waiting."

He gives her an ugly look. "Leave me alone."

Roli and I exchange glances. We've been standing here ten minutes, and Lolo is only getting more upset, though neither one of us can tell why.

"But, Lolo," I say, "I made your name tags and everything. It's like last year. You get to come to all my classes with me this morning and tell them about baseball. I'll take you to the field."

He pivots and walks away from me to the end of the porch.

"*¡Viejo!*" Abuela clips on her earring and loses her patience. "¡Por favor! This is important!"

Without warning, Lolo rushes at her. His face is bright red, and he's opening and closing his fists. "I'M NOT GOING!" he shouts.

I've never seen Lolo talk to Abuela like this. Not ever. It's Abuela who's the yeller. But right now, if I didn't know better, I'd swear Lolo was about to take a swing.

Abuela lets out a little yelp, and Roli jumps in between them in a flash, trying to hold Lolo back. "What are you doing?" he yells. "Stop!"

But Lolo shoves him hard.

"Get Papi," Roli says, still trying to keep them apart.

I'm frozen to the spot for a split second, but then my feet are racing toward my house.

"We need your help with Lolo," I shout into our kitchen window. "Come quick!"

In a flash, Papi comes running over. Mami is behind him, still in her slippers.

Papi steps close to Lolo and starts to steer Roli away.

"Cálmate, Papá," he says quietly. "Take a deep breath."

"I'm not going!" Lolo shouts again. "¡No voy!" And then a string of bad words in Spanish trips out of his mouth, words I'm never supposed to say. You can hear them echo in our yard.

"You don't have to go," Papi says in a quiet voice. "No one is forcing you. Just calm down."

Lolo gives Papi a nasty look, and hurries back to the other side of the porch again like an ogre.

Mami, meanwhile, brings Abuela to the rocker on the porch. Abuela's face is pale and her hands are trembling. "Are you hurt?" Mami whispers. Then she looks up at Roli. "Are you?"

I've never seen Roli look like this. He tucks in his shirt and smooths his hair, but even from here I can see that his eyes are watery. The sight of him makes me scared.

"I'm fine," he says.

Papi clears his throat. "I'll take care of this, Ana," he tells Mami. "Get these two to school."

"But Papi. It's Grands Day. Miss McDaniels and every-body is expecting Lolo—"

"Quiet, Merci." Papi reaches inside his pocket and tosses Roli the keys. "Start the car for your mother," Papi tells him. "You're going to be late."

Roli catches them and stalks off without looking back.

Now it's my turn to stand there, teary.

"¡Ay, Dios mío! . . ." Abuela's hand is still at her throat as she looks at me. "This is a disaster. Give him a glass of water. We can go in a little while when he's calm."

Papi cuts her off. "He's not going, and arguing about it is getting us nowhere."

"Maybe I should stay," Mami says.

He turns to her. "It's all right, Ana," he says. "I've got this. Go."

I'm upset the whole way to school because 1) I am Grandless and 2) nobody wants to explain anything.

"But why was he so angry?"

"Shh, Merci. Let Roli concentrate. We've had enough drama for one morning."

"Did they have a fight? Is he still mad that I yelled at the twins?"

"Quiet, please."

"Was he going to hit Abuela? Or Roli? He pushed him, you know."

"That's *enough*." Her voice is sharp. "Not another word."

I sit back and stare out the window the rest of the way, simmering. When we pull in, Roli hops out and grabs his backpack.

"Coming?" he says.

I turn my head and ignore him. He and Mami exchange looks as I stay put in the back seat.

"You go on," Mami tells him.

I watch him walk up the path as Mami slides into the driver's seat and adjusts the rearview mirror to her height. Then she turns to me.

"When you're calm, you need to get out of the car, Merci."

"I'd like to request a day off, please."

"No."

"But I'm going to be the only one without at least one grandparent here."

"I doubt that very much. Families are very far-flung these days. Not everyone is as lucky as you are to have your grandparents close by."

My mouth drops open.

"Lucky? How is what happened this morning lucky? Lolo was acting plain loco."

"Do not use that word about your grandfather ever again." She closes her eyes and sighs.

"Things happen over time, Merci," Mami finally says. "We grow up and older. We need to respect how things change and adjust."

Her words jumble out of her mouth and make me

angry. "What are you *talking* about?" I say, cutting her off. "It's all blah, blah, blah. Nobody will tell me what's really wrong!"

The car loop volunteer turns to see what's taking us so long. My face feels hot, and my eye is tugging hard into a corner.

"A school parking lot isn't the time or place to talk about these things," Mami says. "For now, what you need to know is that we've had a bad morning. It happens to people every day. Now, *please* don't make things worse. Get out of the car. Try to put this out of your mind and make the most of your day."

Of course, I do *not* enjoy my day.

It's hard enough not to have fancy grandparents whose names are carved into the bricks. But it's even worse to think about Lolo charging at Abuela with that terrible look on his face. Even when I'm having lunch with Hannah's Nana, I can still remember his shout and the ugly twist of his mouth as he said he wasn't coming.

Mami was right about one thing at least. There are a few kids whose grandparents didn't come because they live too far away. In fact, Edna's grands aren't here because they live in California, and Michael's are in Minnesota. And Lena's grandparents are all dead. So everyone sort of shares. When it's time for art, Lena watercolors with Ari's granddad, who wears a bow tie. Edna hangs around with Jamie's Meme and listens to her long stories about being a student photographer in France when there were riots. I catch Jamie rolling her eyes about Meme a couple of times, though. I guess sometimes all grandparents can be embarrassing, or maybe we're just getting too old for Grands Day, after all. Whatever. I stick with Hannah. Her grandmother wears a bright pink track suit because she's a master runner in marathons. She shows us her watch that tells steps, distance, and calories.

All the grandparents are nice.

But none of them are mine.

That afternoon, when I get home from school, I change into my home clothes and wander over to Abuela's house. I move a little like Tuerto when he crosses the street, cautious and listening for sounds as I go to the back yard. Not even the twins are around. I stand at Abuela's screen door for a long while without knocking. Everything is quiet. There's only the low murmurs from a radio on the windowsill.

"Lolo's napping," Abuela says when she finally comes into the kitchen and spots me outside.

She opens the door a little wider and hands me two cookies and an envelope. I can see she's in her house clothes again, but her special pearl earrings are still on from this morning. "Give this to those nice people in the office," she whispers. "A little donation from us." Then she reaches for my hand and squeezes it. "I'm so sorry we couldn't go, Merci."

CHAPTER 19

I'VE BEEN WAITING FOR MAMI in the outdoor sitting area of the Lourdes Killington Residence in Palm Beach for over an hour. It's a fancy place downtown where a lot of senior citizens live, if they can afford it. Last year, the fifth grade sang here near the holidays. After, we had hot chocolate and played checkers, even though it was a sunny day and over ninety degrees. Hannah almost fainted in her Santa hat that day. I'd be sweating to death now, too, except for the wind. The gusts are strong enough that a few of the plastic chairs around me keep toppling. The weatherman said there's a small hurricane out over the water. It's not coming our way, but at least it's making a nice breeze.

Anyway, Mami said we should spend some time together, since she's been so busy lately. She wants to make things up to me, she says. Soccer. The Grands Day disaster. But as usual, everything has gotten squeezed around her work. It's Columbus Day weekend. A lot of people have gone away, but not us. Mami's giving a talk, the one she's been practicing for. It's about how older people can work on their balance so they don't fall. Mami tried to get Lolo and Abuela to practice last night by having them close their eyes and stand on one leg. She didn't get far. I guess no one was in the mood. "We are not flamingos, Ana," Abuela said, and sent her packing.

I wouldn't have agreed to tag along except that Mami promised we could go to the bike shop after. It's only a few blocks from here. I have about ninety bucks saved now.

I'm on a glider in the garden, listening to my music and letting the wind push the swing for me. Mami promised me it would be thirty minutes, but I should have known better. She always loses track of time. I shuffle my favorite songs and play them each twice. But when another fifteen minutes roll by, I decide to go inside and look for her.

The lady at the desk smiles and buzzes me in. She's wearing khaki shorts and a blue polo shirt, like a camp counselor. Her name tag says HI, MY NAME IS GAYLE. She's got art supplies around her and is busy cutting out cardboard pumpkin patterns.

"Good morning," Gayle says. "Are you here for a visit?"

"No, miss. I'm looking for my mom. She's doing a talk here." I point to the flyer that's pinned to the bulletin board. Mami's photocopied face smiles down at us.

"Oh, yes. That's happening in the O'Malley Meeting Room." She uses her scissors to point down a long hall. "You walk straight down this corridor and through the double doors into the next building. Make a right at the first opening. You'll see it on your left."

Except for the handrails that run the length of all the walls, it would be easy to mix this place up with a hotel. Big potted plants. Fancy paintings. A chart pad on an easel announces the Casino Night later tonight and an apple-pie tasting tomorrow. A few people are sitting together in the living area, and a few others are at a table playing cards.

One lady waves to me as I go by. "Hello, darling," she calls out, and I wave back.

I go through the doors that say PHASE II. But when I get to the other side, I can't remember if Gayle said to make a left or a right. I look down the hall and see a nurse's station at the far end, so I decide to go that way and ask directions again.

It's a little quieter in this section, and my sneakers

squeak against the shiny floor. I notice a faint smell, too, like some sort of cleaner. There are rooms on either side of the walkway. The beds are empty in some, but in one, a man is asleep in front of a loud TV, his mouth hanging open. My feet slow to a crawl and then I stand there, staring at him, suddenly thinking of Doña Rosa and how she died by herself.

"Can I help you?" An aide steps out from the room across the hall and startles me. She's wearing blue rubber gloves, and she's holding bed linens and towels. The door behind her has a placard that says MRS. ETHEL BLAIR.

I can't help but glance past her at a small lady who's watching us wide-eyed from her bed. She doesn't smile at all.

"I'm looking for the O'Malley Room," I say.

"Oh, I'll walk you there," the aide says. "I'm heading that way." She calls over her shoulder. "I'll be back with your lunch in a little while, Mrs. Blair." Then she pulls the door closed a bit.

"Are you visiting one of your grandparents?" she asks as she drops the linens in a rolling cart. She pulls off her gloves and drops them in the trash alongside it.

Abuela or Lolo living here?

I can't imagine such a thing. Their house smells like garlic and onions and cinnamon. The sound of Abuela's novelas drifts across the yard at night. Lolo's shoes are always by the kitchen door. Who would cook dinner when Mami's late, or watch the twins? Who would tend the garden?

I shake my head. "No, miss. My grandparents don't live here. My mom is just giving a presentation, that's all. She's a physical therapist."

"Ah." She nods as we get to the fork in the hallway. "Well, the O'Malley is just over that way," she says. "See it? Make a right up ahead."

I'm still thinking about the man in his room and Mrs. Blair after we leave.

Mami and I are walking along the crowded row of new bikes inside the shop while the owner rents some beach cruisers at the register. Everything smells of rubber tires and new vinyl.

"How about this one?" Mami asks. It's a purple one that matches the lavender scrubs she's wearing. "It won't break the bank."

I shrug. "I don't like the flowers on the grips."

She pulls out a few more, including a mountain bike, even though the terrain is flat as a pancake here.

Nothing seems right.

"What's the matter?" Mami says. "You don't seem very excited."

I tap the tires of the bike nearest me and check out the tread, thinking back to the Sunday morning when Lolo fell to the pavement.

Do not tell Abuela, he'd said. *Not a word.*

And then, just as quickly, I picture Mrs. Blair in her bed, watching the world with those frightened eyes. The thought makes my chest squeeze.

"Do those people have nowhere else to go?" I blurt out.

Mami looks confused. "What people?"

"Mrs. Ethel Blair and the others."

"Who?"

"The people who live at the senior center."

Mami plucks at a price tag and pauses.

"Well, it depends. Some people live there because they want to be with others their own age who enjoy the same things. Did you see the activity board? I would get tired having a social life that busy. No wonder it costs so much to live there!" She drags out a bright yellow bike and shakes her head at the price tag. "I paid this much for my first car."

"But it's not all like that, Mami. I saw people who looked . . . alone and sick."

I can see Mami trying to hold her not-that-bad smile. It's like when she told us Tuerto was going to lose his eye after the fight with a raccoon a few years ago.

"Aging isn't the same for everyone. Some older people need only a little support to be independent. But others need a good deal of help over time, Merci. And sometimes it's more than their families can give them at home. They need to be somewhere safe."

I glue my eyes on the bike, thinking about Lolo and all the ways he's been acting strangely. I think again of Doña Rosa and the day she came over to complain about her son, who wanted her to move to an asilo de ancianos. "¡Qué horror!" Abuela said, shuddering. "Those terrible places."

"Are we ever going to send Abuela and Lolo to live there? Are they changing in that way?"

Mami looks at me for a long time. "Merci . . ."

My eye begins its nervous creep. "Are they?"

"Everyone changes, mi vida. Even you are changing. There's no stopping that. But here's what I know for sure. Abuela and Lolo have us to help them," she says. "You don't have to worry about that, at least not right now."

She wraps her arm around my shoulder and leads me to the next aisle, where they keep the discontinued models.

When *will* it be time to worry? That crossing guard is in my head again, stopping me from asking.

I go from bike to bike, trying to look interested, but my heart isn't in it.

"Let's go," I tell Mami after a while. "There's nothing here I like."

CHAPTER 20

AUTUMN IN FLORIDA ISN'T THE WAY you see in books, with people bundled up and colorful leaves blowing off trees in the wind. It happens in small ways that most people can barely notice. The heat starts to break, so we eat dinner on the patio. The snowbird people from cold places like Michigan and Canada suddenly start to wander into El Caribe to make it even more crowded. Abuela and Lolo plant new beds of impatiens to last for the winter.

At Seaward, we know it's autumn when the festival happens. This year, it falls right on Halloween, too, which is perfect. I'll be part of putting it together because the sixth-graders are always in charge of the fairway. Every third-hour class has two weeks to build one of the carnival games. I'm so thankful not to have Mr. Dixon's third-hour math class. He's not much for fun and holidays, which he says "impede student concentration and force him into the role of babysitter." I feel bad for his students. They'll have the most boring stall for sure, same as last year. *Estimate how many pieces of candy corn are in this jar and win it all.* He doesn't even write a new index card with the question. No one wants to go to a festival to do calculations of mass and volume, except maybe Roli, who did, in fact, win last year. He edged out (who else?) Ahana Patel by two pieces.

Ms. Tannenbaum lets us decide the game we want, and we vote on cornhole. The only thing that we can't change is that the game has to have an ancient civilization theme.

"It will be excellent advertising for our Great Tomb Project in December." Ms. Tannenbaum then sweetens the deal. "I also plan to give extra credit for those of you who dress as the gods and goddesses we've been studying," she tells us. "It will come in handy for some of you who struggled on our last quiz." She looks around the room with a knowing glance. "Be prepared to tell us about the deity of your choice."

So it's more or less settled. It takes some haggling to

make a sketch, but in the end, we agree. We'll shape the boards like giant triangles to make them look like pyramids. Lena's dad is donating the wood. I offer some of Papi's old paint. A few others will build them.

After that, we spend most of the class hour deciding on costumes and researching. We get books off the shelf and pull up the sites Ms. Tannenbaum tells us to use. Jackal heads, lion faces, spears — it's hard to choose. Even after, when we're all walking in a group toward math class, we're still making our decisions.

"My brother is in the theater department at Dreyfoos," Hannah says. "They did *Cats* last year. I'm going borrow a good cat mask for Bastet."

"What are you going as, Michael?" Edna says, sidling up to him, which makes Rachel's eyes bulge. I notice that Edna asks Michael something every few minutes. *Do you have a pencil, Michael? What do you have for lunch, Michael? Where do you live, Michael? Have you been to the beach yet, Michael?*

"Not sure," he says. "Maybe Anubis. It's a cool jackal head. I don't know how to make that, though."

There's a mob of kids crowding the exit when we get to the building. One of the doors somehow got locked, and now everyone is pushing and shoving as they try to get out through the only one that still opens.

"Make way," Edna says, but not even Her Imperial Highness can get through this tangle.

Finally, Michael steps forward. He's big enough so that when he stands there, he's a human wall blocking people so we can get by. One by one, we slip under his arm.

"Thanks, Michael," Edna says sweetly as she goes.

I'm the last one through. I squeeze past just as Michael moves and lets the crush of kids finally pass in the other direction.

We start walking together.

"What costume are *you* making?" he asks.

"Personally? None. But my grandmother can sew anything, so I know it'll be good."

"Yeah?"

"She used to own a dress shop." I don't add that it was in her back bedroom.

He stops just as we're about to turn down my hall. "Can she help me with my Anubis costume?" he asks. "I need the extra credit. I bombed that quiz."

A little jolt goes through me, like when one of the twins jumps out to surprise me. I'm thinking of Abuela's salty egg idea, and it makes me look over my shoulder for a second, as if Edna and the girls are right there. Thankfully, they've been swallowed up in the glob of kids. I'm rooted to the spot, with him looking down at me. But here's the thing: if Michael is having funny ideas about me, he can just forget it. My heart belongs to Jake Rodrigo.

"It's a good Sunshine Buddy thing and all," he says, trying to convince me. "Better than busting my face, at least."

"Not funny."

"Uff da! Neither are stitches, Merci!"

The bell rings and everyone scatters.

"Ask her," he begs.

All it takes is three strides for that kid to disappear inside his math class.

Uff da?

I get to Mr. Dixon's class just as he's closing the door. I'm the last one to slide into my seat. I'm flushed, like I've done something wrong, again, but I realize helping Michael will get me some points with Miss McDaniels, especially after the baseball incident. I open my book and get cracking on the problems.

None of us in the family has ever worn a store-bought costume, because Abuela will not have it. Over the years, I've been an angel, a mermaid with a long tail, a lion, a Shasta daisy, a chocolate-chip cookie (Roli was the milk), and a tree, which made running hard. I know that because the twins were puppies that year, and they kept pretending to pee on me.

The only trouble with costume time is that Abuela can get even bossier than usual.

We've just finished dinner outside when Roli tells us to wait right where we are. He walks the twins to Tía's place, and a few minutes later, they come back with a shocker.

"What do you think? We're a mad scientist and his henchmen," Roli says.

Papi glances at Abuela and takes a bite of the last merengue, like he's sitting down to watch the fights on TV.

Abuela looks on, arms crossed, as the twins model their getup. They're wearing lab coats that Roli borrowed from Seaward, old swim goggles, and black rubber gloves that Papi uses when he's working with paint thinner. Their hair has been moussed to peaks with some of Tía Inés's hair foam.

"The sleeves on those coats are too long for the twins," Abuela says.

"Yeah, but besides *that,* with a little blood on their faces and dark circles under their eyes, they're perfect lunatics," Roli says proudly. "Do the laugh," he instructs.

The twins widen their eyes. *"Bwa-ha-ha-ha."*

"I hate to admit how good this looks, Mamá," Tía says. "And it *is* less work for you."

But Abuela still looks injured. "I had the pattern for the piratas and everything. I bought hooks for their hands and was even going to reuse those patches that Merci used to wear for her eye exercises."

I thought I had gotten rid of those, but anyway, this is my cue. I reach into my backpack and pull out the book I brought home.

"Don't worry, Abuela," I say. "*I* still need lots of help on my costume. It's for the fall festival—and for extra credit."

Tía looks at the page I marked in my textbook. "Ooh, Egyptian goddesses! I think I have a wig that's a pageboy. You'll look so pretty."

I roll my eyes. That's exactly what I'm trying to avoid. Cloth wound around me tightly. Wigs. Eyeliner. Jewelry. *Blech.*

"Actually, I want to go as this one." I point at the picture of Ammut. It shows the head of a crocodile, the body of a lioness, and the rump of a hippopotamus. "She's a demon."

Abuela crosses herself and looks up at the sky. "What are you saying? I'm not turning my only granddaughter into something evil. ¡Dios, nos ampare! It's bad enough that the babies are going as madmen." She gives Roli a pointed look.

"Mad scientists," he corrects. "Specifically, evil henchmen."

"But Ammut wasn't evil," I say. "She ate the souls of those who had been wicked in life. Plus, there are super-powers to consider. She was immortal *and* could be in two places at one time."

"Now that's a superpower I wish I had." Mami has been looking tired all day. She got three new patients this week.

Tía studies the picture and points at the haunches. "There's some serious booty on this costume," she says.

"It's all the rage," Mami says as she scrapes my plate clean and stacks it on hers. Then she pulls out her tissue and wipes her nose.

"Stay put, Ana," Papi says, taking the stack from her. "I'll clear the dishes."

Abuela looks at Mami. "Ana. You're her mother. Are you saying that you approve of this costume?"

I put my hands up in prayer and do a silent plead.

Mami blows her nose hard. Then she shrugs and smiles. "What's the harm?" she says. "Merci is old enough to choose what she wants."

"No. She'll always be my little preciosa," Lolo offers from the head of the table.

"Lolo," I say. My voice is sharp. I know he's trying to be sweet, but his pet name for me suddenly feels annoying, like a box I want to get out of.

"This is a little complicated . . ." Abuela mutters. She clicks her tongue and studies the image more closely. "I'll need to get some foam for that bottom . . . and maybe cardboard for the crocodile head . . ."

"Um." I lower my voice. "I have a kid in my class who needs some help, too."

"Yes?"

"Michael Clark wants to go as Anubis." I point to another picture. "He'll need a jackal head."

"¡Un chacal!"

Tía's ears perk up. "Michael Clark? You mean the kid you didn't want to be nice to?"

"The boy from the movies?" Papi adds darkly.

"The one whose face she busted," Roli says.

"Yes, OK? Michael," I say.

"Well, he'll need to come for a fitting," Abuela tells me.

"You mean here?" I ask.

"How else can I make something that fits correctly?"

"But that means he has to come home with me."

"Well, obviously. And it needs to be in the next day or two, Merci. These things take time."

I stand there, blinking.

"Do you want my services for this costume or not, niña?" Abuela says.

"Fine. I'll ask."

I pull my phone from my pocket and text his number.

Can you come over tomorrow to work on your costume?

I press send and stand there staring at the screen as I wait.

A loud squeak behind me makes me jump and turn around. La Boba has appeared mysteriously from the sewing room closet. She has a sheet slung over her decapitated neck to make her look like a ghost.

"Ooooo-oooo . . . Bring me the head of Michael Clark . . ."

I chase the twins under the folding table, where they hide between Lolo's legs. They're screeching louder than La Boba's noisy wheels as I try to grab them. But just then my phone vibrates. When I check, an even bigger jolt of fear shoots through me.

He says he can come.

CHAPTER 21

I HONESTLY DON'T KNOW WHAT makes me more nervous today: Michael coming over to get fitted for his costume, or the fact that Roli is driving us home from school. Mami woke up sick. She has fever, chills, aches—the whole tamal. When we walked into her bedroom this morning, we got hit with the smell of Vicks VapoRub. The scent was strong enough to melt your face. Mami's gaze was glassy, and she had the ends of a tissue shoved in her nostrils. Papi was already gone; he'd left early for a job.

"The keys are hanging in the kitchen," she told Roli. She rolled over with a groan and pulled the blanket to her chin.

We pull into Seaward at our usual turtle crawl, but thankfully in one piece. I've only got a minute to get to class, though. The lot attendant points us to the visitor section since we don't have a parking sticker, which means a long walk to my building. Miss McDaniels has strict rules about who parks where. If she notices that a car is in the wrong place, she'll order a tow truck in no time flat. I've seen it with my own eyes.

"Meet me here at three fifteen sharp," Roli says.

I grab the two cans of paint that Papi left for me and start my mad dash to homeroom. The paint was from a job in Boynton Beach, a baby's nursery. All I can say is, poor kid; he's probably blind by now. The color is screaming yellow, like an egg yolk. On the upside, it's just the right shade for painting our cornhole game for the fall festival booth.

I'm almost to my building, huffing and puffing, when Edna and Jamie approach me on the path. They don't look happy, although maybe that's because their matching high ponytails are pulled too tight.

Edna steps forward and cocks her head. "Michael Clark is going to your house?"

"Today?" Jamie adds.

I stand there breathing heavily. News travels fast, I see.

"He wanted help with his costume, and my grandmother can sew."

They exchange looks.

"He likes Edna," Jamie says. "Not you."

He *maybe* likes Edna, but I know better than to point out the difference.

"What does that have to do with anything?" I say. "It's just a school project. Plus, I need something to tell Miss McDaniels for Sunshine Buddies."

An awkward silence follows as I stand there. Edna looks more sad than angry, and I don't know why. I don't like Michael, at least not that way.

The paint cans are getting heavy, and it feels like my arms are being pulled like one of the twins' stretch toys. "We're going to be late, and these weigh a ton, so . . ."

I can feel their eyes on me as I walk away.

All day, Edna's mojo is especially potent.

I go over things in my mind to see exactly what I've done. Our fun at the movies seems like a million years ago instead of just a few weeks.

At lunchtime, she won't look at me, and I notice that the other girls get kind of quiet, too. Only Hannah waits for me when the lunch bell rings. And then in PE that afternoon, we play lacrosse and Edna doesn't pass to me once, even when I'm clear and have a perfect shot on the goal.

And worse, after school, Edna and Jamie are standing

around the bike rack near where Roli parked. I can see them whispering as I run to join Michael, who's already waiting by our car. Roli is hurrying across the parking lot, too.

"Sorry!" Roli says when he reaches us. "We were ordering the cow eyes for next week."

"Don't ask," I whisper to Michael.

He takes off his red blazer and tie and starts to climb into the back seat. The back is tiny, though, and that's never going to work with his long legs.

"I'll get back there," I say.

My phone buzzes almost as soon as we pull out of the parking lot. It's a snap. When I tap it open, I see a picture of Edna crossing her eyes at me and letting her tongue hang out. Is she making fun of my eye? If she weren't mad at me, I'd say no. Everyone sends dumb snaps all the time, right? It's just something we do occasionally, like wearing 3-D glasses for a movie, like eating ice cream too fast on purpose to see who gets a headache, maybe even like stealing each other's lunches.

But now it feels different, meaner.

I'm still deciding what to think when the snap disappears. I stare at the screen. Everything has evaporated, like it never happened at all. The only way I know it's real is by the sweat on my palms.

I turn my phone off and slide it into my backpack.

Roli tries to hurry along the side streets, and by that, I mean he drives at twenty-six miles per hour, but we still get stuck at the drawbridge at its scheduled opening. There's a long line of cars waiting for the boats to pass underneath. It makes me wonder if any of them are Frackas yachts down there.

"Look, Roli," I say, pointing. "That one over there is called the *Sea Señorita*. Lolo would love that."

"Who's Lolo?" Michael asks.

"Our grandfather."

"Does he have a boat?" Michael asks me, turning around.

"Who, Lolo?" Roli snorts. "No." He scrolls his phone for some music to pass the time.

"Oh."

"We like renting charters a lot better," I say quickly.

Roli looks up at me in his rearview mirror. I'm stretching the truth and he knows it. We've only ever rented a boat once.

"Do *you* like boating?" I ask.

Michael shrugs. "Yeah. We used to take the Johnson boat north in summer, but we sold it when we left Minnesota. We'd go ice fishing for winter break, too. Not much of that here, I guess." He sounds a little sad.

Roli looks at him. "Um, no, Lake Okeechobee doesn't freeze over." He keeps his voice calm, like when he's trying to tutor someone who is a blockhead.

"Lake Okeechobee? Where's that?"

"It's the enormous blue spot on the map of Florida," Roli says. "It's west of here, past the sugar cane," Roli says. "Which is the problem, of course."

Oh, no. Before I can stop him, Roli starts in about fertilizer that runs off into the lake and how that eventually leads to the toxic algae in the ocean that closed the beaches a few years ago. "It's a green slime that smells like farts and can double its biomass in a day." He actually says this.

I cut him off before Michael's head explodes. "But there's other fun stuff to do near the beach," I say from the back. I kick Roli's seat hard and he goes back to picking music.

I tell Michael about the time Lolo took us on a night fishing trip on a charter boat and we caught a twenty-pound tuna in the moonlight. I tell him about the Save the Manatee Club, and the sea cow named Tubby that our class adopted last year.

Michael seems a little happier after that. When the bridge finally closes, he sits back. Then Roli's favorite song comes on, and we head for home.

I'm jittery when we pull into our driveway. It's strange to have someone from Seaward here. The truth is, nobody outside our family comes over. We just meet our friends at school or at the places we're going. We've never talked about why, but somehow we both know that's our rule. Nobody else at school lives with their whole family like we do at Las Casitas. And brothers and sisters don't share rooms, so our friends might think we're weird or poor, even though what are you supposed to do if your house is small? Other people's houses seem to have more of what's fun, too. There's no pool in our backyard, just the one at the condos across the street that we used to sneak into when Doña Rosa loaned us her gate key. There's no Dance Central video game here, like at Hannah's. No Echo speaker that can search the web and answer your craziest questions, like Rachel has. It's just plain here.

Abuela is waiting for us on the front patio, measuring tape already strung around her neck. Lolo is there, too. He's standing up and he looks fidgety. Has he been pacing, I wonder? I glance at Michael, but he doesn't seem to notice anything. I don't want him, or anyone else, to see Lolo acting weird.

"About my grandmother . . ." I tell Michael when we finally pull under our carport. "She can be a little picky.

And bossy." I don't say anything about Lolo, though. Roli and I have worked out a plan just in case.

Suddenly the twins come racing across the yard at our car. They're screaming like lunatics and pressing their faces against the car windows.

"Do they bite?" Michael asks.

I lean toward him in the front seat. "Not usually. But if either of them offers you anything to eat, definitely check it or show me first," I tell him.

"Um, OK."

The twins stare up as Michael gets out of the car.

"Are you a ghost?" Axel asks.

"Or a giant?" Tomás adds.

"Don't be rude," I say.

"Get back from our guest, boys," Abuela calls, motioning to them.

Roli grabs Tomás just as he's about to fish inside Michael's backpack and follows us to Abuela's porch.

Lolo has stuffed his hands in his pockets and jiggles the change nervously. He says hello to us when we reach them, but he seems distracted. Then he turns to Michael. "Ana is feeling sick today. Very sick."

Michael looks at me, unsure. "Who's Ana?"

"My mom," I say. "She's got the flu." I turn back to

Lolo, my stomach already doing nervous flips. I wonder if maybe he's been worried about Mami all day. I smile, trying to act like nothing's wrong.

"Lolo, this is Michael," I say.

It's as if he doesn't even hear me. "Ana is sick today," he says again.

Abuela steps closer. "She'll be fine, viejo," she says. Then she offers Michael a big smile. "Hello there."

Roli glances at me and takes his cue without me having to pinch him. "How about some dominoes?" he says to Lolo. "My place. Mami might want some company."

"Dominoes!" Axel shouts. And the twins tear down the path for our door. Lolo follows.

Michael stands in Abuela's kitchen a few minutes later, unsure where to sit. My eyes scan the plastic flowers near the sink, the faded wallpaper that Tía keeps telling her to take down, the wall clock shaped like a stopwatch, the teeny ants zigzagging near the leaky faucet. When I sit down at the table, I stuff my toe under the table leg to make sure it doesn't jiggle too much.

Abuela has snacks ready, of course—a spread of things from El Caribe. I start to reach for a couple of ham croquetas when I notice Michael taking a cautious look.

"What are these?" he asks.

I tell him the names and which ones are ham, cheese, or sweet. "They're good," I say, but I can see that he still looks unsure. "My aunt might have Oreos next door, if you want those."

"No. That's OK." He chooses an empanada, sniffs it, and bites in. He chews slowly, thinking. "Well, that's interesting," he says at last. "It's kind of like fry bread."

We finish our snacks and Abuela leads us to the sewing room. "Excuse the mess," she says. Bits of foam and cardboard litter the floor. "See what you think of those," she says, pointing. She's drawn her costume ideas on a torn sheet of pattern paper and taped it to the wall.

The sketches look almost exactly like what's in our book. Michael squints and looks closer. "But wait. I'll be wearing a skirt?"

"More or less," Abuela says. "It's not up to me to change history. But I'll make it reach to your knee so you're decent. On the bright side, my granddaughter said you might need this." She reaches behind the ottoman and pulls out the most amazing mask. It's not quite finished, but you can see the shape of the jackal head, with beaded eyes and a thin, sharp snout. The mouth even opens and closes with a hinge she made from round head fasteners.

"Holy buckets!" Michael slides it on carefully. "How does it look?" His voice is an echo—perfect for the god of the afterlife.

"Fierce!" I say.

"Thanks!" he says to Abuela. "It's perfect!"

"You'll have to paint it and add the details," Abuela tells him, "but you've got the basic form."

She can barely hide how proud she is, but I can see that she may have overdone it today. She's rubbing her hands the way she always does when her arthritis is bothering her. Sometimes Mami wraps Abuela's hands in warm towels and pulls gently on her fingers to make them feel better. I make a note to do that for her later, after Michael goes home.

"It must have taken all day," I say to her. "Thank you."

She bows her head a little. "Well . . . Lolo was underfoot, como siempre, and there were the twins to pick up . . ." Her voice drifts a little, and I suddenly wonder if maybe she ever gets tired of caring for all of us.

She points to the ottoman.

"Get up there, please, Michael. Hold your arms out, like so." He does what Abuela says. I swear, with that mask on, he looks just like a scarecrow. I snap his picture and turn him into one before sending it to his phone.

Then I pretend to read *People en Español* so I don't have to look at her measure his chest and waist.

She finishes with Michael and then motions to me. "You're next, mi vida," she says, stifling a yawn.

My face flushes. Is she going to wrap that measure around my chest right here in front of him?

"Why don't you rest, Abuela? You look tired. We can work on mine this weekend."

I turn to Michael. "Come on. I'll show you our one-eyed cat before you have to go."

CHAPTER 22

"ALL RIGHT, EVERYONE. I'D LIKE you in pairs," Ms. Tannenbaum says on Monday morning. "Try to find someone you haven't worked with in class before."

We all groan. If we haven't worked with someone, it's probably for a reason, right? And now, since a lot of the girls have already worked in groups together, it leaves the boys as our main partner options.

When nobody moves, Ms. Tannenbaum sets her phone's timer. "Come on, now. We have a lot to cover. I'll give you exactly one minute to pair up. Go."

Everyone rushes around the room looking for a partner, but my feet feel nailed to the floor as I try to decide which way to go. Each time I head toward someone, it seems like they're snatched by someone else.

"Ten seconds!" Ms. Tannenbaum says.

Just as I start to panic, Michael walks over.

"Hey," he says.

"Time," Ms. Tannenbaum says before my lips can work. "Pull two desks together and please tap on the religion folder on your screen."

"No fair, Ms. Tannenbaum," says Edna, pointing at us. She's standing next to Lena near the front of the room. "Those two are working on their fall festival costumes together."

Ms. Tannenbaum looks over at us. "True?"

I nod.

But Michael only shrugs. "You said to find a partner we haven't worked with in class, though. We did the costume at Merci's house."

Ms. Tannenbaum hesitates a second. "Fair enough."

Edna pulls her face into a frown that worries me. I don't know if it's because she doesn't like working with Lena, or because she's mad that Michael picked me. All I can think of is that ugly snap Edna sent me last week when Michael came home with Roli and me. Suddenly I wish he had walked over to someone else.

Ms. Tannenbaum turns back to the class and starts

the lesson. "So, let's look at the role that religion played in everyday life. What benefits would religious beliefs have in their world?"

It turns out that Michael and I work well together. We breeze through the worksheet, mostly because I read the chapter last night and because he doesn't mind typing our answers. When we finish I'm surprised to realize we're the first ones done. Everyone else is still working, even Lena and Edna. When I ask, Ms. Tannenbaum lets us visit her stash of board games. We borrow the mancala game and play quietly while the others finish.

"Hey, is your grandmother done making our costumes?" he asks. " I still need to paint it."

"Almost." I drop my marbles in the spaces around the board. "She's been kind of busy this week, but she'll get it done."

It's true. With Mami down with the flu, Abuela has been busy cooking dinner for us every night. And it's been hard for her to sew during the day like she used to because Lolo gets bored and wants to go for walks, which she insists on taking with him. So she's been staying up late to finish our costumes. Last night, I fell asleep to the whir of her sewing machine through the yard.

"Good," he says. "I need the grade. If I get all As this

semester, we're going to Disney over winter break." He scoops up marbles and takes his turn.

"Lucky," I say. Good grades never come with perks at our house. Roli has ruined that curve forever. "Don't worry, though. You'll get an A."

CHAPTER 23

A WEEK LATER, I WAIT at the front desk. Miss McDaniels is on the phone, so I put down the jackal mask while she finishes. Roli drove us to school again, or should I say *crawled* us here. No surprise, the slowpoke made us late. He's still parking the car, or trying to.

Miss McDaniels hangs up and comes to the counter. She turns the sign-in screen in my direction.

"Overslept?"

"No, miss." I tap the icon for tardies and add my name to today's list of shame. "My mom is still getting better from the flu, so my brother drove. He has a speed impediment."

"Set your alarm earlier," she says. "I won't consider it excused next time."

She prints out a pass, and I glance down when she hands it to me.

"Can you add a few minutes to this, please? I need to drop off a project in Ms. Tannenbaum's room." And then for good measure: "It's for my Sunshine Buddy. Michael and I worked on costumes for the fall festival together." I hand her my weekly report and smile.

Miss McDaniels hesitates, making sure I'm not conning her.

"Very well." She writes a new time in pen and initials it. "Five minutes granted."

When I get to Ms. Tannenbaum's classroom, I find that it's empty and the lights are off. I forgot that she has her first period free. For a second, I wonder if I should leave Michael's costume in the front office with Miss McDaniels, but I won't have time. I try the door, and, luckily, it's open.

I put the jackal mask and toga on Ms. Tannenbaum's desk and search for paper and pen, but I don't see any. So I grab a dry-erase marker and write her a big note on the whiteboard.

MS. T—I AM LEAVING THIS MASK HERE
BECAUSE IT IS TOO BIG TO FIT IN MY
LOCKER OR LUG AROUND. IT'S FOR
MICHAEL CLARK.
—MERCI, PERIOD 3.

I look at the mask one last time. Michael is going to look perfect for the fall festival, so I hope he does a good job painting it and presenting his god. Now that this one is done, Abuela and I can finish up mine tonight. It has an enormous hippo booty made of sofa-cushion foam, and my crocodile head is going to open and close on hinges, just like Michael's.

There are only two minutes left on my pass. I hoist my backpack over my shoulder and shut the door behind me on my way to class.

I'm standing at my locker, collecting my things for social studies after second period. "Did David and them finish making the game board?" I ask Jamie. That's who was in charge of sawing the holes in the plywood and painting it.

She's standing right next to me, talking with Edna. When she doesn't answer, I say it louder. "Jamie, is the game board done?"

But she doesn't so much as turn. They just keep talking with the other girls. It's as if I'm a ghost. That's how I know for sure that something's up.

"Everybody can ride home with me after the festival tomorrow," Edna says. "And if you can't, just get to my house by nine o'clock. That's when we're watching the movie."

"But I'm not allowed to watch that," Hannah says irritably. She yanks her lock but it won't open. "It's rated R, isn't it?"

"You have to watch scary movies on Halloween," Edna says. "It's the rule. Besides, how's your mother going to know?"

"Hello? She's going to ask your mom," Hannah says.

"Well, my mom won't know either. David is bringing the DVD over from his brother's slasher collection."

I stare dully into my locker, pretending to look for something. No one has said anything to me about a party at all.

"The boys are coming over, too?" Rachel says. "Michael and them?" Her eyes bug out.

Edna looks right past me. "A few. For the swimming and beach bonfire—and the movie. Not for the sleepover part on the terrace. Obviously."

"Obviously," Jamie says, giggling.

My eyes slide over to Hannah. She glances at me and turns bright red. "I hate this stupid lock," she mutters, giving it a savage yank.

My locker suddenly seems small and crowded with papers and notebooks. I pull out the wrong textbook, and then my science folder spills to the floor. I shove them both back inside the mess.

Edna keeps talking. "Don't forget to bring a note if you're riding home with me," she calls over my head. "Never mind. I'll do a group text to remind everyone. You, too, Lena."

Lena, who is never invited to anything, looks up but doesn't answer. When they're gone, she turns to me.

"I think I saw David carrying the cornhole boards from the car loop this morning," she says quietly.

"Oh," I say. "Thanks."

I slam my locker shut and walk to class, pretending I don't care. And maybe I don't. Who wants to be at Edna's stupid party? Not me.

But even as I try to convince myself, I start to wonder if Michael is one of the boys who was invited or if she's mad at him, too. If he is, will he go? When I realize the answer might be yes, I get even madder.

I toss my things down as soon as I get to social studies. At least Michael will get to see his Anubis costume now.

But the costume isn't on his desk.

And when I look toward the front of the room, I don't see it on Ms. Tannenbaum's either. Or on the windowsill. Or anywhere.

I get up and walk toward Ms. Tannenbaum. When I get close, I spot a piece of cardboard sticking out of her garbage can. Dread crawls up from my stomach as I look more carefully. Sure enough, when I pull it out, I realize that the jackal mask—or what's left of it—has been crammed into the trash. It's in two pieces now, ripped apart at the jaws. The cardboard has been stomped flat, too. The toga has been slashed with marker and is balled up underneath.

"What happened?" I ask Ms. Tannenbaum. My voice must be louder than I intend because she looks up and frowns.

"Excuse me?"

"Michael's costume for the festival." I hold up the two pieces. "How did it get broken? I left it on your desk this morning when you weren't here. Didn't you read my note?"

But when I point to the whiteboard, there's nothing there at all, not even a trace of my writing. Somebody has erased my message.

"I didn't receive a note," Ms. Tannenbaum says. "And this is the first that I'm seeing this." She knits her brow. "I'm so sorry, Merci. I have no idea how it got damaged."

The bells rings, but you can hardly hear it. All around us, people's voices are loud with excited talk about the festival tomorrow.

"All right, everyone. Calm down and take your seats. EVERYONE!" Ms. Tannenbaum turns to me, flustered.

"We'll have to see about sorting this out later," she says. "There's too much commotion now. But don't worry. I'm sure it can be fixed."

But I can see it's beyond repair. Michael will need to start all over again. And even if he were good at art, he'd never be able to do it by tomorrow.

"Hey," he says to me as I go by his desk. "Did you bring the costume?"

I put the smashed mask on his desk and swallow hard. "I did, but it got broken."

"*What?* But the festival is tomorrow!"

"Somebody ruined it. I left it in here this morning."

"In your seats, please, everyone," Ms. Tannenbaum says again, louder.

I drop into my chair and glare at the one person horrible enough to do such a thing. Edna is busy taking down the homework assignment, just like we're supposed to at the start of class.

All hour long, she doesn't look my way.

CHAPTER 24

IT'S LUNCHTIME, BUT I'VE COME to the science lab instead of the cafeteria, even though they're serving free Halloween cupcakes decorated with spiderwebs for dessert. As we get closer to Halloween, the chefs try to get creative. Yesterday, they arranged black olives on little balls of white cheese to look like creepy eyeballs staring out from the tacos. But I'm not hungry now, and even if I were, I wouldn't want to sit at a lunch table with Edna.

Maybe Roli can tell me what to do.

I find him at one of the lab tables with Bilal, hunched over stacks of bubbled answer sheets, sorted by class hour. As soon as Roli looks up at me, everything wells up. My eye cuts loose, and my bottom lip starts to quiver, even though I'm trying my hardest not to cry.

"What's wrong?" he says.

I swallow hard. I can't talk.

Bilal gets up. "I'm going to start these at the Scantron," he says, scooping up a stack of tests.

When he's gone, I start to cry, explaining the costume catastrophe.

"I think it was Edna who ruined it," I say. "She's been mean all week."

"You're probably right, but what proof do you have?" Roli asks.

"Who else could it be? She's the only one who was mad about me working with Michael. I'm going to tell Ms. Tannenbaum."

Roli shrugs and hands me a tissue. "Do what you want, but it might not go your way if you snitch. For one thing, you're jumping to conclusions without evidence. But more important, you're accusing Dr. Santos's kid. Who's going to believe you, Merci?" he says. "Without proof, it's your word against hers."

I glare at him, knowing that, as usual, he has a point.

"Look, I've got to get Ms. Wilson's quizzes checked before the end of the period." He grabs his stack and walks me to the door. "We'll talk on the way home."

There are still ten minutes left to my lunch period, but I don't have it in me to be in the same room with Edna. So I walk across to the courtyard, where it's always quiet. Only a couple of kids are out here, including Lena, who's reading as usual. She looks up at me and smiles. I wave, but I don't join her. Instead, I find a bench by myself in the shade and try to eat some of my sandwich.

When the bell rings, everyone files out of the cafeteria. I ball up my lunch bag and toss it in the trash bin.

"Hey, Merci!"

I turn to see Michael jogging over. A piece of the broken mask is sticking out of his backpack. The sight of it makes me want to cry all over again.

"So what happened to this thing?" he asks.

"I told you. I left it on Ms. Tannenbaum's desk this morning and it was fine. Somebody wrecked it."

Michael frowns. "On purpose?"

I look at him, trying to keep my gaze steady. I could tell him that I think it was Edna, but then I'd also have to explain why she's mad at me. And what if I'm wrong like Roli says? It could have been somebody else, maybe someone just looking to do something stupid.

"I don't know for sure who messed it up," I tell him. "Maybe you can put it back together with duct tape or something."

"I'll try, but it's going to be tough," he says, shaking his head. "It's pretty wrecked. Now I don't have a costume for Edna's party either."

I blink.

"You'll be able to fix it," I mumble, and then I hurry away from him, wondering if he's being mean or if he just doesn't know I'm not invited.

Up ahead, Edna and the others are walking, boys and girls together. They're laughing and talking as if nothing is wrong at all. They're probably all planning the fun at her house tomorrow night.

"Hey, wait up!" Michael calls. I turn, but it's not me he means.

I watch as he dashes after the others.

CHAPTER 25

ONCE EDNA PROMISED TO TAKE me to Coral Cove on her boat.

It was last year, my first week, so I didn't know her very well. We were walking to class that day and had stopped to look at the glass display outside the art room. The fourth-graders had taken photographs of sea creatures during a class trip to go snorkeling at MacArthur Park. I'd only seen pictures like that in magazines.

"You've never snorkeled?"

"Not off a boat." I didn't mention that it was a long time ago, near the water's edge, when I was little and Lolo bought us those cheap masks and flippers from Walmart.

"I'll take you sometime," she promised, showing me some pictures on her phone. "It's so fun. We can go to Coral Cove."

I was so excited; I told Mami I needed a new mask and everything. Well. I waited, and I even hinted to Edna a couple of times, thinking she forgot. But the invitation never came. Mami told me I shouldn't mention it anymore. "People say things to be polite sometimes," she told me. "She was trying to be nice."

I thought about that last night as I tossed and turned. It was hard to wait for something that never came, but this feels even worse.

I'm picking at my breakfast when Abuela comes over, carrying the bag with my costume.

"Here you go! The best demon costume just for you!"

"Thanks," I say.

"¿Qué pasa?" She frowns at me. "Are you coming down with the same thing your mother had?" She puts her hand on my forehead. "You look terrible."

"I'm not sick," I say.

"What's the matter, then?"

I don't have the heart to tell Abuela what happened to Michael's costume. I don't even want to mention Edna's party. I know Abuela won't understand. She'll just say it's not important to be friends with someone who's rude to you. It makes me ache for Lolo even more.

"I just get stage fright in front of people," I tell her. "And we have to give our oral reports today."

She waves her hand. "¡Qué bobería! That's nothing to worry about. With *this* costume, you'll be the best-looking demon in school. Now finish eating. Your brother's waiting in the car."

So here I am sitting in social studies, still mad. We're in our costumes, buzzed on Halloween candy and trying to sit through our presentations until it's time to go to the festival.

"I am Isis, queen of all gods, but you may call me the Divine One."

It's Edna's turn to present her costume to the class. She's wearing a short black wig with straight black hair and bangs, shiny and fake like a Barbie's. Her eyes are rimmed with liquid eyeliner. She's wrapped tightly in a white bedsheet and has a carpenter's square on her head. Shiny bracelets decorate her arms. She looks pretty in the way that older girls do. *Wonderful report, very detailed,* according to Ms. Tannenbaum, and it's true that Edna delivers it like she's in a school play. People clap when she's finished.

253

But not me.

I doodle in my notebook, trying not to get nervous.

Michael is next. He was right; he wasn't able to do a very good job of fixing the mask. The duct tape shows everywhere, and the jaws don't move anymore. Lucky for him, Ms. Tannenbaum isn't grading hard on the costume portion. It's mostly about the quality of your report. He has a lot of interesting things about Anubis in his speech. If he's lucky, maybe he'll still get that A and go to Disney after all.

"Lena Cahill? You're next."

Lena cracks all ten fingers and walks to the front of the room. Then she turns around to face us all. She's wearing a blue top that matches her spiky hair. Sheer scarves are pinned to it. She takes three deep breaths before plugging her iPhone into a portable speaker that she props on Ms. Tannenbaum's desk. The sound of flutes fills the room. Lena closes her eyes and concentrates. In a few moments, she starts to sway to the odd music. It's almost as if she can't see any of us anymore.

"I am Nut," she begins.

A few kids snort. "No kidding," someone whispers behind me.

"Mother of Osiris, Isis, Seth, and Nephthys."

She moves each of her arms and legs in slow arcs, her

eyes following them, like a dancer in slow motion. "I am everywhere: north, south, east, west."

"I am the sky over the whole world." She bends forward and puts her hands on the floor. Her hips jut high, so she looks like a mountain. "At night, I swallow the setting sun. I give birth to the light each morning."

The music finishes and she lifts herself out of her pose slowly.

We all sit there blinking as she unplugs and sits down.

"Lena, that was amazing," Ms. Tannenbaum says in the quiet that follows. "I didn't know you were a dancer."

"Everyone is a dancer," Lena says.

"Well, you gave an absolutely brilliant interpretation. Excellent! Thank you!"

Finally, Ms. Tannenbaum checks her grade book and turns to me.

"Last but not least, Merci Suárez. You're on. It's a tough act to follow . . ."

I slide on my mask. At least it will stop people from staring at my eye. Oohs and aahs follow me as I go to the front of the class in my costume. It's hard to walk in a big hippo booty. My rump bangs into people's desks and knocks their books to the floor.

I turn around and take a deep breath. Behind this

mask, I'm willing myself to be someone else, someone braver.

"My name is Ammut, and I'm a demon, devourer of the dead." My voice echoes in here. "I have the head of a crocodile, the body of a lion, and the bottom of a hippo.

"You will all meet me when you pass into the afterlife. But you don't have to worry—unless you have been evil. That's because I work with my friend, the goddess Ma'at. After you die, your sins will be put on one side of a scale, and Ma'at's feather will be put on the other." I hold my hands like a seesaw. "Beware: If your bad deeds outweigh the feather . . ." (here I look straight at Edna and snap my jaws hard) "I'll make a meal of you. You have been warned."

I waddle back to my desk, tears welling up, wishing I really could be brave without a costume, wishing I really could chomp Edna to bits.

I sit at my desk, but I keep my mask on for a few minutes longer until my tears go back to where they belong. When I finally pull it off, Lena turns around and smiles.

That afternoon, the quad becomes a fairway with the booths made by all the classes. Our stall looks the best, I think. Just as I predicted, the yellow paint is so loud, you can't miss it. And Ms. Tannenbaum brought in temporary tattoos of the Eye of Horus to use as prizes, so lots of people stop at our booth to get one.

But the festival isn't fun, at least not for me. I'm too busy thinking about everyone going to Edna's house afterward without me.

I roam around for a while, eating kettle corn and playing a few games at the other booths. Roli told me what to guess for Mr. Dixon's boring estimation jar, so I drop in my prediction, knowing I'll win all the candy corn at the end of the festival. Then I wander over to the fields and watch the fifth-graders play their kickball game. Miss Miller is dressed in jeans and a striped shirt like Waldo, and she's pitching for both teams. I pull out my camera and take a picture of her as she plays, although something about the sight makes my heart squeeze. She's not my teacher anymore. Now I have lots of teachers—a whole collection of people who somehow know me less. Miss Miller always said she loved having us. Does she love these new kids as much as she loved us, I wonder? Nobody says gooey things like that to sixth-graders, not even Ms. Tannenbaum.

I steal another glance at Edna. I hate myself for it. Her group—which includes Michael today—looks like they're having a great time. They laugh and play all the fairway games, and then I see them slip off to hang out near the football bleachers. It's where the varsity cheerleaders shake their pom-poms during Friday-night football games and make their human pyramids.

I wonder what would happen if I told Michael that I think Edna ruined his costume? Would he believe me? Or would her mojo still win out?

"Enjoying the festivities?"

Miss McDaniels's voice makes me jump. I almost don't recognize her without her blazer and pumps. She's wearing jeans and sneakers, and a headband that has springy bats wobbling from it.

"Yes, miss."

"And where is your Sunshine Buddy? I'd think this would be the perfect opportunity to spend time together."

I swallow hard. "Oh, he's having fun around here somewhere."

"Oh?" She gives me a doubtful look and then glances past me. It doesn't take her long to notice what I've been looking at. Her eyes narrow, and I can see she's thinking.

I pretend to check my phone. "I have to go, miss. It's almost my volunteer time in the booth."

She nods at me and reaches for her walkie-talkie. I hear her voice as I move away. "A PTO volunteer is needed to supervise the bleachers, please. I'm on the way to retrieve some students now."

———— ✳ ————

After the festival, while I'm waiting for Roli in the parking lot, I see Jamie and Rachel pile into Mrs. Santos's minivan (license plate: *FUT–Z 2*). I can't see who's already inside. Probably everybody in the whole world, all jammed in like one of those clown cars. Then Michael comes up along the path.

"Hey. You won the candy corn?"

I hold out the bag and he takes a handful.

"Thanks! My favorite," he says, digging in. A car horn beeps. It's Edna signaling to him. "Oops." He starts to jog away. "See ya, Merci," he says. "Watch out for zombies!"

CHAPTER 26

WE'RE A FEW BLOCKS FROM our house, just across the road from the strip mall that has El Caribe and the big Walgreens. It's right by the bus stop where Lolo and I rested after his fall.

"Good song," Roli says, and turns up the volume. We're tossing back candy corn and blasting music. The bass is making the car shake and buries anything you're thinking about except the beat. At each light, people stare in a way that for once I don't mind.

I check my phone for the fourth time since we got in the car. But there's no message bubble. No one has tried to reach me to say, *Hey, Merci, where are you? You were invited, too!* There's not even a prank message. There's just a stinging quiet.

I close my eyes and listen to the music. Maybe I can talk to Lolo about it in the morning. He's clearest then. *Don't worry about Miss Santos, Merci,* he'll probably say, and he'll make me forget all about dumb Edna. We'll take a walk or share a tropical smoothie. He'll tell me an old story or we'll bat some balls across the yard.

At least there's trick-or-treating to save the rest of this day. I'll walk around the neighborhood with Roli and the twins as soon as the sun sets. Those two are probably foaming at the mouth about now. They hate to wait for anything, much less trick-or-treating. It's not that I blame them. Everybody knows that you get the best candy early. Plus, the older kids come out with eggs and shaving cream when it's late, so Tía likes us to be home. Lolo might be able to help Tía keep them calm until it's time to go. He'll pretend he's a hypnotist, opening his eyes wide and lowering his voice the way he used to do with me. He'll move his long fingers in a pulsing motion like sea anemones. Look deeply. Nos concentraremos . . . You will do as I say . . .

I'm thinking of all that and watching the rush-hour traffic on Military Trail when I spot something strange up ahead. At first I think it's a mirage, just my thoughts mixing up my eyes. But no. Through the three lanes of traffic moving in each direction, I see Lolo. He's standing on the median that's perpendicular to ours, and he's holding a plastic shopping bag from Walgreens with what looks like bags of Halloween candy inside.

But where's Abuela?

"Look." I nudge Roli and point.

Lolo isn't crossing the street. In fact, he looks uncertain, as if he can't decide what to do next in the heavy traffic. It's the same look he wore at the pier, and suddenly my stomach plunges.

"What's he doing out there?" Roli asks. He lowers his window. "Lolo!" He waves. "Over here!"

Lolo turns, but he doesn't smile or even look like he recognizes us. His worried frown is still there.

"Wait there!" Roli calls out. "We're coming around."

But just then the light changes, and the traffic starts moving in the through lanes near Lolo. We catch glimpses of him as he paces back and forth on the median, impatient.

A driver waiting in the turn lane closest to him looks like she's trying to talk to him, but he doesn't answer her either.

"He's in trouble, Roli." My hand goes to the door.

"Stay in the car," my brother snaps. He checks his

rearview and side mirrors, trying to edge out safely. He'll need to move us way over to the right lane to turn around.

"Let me in," Roli mutters. Sweat is beading on his top lip. Drivers lay on their horns, and one guy leans out his window and shouts at us angrily.

Meanwhile, Lolo is still pacing. He's wringing the bag's handles as he walks back and forth. The bass in our car is still *boom, boom, booming.*

I keep my eyes on him like a hypnotist, willing Lolo to stand still with my mind.

I force myself to believe it will work the way I used to believe in unicorns and Santa Claus.

Concentrate. Wait there. Don't move, I say over and over in my mind, even as my heart pounds.

But it's no use.

Everything happens in a flash. Lolo steps off the median, and Roli lurches us out of the lane. Tires screech as cars swerve to avoid us. And then a huge jolt sends me forward as we're hit from behind and go spinning across the lanes like a top.

CHAPTER 27

THE BASS OF OUR RADIO kept thumping.

Every time I close my eyes, I hear the pounding beat and then the ambulance sirens from far away. I hear the shattered windshield crunching under my sneakers. I smell the burned tires and gasoline. I can see people staring, their mouths hanging open the way Rachel's does.

The back end of Mami's car was crushed into the back seat. At least no one was sitting back there. Not like the day we had Michael.

"You're lucky," one of the nurses said as she picked glass out of my curls in the emergency room. "God was looking out for you today."

But I don't feel lucky, not at all.

And as for God, why wasn't he looking out for Lolo? Why did he let him get confused on that median? Why did he put him in so much danger? Why did he nearly kill Roli and me?

Our bedroom feels different tonight. I listen for Roli's breathing on the other side of the curtain. When we were little, I could crawl into his bed if I was scared. Not now, of course. We're too big. Nothing is the way it used to be, not with Roli, not with school, not with Lolo.

I slip out of bed and stand by the window. Lolo and Abuela's house is dark, and there's no one on the glider. Papi is sleeping in the sewing room over there to make sure Lolo is OK. He and Tía helped get him to bed tonight. Abuela was too upset to do it. Too angry. Too tired, she said, crying. Too everything.

"¿Pero, cómo? How could this happen?" she kept asking. "It was just a moment."

But nobody had an answer, or at least not one they would say. Not even Lolo himself could explain how he slipped away from her at the drugstore or why. But that's what happened. They had gone to get more bags of Halloween candy because the twins had already eaten all of theirs. Before Abuela even noticed he wasn't beside her, Lolo was walking home.

Roli's bed creaks, and then the curtain slides open.

His hair is all points. There's a nasty cut over his eyebrow where he hit the rearview mirror.

"Are you OK?" I ask.

He nods as his finger drifts to the stitches at his forehead.

"What's wrong with Lolo?" I whisper. "Why is he acting like this?"

Roli looks at me for a long time. Finally, he crosses to his desk and signals to me to sit in the chair.

"Come here."

He flips on the desk lamp and reaches for his paperweight. It's the model of a brain he got for Christmas a couple of years ago. At the time, I told him it was the dumbest gift ever. He insisted that he wanted it.

It's life-size, the width of two fists, and it comes apart like a 3-D puzzle. He pulls it in front of me now, and in the dim light, I see that he's labeled all the parts with long words that jumble in my mouth when I try to say them.

"A human brain weighs about three pounds, and it has three main parts," he whispers.

"Roli—"

He talks over me, his watery eyes on the model. "There are sections that manage how we talk, how we decide, how we remember, all like little departments that make us who we are."

He puts it down. "Lolo's brain has gotten sick," he says. "It's shrinking a little every day, and so the parts aren't working well anymore."

I stare at him. "Shrinking?" The thought is eerie. "Well, how can we make it better?"

He looks at me squarely, the lamplight reflected in the lenses of his glasses. "He's not going to get better, Merci. He's going to get worse."

He can't be right. "How do you know that, Roli?"

"Because he has something called Alzheimer's disease, Merci," he says. "He's had it for a few years, but now it's advanced."

The word *disease* hangs between us. It's a word that has bats and beetles all over it. A word that means sickness and worse.

"Lolo has had a *disease* for years and you didn't tell me?"

He stares at the brain model, his face bright red. "Yes."

I push him but he stands his ground. I shove him again as everything starts to make sense. Lolo's falls. His questions. How he wanders. His confusion. The day he almost hit Abuela. All along there has been a big secret in the Suárez family, and no one told me.

"Merci," Roli begins.

"Quiet," I say, glaring. "Why didn't anyone tell me?"

267

I grab the brain model and angrily peel back layer after layer on my own, the complicated names sticking on my tongue as I practice them. Roli watches as I put it together and peel it apart, again and again, stumbling over the words until I can say them all perfectly.

We sit together late into the night with that rubber brain. And when I finally start to ask all the questions I can think of, Roli answers every single one. For once, I don't mind all the details.

CHAPTER 28

MAMI KEEPS US HOME on Monday.

Are you dizzy? Are you feeling nauseous? Did you vomit?

These are the questions Mami asks us every little while all weekend until Roli finally puts on his headphones and draws the curtains. The cut above his eye has seeped into a bruise that runs along his eye socket, just like Lolo's old bruise. If he wanted to be a mad scientist today, he wouldn't need makeup at all.

Mami's nose is still chapped, and her face has the pale color of someone who's just been sick. But that hasn't stopped her from getting out of bed today to light a candle in the living room. Abuela says novenas, but not Mami, who has never been one for church. When something big is wrong—like when the twins were born so small and couldn't breathe on their own—she lights our Caridad del Cobre candle and says her prayers in her own words. "God hears everything, everywhere," she says.

I watch her from the doorway without her knowing. Her lips move quietly. Other times when I've been sick, Mami has let me crawl into her bed and watch game shows or read. Abuela has made me broth. But today, I still want to keep my distance. She knew . . . everyone knew . . . that Lolo was sick. And no one told me. I'm so angry that they kept it a secret that I can barely look at her. It's one thing not to tell the twins, who can't understand yet. Even when we came home from the hospital, they were still red-eyed and grumpy that they missed Halloween. Tía let them open every bag of candy we had left to keep them quiet.

But I'm not five. I'm eleven!

There's a knock at the screen door in the kitchen. Mami's eyes snap open in the middle of her prayers. "Merci," she says, surprised to find me watching her.

I turn away without a word.

Lolo and Abuela are outside the kitchen door. They've never knocked before. More or less, we all call out and let ourselves in. But I locked the door, like another boundary between us.

Abuela looks like she hasn't slept a minute in days. "Are you feeling all right this morning?" she asks.

"Preciosa," Lolo says through the screen.

I just stare at them. It feels as if I've lifted a whole house by myself. Everything hurts.

After a minute, I unlock the door and Abuela wraps me in a big hug that lasts too long and that I don't return. When she pulls back, her eyes are wet, and the sight of her so sad makes me stand back, afraid. I can't find any words to say to her. All that's banging around in my head is: *Liars. I live in a family of liars.*

I stalk off to the living room, mute, right past Mami, who has come to see who's here.

"Merci," she calls after me. "Come back."

"Déjala," Abuela says. *Let her be.*

I don't know how long I'm in the living room, but a little while later, Lolo comes to find me. He's showered and shaved, and his hair is neatly combed, the way Abuela likes, but I can still see that his eyes look tired, too. There's not a scratch on him, though, nothing to say that he was almost hit by a car on Friday or that he caused an accident that was serious enough to be reported on the late news. It's like the whole thing could have been a dream, like he's not changing the way Roli says, but I know he is.

271

Lolo sits down on the edge of the sofa and puts his tin of dominoes on the coffee table.

"In case you were bored and wanted to play," he says.

Neither one of us makes a move to open the lid. Instead, I stare at the candlewick as it flickers against the Virgin's calm smile. Normally, Lolo and I are easy with each other, pals. But not now. Everything feels stiff inside me in a way I don't like. Everything is diseased.

His brain is shrinking and it's changing him. Everyone kept it a secret from me.

It's an angry loop.

Lolo looks up at the ceiling and clears his throat. "I want to talk about something, preciosa."

I stay very still. Out in the kitchen, the coffeepot gurgles, and the smell of afternoon espresso snakes its way through the house. Roli is back in our room, sleeping. Maybe. Or spying. I just can't tell anymore.

"I am so sorry. I don't know what happened. I got confused and nervous and suddenly . . ." His voice drifts off.

"Roli told me what's going on," I say. "You *do* know what happened. You don't have to lie to me anymore. You have Alzheimer's."

Lolo folds his hands in his lap. They're trembling a little.

"I suppose that's true," he says after a few seconds.

"You should have told me," I say. "You kept a big secret, and we're not supposed to have those in the Suárez family."

Lolo sighs. "You're right," he says.

My voice is shaky as the anger in my belly swells. "Why didn't anyone tell me? It's not fair to treat me like that. You should all be grounded forever."

"Blame me," Lolo says. "Not anyone else. I made them all promise a long time ago not to tell you until we had no choice."

It feels like he's slapped me. Lolo and I have always told each other everything—or at least, I thought so. But now I see that he was the one to cut me out on purpose. My eyes fill up.

Lolo stares into his hands and continues. "I wanted to enjoy our time the way it has always been for as long as possible. What's coming is coming, mi cielo. Why think about drowning before we reach the river?"

Is that what losing your memory is like, I wonder? Drowning? The whole idea makes me shiver. Lolo is right here, talking to me, the same as always, but he's disappearing a little bit at a time. How can a grown-up forget how to walk across the street, and come to explain himself the next day?

I stare at the tin of dominoes, blind anger rising

suddenly from my toes. Roli's words crowd inside my head, making me hate this game. Lolo will forget how to count and match the tiles one day. He'll forget all the rules. *In the next few years, Lolo might not be able to remember us, Merci. He won't even remember himself.*

My eye pulls to the edge, but I don't even try to coax it back. There's no cure for what Lolo has, no pill that can take this away forever. Even if Roli becomes the best scientist in the world one day, he won't have time to fix Lolo the way he wants to.

My thoughts race faster and faster, balling up into an angry fist. Who will go to the twins' Grands Day? Or walk the twins? Or help Papi on the job? Who'll crack bad jokes at El Caribe and dance with Abuela?

With one sudden swipe, I send the tin flying away from us. The clatter of the tiles spilling on the floor sounds like glass shattering.

Mami and Abuela come running into the room. When she sees what I've done, Mami is on me in two steps. Her hand clamps down on my shoulder.

"That's enough, Merci," she says. "I want you to pick this up right now."

Lolo steps forward. "Let her go, Ana," he says softly.

I back away from them all. "This is what it's like when someone changes and scares you. How do *you* like it?"

Lolo has a broken expression on his face. He steps forward slowly. "You're frightened," he says.

I stand there, gaping. As soon as he says it, I know that it's true. I know that one day Lolo will look at me and not remember who I am at all. There won't be Lolo and me. I'll be forgotten with everything else.

My shoulders hunch as I start to sob the way I used to when I was little. I feel Lolo's arms close around me, but I don't have any energy left to fight or squirm. He lets me cry, waiting until the last drop is out of me.

When I'm finally sucking in ragged breaths, he kisses my head.

"I am frightened, too," he says. "We all are. But we are the Suárez family, Merci. We are strong enough to face this together." His words echo inside his chest as I listen. Already he sounds far away.

CHAPTER 29

EDNA IS COVERED IN sea lice bites.

Her arms and neck are bumpy with flaming welts that are almost a perfect color match to our blazers. It looks like acne—the kind that needs a doctor to cure. The calamine lotion that's smeared all over her legs doesn't seem to be helping, either. She's constantly scratching under her desk. Then I notice that it's the same for Jamie, Rachel, Michael, and a few other kids, who are all scratching at themselves miserably. It must have happened when they went swimming at her party. Hannah's overprotective mother finally came in handy. When Mrs. Kim saw the blue flags posted in the surf report, she kept Hannah home. And Lena didn't go, either, I guess.

Ms. Tannenbaum stops at my desk.

"I was so sorry to hear about your car accident," she whispers to me, kneeling near my desk. "I happened to be in the office when your mother called yesterday morning to excuse your absence. Linda McDaniels shared the details. We're all so glad that you're all right."

I suddenly feel everyone's eyes on me from around the room.

"This is for you." Ms. Tannenbaum hands me an envelope. "Your fellow scholars in third hour wanted you to have this."

It's a card.

Accidents Happen is on the front, along with a picture of a puppy that has a bag of ice on its head and a thermometer in its mouth. Inside it reads, *Glad you're OK.*

My whole class has signed their names, even Edna and Jamie in their matching swirly script.

My face flushes and a knot rises in my throat when I see all those names. I can't help but wonder if Miss McDaniels made them all sign. She's no stranger to forced notes of apology, after all.

Still, I tuck the card inside my notebook for safekeeping.

Ms. Tannenbaum lowers her voice even more. "And I don't want you to think that I've forgotten about your costume, either. We'll try to get to the bottom of things in the coming days when things settle down."

I look up at her blankly. I hadn't thought about the ruined costume—or Edna's party—since Friday at the fall festival. It seems like a million years ago now instead of four days. It's the kind of thing that belongs with old toys that I've given away. In fact, if I were Miss McDaniels, I might file it in my Utter Nonsense folder.

"Michael's costume, you mean," I say. "It doesn't really matter anymore."

She nods and pats my hand as she straightens. "I suppose perspectives change based on events. What's most important is that I hope this week will be better."

I glance at Edna, who's squirming in her seat. She's jammed her pencil inside the back of her shirt trying to reach a spot between her shoulder blades.

"Yes, miss. I think it will be."

I still like Ms. Tannenbaum, but I'm not so sure about social studies anymore.

I don't want to talk about anybody's death, not my own near experience that everyone keeps asking about. I don't even want to talk about Egyptians who died thousands of years ago. Corpses, tombs, or burying treasures with important people. No matter what, all of it comes back to death, which comes back to Lolo being sick, and *that* makes me so sad that all I want to do is stare out the window.

So I stay quieter than usual and answer questions only when she calls on me. I ask for a lunch pass to the library, too, so I don't have to get grilled at our lunch table. (Was Roli drinking? Were we speeding? Did it hurt? Was anyone killed?) I just want to be by myself for a while. I sit at a computer and look up everything I can find about Alzheimer's disease. Some things make me feel better, but others make me feel worse, especially the interviews with people who know they're getting sicker every day. No place I look says there's a cure.

Today Ms. Tannenbaum announces that we're finally going to start building our Great Tomb. We'll work on it for the next few weeks, she says, right up to the winter break. On the last day, our adoring public — meaning Dr. Newman, our whole school, our parents, and even a reporter from the *Palm Beach Post* — will come see what we've made. So it's got to be our best work.

I'm barely listening when the peace in our class is shattered by what she says next. She announces the person in charge of the mummy committee this year.

"Congratulations, Lena," she says.

For a second, there's total quiet while it sinks in. That's the most important job. Without a mummy and sarcophagus, there is no Great Tomb Project at all. It's the spotlight job. The mummy maker almost always gets their picture in the paper with Dr. Newman and Ms. Tannenbaum. Like everybody else, I more or less assumed it was going to be Edna. She has the highest grades, and she can get people to do what she says.

Which is probably why Edna raises her scabby hand right away.

"Shouldn't Lena at least have a cochair, Ms. Tannenbaum?" she says. "Someone who has, you know, good grades and stuff? Our whole tomb depends on it. No offense, but you can't give that job to just anybody."

"Just Anybody" Lena doesn't even flinch.

Ms. Tannenbaum takes a deep breath.

"I have every confidence in Lena. But as it happens, she *will* have help because, you are right, creating our mummy is a very big task. And since Lena will be the committee chair, *she* will have the option of choosing her assistants," Ms. Tannenbaum says. "Lena, you may pick two associates."

Edna turns to face Lena and crosses her arms, waiting to be picked first. Lena doesn't change her expression, though, even when everybody starts to whisper, "Pick me!"

"Would you like to think about it?" Ms. Tannenbaum asks, because it's taking a little long.

Lena shakes her head. She closes her eyes the way she did during her interpretive dance for the class. The blue points of her hair quiver a little, like a porcupine's quills on alert.

"Merci." My name rings out clear as a bell. "Hannah, too."

"Oh my *God*," Rachel says.

CHAPTER 30

LENA'S BLUE HAIR MAKES PEOPLE notice her now, which is strange for somebody who mostly seems to want to keep to herself. In fact, she is the only kid who walks around alone and never looks lonely. Maybe that's why we haven't really been friends. But now that I *am* working with her, I notice that she's kind of interesting. She's a notebook doodler, and she's so quiet that you can walk by her and not realize she's there. Once, I saw her doing a yoga stretch near the Sierpiński sculpture even as people were walking by. She's always reading something that looks good, too, like a comic book or graphic novel with the words in another language. "How do you know what it says?" I asked her.

"I read the pictures."

Still, I really wish she hadn't picked me yesterday. Our main job is to make the dead body and the coffin. This is about as death-ish as you can get.

Hannah looks uncomfortable, too, but not because she doesn't want to think about dead things, the way I don't.

I think it's because she's not working with Edna and Jamie, who've been assigned to the scribe committee. Hannah's eyes keep sliding over to the cafeteria windows to gaze at our usual lunch table, which I suppose is where she really wants to be.

"Hannah," Lena says, "what's your idea for the mummy?" The three of us are eating lunch in the court-yard at Lena's spot, so that we can plan in peace.

"Sorry," Hannah says, finally looking at us. "Why don't we just wrap someone in toilet paper?"

Lena takes a sip from her juice box. "It rips too easily," she says. "Plus, we'd have to wrap a new mummy every day. What's your idea, Merci?"

I shrug. "Why don't we make a model with a doll or something?" I take a bite of my sandwich, which is even drier than usual. I could offer to use La Boba, but the thought of making her a mummy scares me. What if that gives her devilish powers for real?

"But a doll is too small." Hannah's eyes dart to Edna's table again. "I don't have any left anyway."

Lena dips a baby carrot into her hummus and takes a loud bite. "I think we should use a *live* model," she says. "We can use plaster of paris. The model would have to lie still and be totally quiet—but only until it sets. It doesn't take long. Then we can let them out."

"They'd have to play dead?" Hannah asks, giggling. "Creepy."

I shift in my seat and stare up at the clouds. It's breezy today, and shapes move across the sky much faster than usual. Dragons, clowns, whales, a man's face. I pull out my phone and scroll to video.

Lena looks up, too, and gazes for a few seconds as I film. "Oh! Did you get the guy with a beard?" she says, pointing.

I nod. Then I stop recording and turn to her. "I don't want to pretend to be dead," I say quietly.

Lena looks at me as she chews.

Hannah blushes and tries to change the subject. "Why don't we work on the sarcophagus first? I have gold paint and beads. We can put gems on and glitter to make it shiny and—"

"Focus: mummy," Lena says. "We can work through the problem. Why don't we get a volunteer from the class?

Somebody will want to do it. They'll be immortalized in plaster, remember? That makes them the star of the whole tomb."

All three of us turn to look inside the lunchroom. Edna is showing what's left of her rash to anyone who wants to look.

Hannah breaks into a grin and balls up her trash.

"Wait here," she says. "I know just who to ask."

CHAPTER 31

THE GIRLS' SOCCER TEAM HAS its first home scrimmage after school today so the team got to wear their jerseys. The buses from The King's Academy roll into the parking lot at dismissal time, just as Mami beeps and waves at me from a loaner car that I don't recognize. For once, I'm happy to go home to the twins so I don't have to watch.

I'm starving as usual, but Mami only leaves chia-seed pudding as a snack before she goes car shopping. So I head over to Lolo and Abuela's to see if there's something better. Besides, I need to get beads and buttons for the sarcophagus, if Abuela can spare some.

Tía Inés is hanging the twins' laundry in the backyard. It's weird that she's home, especially this close to

Thanksgiving, when the orders for cakes and special pastries start pouring in to El Caribe.

"You're not working today?" I say. Tía is usually on until at least four, which is why I have to help babysit every day.

"Somebody had to get the boys from school." She shrugs. "I've got Irma covering until I can get back."

"Where's Lolo and Abuela?"

"They're not home right now." She pins a pair of overalls to a shirt on the line. "Your dad took them to the doctor. It was his turn."

I glance over at her, trying not to think about the doctor, about all the appointments filled with information that nobody gave me.

The twins are already in their play clothes, barefoot, and trying to catch lizards in a plastic jar. They're terrible at hunting. Even Tuerto is better. They've only ever managed a capture once that I can remember. They named the poor thing Seymour and said he was a baby dragon.

"You OK?" she asks. "You're moping again."

I give her a look. I don't have the energy to tell her about what's been going on with Edna or anything else. Lolo was the one who always used to help me with stuff like that.

"I'm just getting a snack," I say, and let myself into Lolo and Abuela's kitchen.

I haven't been over in days, which has almost never happened before. Now, even though everything is in the same place, it feels like I'm stepping into a strange house. With the lights off and no one home, the place feels too still.

The Gilda crackers are on the counter in a plastic bag. I'm not supposed to have those. They're made with shortening, which Mami always points out is a death sentence. But I don't care about that. They're delicious with butter — even better dunked into Abuela's sweet coffee. I fish a couple out of the bag and bite into one dry.

I start down the hall for the back door, straightening a few of the framed pictures as I go. Abuela likes to say that I take after her because I'm "artistic." She might be able to turn a thousand scraps of fabrics into a beautiful dress on her sewing machine, but she can't figure out how to take a picture like I can. The walls are cluttered with the headless pictures of our first days of school every year, our Communions, our family trips, Roli's prom.

There's only one set of photos that's any better: the ones in their bedroom — because Abuela didn't take those. Two years ago, we got a special package in the mail. I knew it was from Cuba right away because of the funny stamp and the Spanish words in the return address. *Quemado de Güines, Villa Clara.* Inside the big envelope were dozens of loose photographs, old ones in black and white and in faded colors. One of Abuela's cousins, who still lives in their old house, had found them at the back of a closet where Abuela had hidden them before she left. Bugs had bored holes right through some of the faces, and the photos smelled a little like mold. But Abuela made a big fuss and got teary. She bought frames for them at the Dollar Store and made Papi hang them over her bed. That's how we have pictures of her mother on her wedding day in 1930, of Lolo with his father, who came from the Philippines, and of a young and skinny Abuela holding baby Tía Inés in her arms.

I walk farther into their bedroom and stand in front of my favorite photograph. It's Lolo on a bicycle. It's not the bike he has here. This was the one he rode in Cuba, which he used every day, since he didn't own a car. His hair is slicked back and he's laughing, like someone just told him a good joke. I notice a bouquet of flowers resting in his basket, which makes me wonder if they were for Abuela or maybe someone else. He looks completely happy, squinting into the sunshine.

"If it weren't such an old shot, you might swear it was Roli, right?"

Tía Inés's voice startles me. "Sorry," she says.

"You shouldn't sneak up on people," I say.

"You were taking a while, so I came to check before I left for work again."

The twins' voices rise and fall as they keep up their chase outside. Tía glances out the window as I take a bite of my cracker. I offer her the other but she waves me off. Instead, she sits on Lolo and Abuela's bed and smooths the quilt over the lumps, the same way Abuela does.

"Are you still mad at all of us?" she asks.

I shrug.

She nods, thinking. "I don't blame you. We should have told you. To be honest, I'm mad, too."

I give her a side-eye. "What are you mad about? Nobody lied to *you*," I point out.

"No. But I'm sad, too," she says sharply. "My father is sick, and I worry about taking care of him as things get worse."

I haven't given much thought to how this is for her or Abuela and my parents. Mostly, I've been thinking about how this feels for me.

"There's no use pretending anymore. A lot of things are changing fast," Tía says.

I throw myself back on the bed and stare at the

ceiling. "I'm sick of change. Nothing makes sense anymore. Not Lolo or the kids at school or anything."

She looks down at me with an arched brow and starts to detangle a knot I hadn't noticed in my hair.

From down here, Tía looks pretty. She has almost no makeup on at all, and I can suddenly see that long-ago baby in her face.

"Hold still." I pull out my phone and snap a picture.

"Ay, niña," she says. "I'm a fright. Delete that."

"No." I hold out the screen to her and she rolls her eyes.

Outside, one of the twins starts shrieking. Tía crosses to the window and peers out. "They've either finally caught something or they're murdering each other," she says. "I'd better get back out there and see which it is." She turns to me from the doorway. "Anyway, I just wanted to say I'm sorry, Merci. We're all sorry, and that's the truth."

"Don't go yet." I walk to her and position my phone. "Stand here with me."

Her hands fly to her hair. "Come on. Not like this!"

"Smile," I say.

We put our heads close together as I take a selfie. When we check the picture, it's plain to see that neither of us looks great. My barrette has opened, and there are cracker crumbs on my chin. Tía's blouse has a stain near the collar. Abuela will probably say we don't look decent. I fiddle with the color and blanch us out to black and white. The picture looks totally different. Suddenly you notice what's important in the picture. Little lines around Tía's eyes. The tilt of my glasses. How our smiles are kind of the same, even though I never noticed before.

"What do you think?" I ask.

She looks at it and kisses my head.

Later that night, everyone comes over to our house. Lolo and Abuela. Tía Inés and the twins. They sit in our living room, the twins dozing like puppies on my favorite blanket near the TV. This time, there is no whispering in the kitchen. They talk about what the doctor said even when I wander in to get a snack. I don't understand everything. But I hear it all as I sit in the corner and snap photos with my phone to pass the time. *More rapid decline. Drug trial. Accessing assistance.* Smiles and sad faces and a few tears. Lolo closes his eyes from time to time. Abuela holds his hands.

I click and click and capture us the way we really are right now.

CHAPTER 32

"AND WHAT, MAY I ASK, is this?"

Lena, Hannah, and I have made a huge pile of buckets, garbage bags, masking tape, and drop cloths in the main office. Miss McDaniels is standing with her arms crossed, giving us her I-am-not-amused look.

"It's official business, miss," I say. "We're collecting materials for our Great Tomb Project. We'd like to keep our things here until we need them. We're mummifying someone this week."

Her eye twitches. "It's quite a mess, ladies. What's wrong with putting it in Ms. Tannenbaum's room?"

I exchange glances with Hannah and Lena. That's what

they suggested. I was the one who insisted that we keep our things in the office. "We want our stuff safe," I say.

Miss McDaniels arches her brow. "Pardon me? Why wouldn't your 'stuff' be safe in her classroom?"

I shift on my feet, unsure what to say. I don't want to tattle, so I keep things brief. "It's just that last time I kept something there, it didn't work out." She looks at me doubtfully. "It was the mask and costume for the fall festival. I brought it in for my Sunshine Buddy and left it in Ms. Tannenbaum's room — remember, miss? When I went back, it was smashed to bits."

Her face becomes a stone. "I see."

This is how I find out that Miss McDaniels has yet another pet peeve besides lateness, wasting valuable time, and utter nonsense.

She fishes under her counter and pulls out an official-looking form. Then she hands me a plastic daisy pen. "You'll file an incident report," she says.

I glance at the sections marked *Victim Statement* and *Estimated Value of Damaged Property.* "Oh, no, miss. That's OK. It doesn't really matter anymore," I say.

"Incorrect," she says, holding my gaze. "What happened is called destruction of personal property. And it is unacceptable at Seaward Pines."

She slips the sheet onto a clipboard and hands it over.

"Sit over there and fill this out. Press hard. It's in triplicate."

"It doesn't have to be a boy," Edna insists. "Ancient Egypt had famous queens, you know. Duh, Nefertiti—who was gorgeous, by the way."

"Very good point!"

Ms. Tannenbaum's eyes are shining with pleasure. She's enjoying the class discussion (aka argument) about who gets to be the model for our mummy. She claims that a good debate gets her blood pumping. In any case, we weren't expecting that more than one person would want to be the mummy. We asked Edna, but other people volunteered, too. Right now, the contenders are, of all people, Michael Clark and Edna, which has split the class into boys versus girls.

"But nobody's ever found her tomb," says Michael. "It said so in the homework video."

The girls boo.

"And besides, King Tut is cooler," he says.

"Says who?" Edna says. "He's overdone."

"Way overdone," Jamie adds.

"And Ms. Tannenbaum says we've never had a queen's

tomb. It's a girl's turn," Rachel says. She raises her fist in a power sign, but when no one joins her, she lowers it again and blushes. "Sorry, Michael."

"The layout would have to be slightly different for a queen's tomb, so the archaeology team will have to do further research," Ms. Tannenbaum says, which is welcomed by a faint groan from the back of the room.

Lena is doodling in her notebook and listening. I can see she's drawn King Tut's famous mask and the bust of Nefertiti, too. It looks almost the same as what's in our books.

Edna folds her arms. "We should be practical. Face it, I am a much better size as a model." She smiles sweetly at Michael, who is towering over all of us. "*And* I am yoga trained in slow breathing. I won't move a muscle."

The arguments erupt again, until finally Ms. Tannenbaum raises her hand in the quiet signal. "Committee?" she says, turning to us at last. "What is your decision?"

Lena, Hannah, and I get up and do a football huddle in the corner.

"What do we do? Edna really wants the job." Hannah looks like she wants to throw up. Making decisions has that effect on her, and Jamie's laser eyeballs on her aren't helping.

Lena looks at me. "By my calculations, Michael will take up too much plaster," she says. "Plus, we'll need a lot more wood to build the sarcophagus around him. Unfortunately, I think Edna has a point."

I give her a pained look.

Lena nods thoughtfully. She's no dope. "Think of it this way: she'll have her mouth plastered shut for at least half an hour," she says. "That's something."

So that's how it ends up that Edna is going to get immortalized.

She comes to school in her gym suit on the last day before Thanksgiving break. She had to clear permission from Miss McDaniels, of course, since she'd be "outside of regulation attire," not to mention the fact that we'll all be missing math class today while the mold hardens. Apparently, Miss McDaniels peppered her with questions.

"God. She's so nosy! No offense, but why does she have to know everything about all of our projects? She's the school secretary." She rolls her eyes and steps into the garbage bag I hold out for her.

Our work plan is simple. We're going to wrap Edna into a human burrito using plastic bags, then plaster her with two coats of paper strips. Lena says the main thing is

297

to tape everything very close to her, otherwise we won't see the shape of her body. "It will look like a big pile of doo," Lena warns.

Lena lays Papi's drop cloths over the desks that we've arranged like an operating room table. Meanwhile, Hannah does Edna's hair for the big event. She twists the pieces into a braid and then wraps them up first in a towel and then a plastic bag over that. She even brought two cucumber slices in a baggie to put on her eyes. In the end, Edna looks like one of those ladies getting facials at a spa.

The other committees are working all around the room, too. Jamie and the remaining scribes are painting the story of our queen. The engineers are figuring out how to arrange the cardboard dividers inside our tomb to make chambers. Artisans are working on vessels and statues.

"I've got to mix the plaster strips," Lena says. "Can you prep her face, please?" She hands me a big jar of petroleum jelly. But when I scoop out a glob, Edna speaks up.

"Not so fast! *That*—on my face?" she says. "I'll break out."

"Well, would you rather we put a plastic bag over your head?" I ask. "You'll suffocate, of course, but if you insist . . ."

"Don't worry, Edna," Lena says, cutting in. "We're

going to leave big holes for your nose. And the whole thing will be dry in less than forty minutes. You can wash your face right afterward. Promise."

"Fine." Edna leans back and puts the cucumber slices back on her eyelids. "The sacrifices I make."

I start gooping her up, following the line of her cheekbones and her chin, all the way to where the plastic bag touches her neck. I try not to miss anything as I go. This close, I can see that Edna's face is covered in little bumps and blackheads, like mine. If she does break out, we'll never hear the end of it.

"Step on it, Merci," she says. "It feels gross."

I slather on what I can and call it a day.

"OK," Lena says, pausing over Edna like a surgeon. "We're going to start plastering, so don't move or talk. We don't want it to crack."

"I am going to the afterlife," Edna says dramatically. Then she takes several cleansing breaths.

I hate to admit it, but she doesn't move a muscle. Lena hoists a bucket of water onto a desk and puts it next to our pile of plaster strips. We dip each one and crisscross them in place. I work on Edna's head, while Lena and Hannah work the larger pieces on her body. It doesn't take long to finish the first layer, but you can still see through it in spots.

"You OK, Edna?" Lena asks.

"Mmm-hmm," Edna says.

We point the fan at her and wait for fifteen minutes before starting layer number two. This one is trickier. Lena shows us how to use our thumbs to smooth the slime down around the edges as we go.

"How do you know so much about art?" I ask her as we work.

She shrugs. "I've always done it. My grandfather was a painter."

"Hey, mine, too," I say. "Sol Painting, Inc."

"Not the same kind, probably. Mine painted portraits, the ocean, that kind of stuff. My dad has some of them still hanging in his gallery in Delray." She shrugs. "I'm not as good, but I like the quiet when I paint. And the colors."

"Same here," I say. "It's not that different painting rooms."

Lena thinks about that and smiles. "You're right."

We work together, all three of us. Hannah tells us about her grandfather, too, who lives in Miami and is married to someone very young. He and her Nana don't get along.

It takes us most of the class hour to finish everything. But by the time the bell rings, we have a pretty good-looking cast of our dead queen.

Ms. Tannenbaum turns the fan on again to dry her faster and nods in approval.

"Good work, ladies," she says. "You, too, Edna," she adds loudly. "Very professional."

Everyone gathers to see what we've done. Even though it's still gooey, we can see that it's going to be perfect.

Lena checks the clock. "She'll be completely ready in fifteen more minutes."

"That's a wrap!" Hannah says, and we throw little pieces of plaster at her.

Then we get busy cleaning up the soggy drop cloths and dump the buckets of gray water in the grass outside.

Edna stays still as a stone the whole time.

Lena turns off her beeping watch and runs her fingertips over the surface. It's rock hard and smooth. "I think our queen mummy is ready."

Ms. Tannenbaum unplugs the fan. "All right. Why don't you girls remove the mold while I get this back to Mr. Shaw's art room? I'll be back in a flash."

"Positions," Lena says.

I stand at the head, just as we planned. Hannah and Lena get on either side of the cast. We'll have to lift the cast at exactly the same time so it doesn't break apart.

Lena leans down and talks near Edna's ear. "OK, Edna, I want you to wiggle your fingers and legs and face very gently. Not too much; we just want to loosen the mold a bit."

The rest of the kids who are still working stop what they're doing and come to watch. It's a little creepy to see the cast start to move. It's like those horror movies about the undead.

"That's enough." Then Lena turns to us. "When I say *three,* we lift together slowly." The room gets very quiet in anticipation. "One . . . two . . . three."

The feet and sides loosen as we lift together. I pry the sides of the face mask away easily and pull upward. But suddenly, I hear Edna cry out from below.

"OUCH! Stop!"

We all freeze. "What's the matter?" I ask.

"My face is stuck."

"That can't be," Lena says.

But sure enough, when I peek underneath, I can see that Edna's eyebrows are pulling up with the plaster.

"Uh-oh."

"Uh-oh what?" Edna says. One of the cucumber slices slips off, and she give me a side-eye as best she can. "What do you mean, 'uh-oh'?"

"Hold on a second," I tell her. Then I stand up and whisper to Lena. "A little problem below, chief."

She bends down to look and her eyes grow wide. "Hang on," she tells Edna. Then she whips back to us. "Didn't you use the Vaseline?"

"Of course I did."

"Maybe you didn't use enough? Or maybe you didn't get close enough to her eyes?"

"I was hurrying," I say, trying to remember. "She was rushing me."

"You must have missed her eyebrows!" Lena says.

"Well, now what do we do?" asks Hannah.

"Get me out of this," Edna calls to us.

"Just a second," I say. Then I turn back to Lena and Hannah. "Let's rip it off fast," I suggest. "My aunt gets her eyebrows waxed all the time. How different can it be?"

Hannah's mouth drops open in horror.

The boys start cracking up, especially Michael.

"Oh my *God*!" Rachel says, when they tell her what's so funny. "Is Edna really stuck?"

"Quiet," I snap.

"I'm *stuck*?" Edna shouts. "Who said that? Is that you, Rachel?"

"Let's try one more time," Lena says quickly. We pull

up as gently as we can, but the skin under Edna's eyebrows just stretches up with us until she yelps again. "You're killing me!"

"She's glued in, all right," says Michael. "Glad it wasn't me." And then the boys just double over in hysterics.

"Help!" Edna says.

"We'll have you out in a second," Lena says. "Quick. Come here and hold this side up," she says to Rachel. Then she jabs her fingers into the petroleum jelly. "Hold still, Edna. I'll try to loosen you."

But there's no such luck. We use the whole rest of the jar of Vaseline, but when we pull again, Edna swats at us with her free hand.

"OW!"

Lena looks at me gravely across the plaster we're all holding. "There's only one thing to do," she says. She walks slowly to Ms. Tannenbaum's desk and fetches a pair of scissors from the pencil cup. She swallows hard. "Close your eyes, and don't move a muscle," she tells Edna.

"Wait," I say. "I messed it up. I'll get her out."

"Are you sure?"

I nod and take the scissors.

"What are you doing?" Edna says when she sees me zeroing in above her eyes.

"It's the only way, Edna. Now hold still."

It's hard to keep my vision in focus, especially since my eye is doing its nervous crawl. My hands are shaking as I *snip, snip, snip* along Edna's brows.

Finally, she's loose. We lift the cast carefully and set it on the floor. Edna sits up and yanks the plastic bags from her body. Her face is shiny with grease, and the skin around what's left of her eyebrows is bright pink. Hannah takes one look at her and covers her mouth. The boys go into more laughing fits. It makes me want to slug them.

"Quit it," I say.

Michael Clark is the first to catch his breath enough to speak. "Your eyebrows look weird," he says, wiggling his own.

Edna scowls. "Mirror!" she says.

Jamie fishes in her backpack and hands her a compact with kitten ears on it. Edna flips it open. All I hear after that is her scream.

That's when Ms. Tannenbaum rushes back in. "What on earth is this racket about? I could hear you down the hall!" she says, frowning. "Boys, quiet down at once!"

No one has time to reply. Edna hops down from the desks and snatches off the rest of the plastic bags. "Look what this idiot did to my eyebrows after all the help I gave them!" she says, pointing. "Just look! They're ruined!"

She's not wrong. I tried to be careful, but I had to cut

close to the skin with those big scissors to free her. Now her brows are patchy and crooked. Half of the left one is mostly gone. What stubble is left is covered in little balls of plaster, too.

Ms. Tannenbaum's face darkens. "Oh, no . . . no, no, no, no, no, no, no . . ." She takes Edna's face in her hands to inspect the damage.

I try to explain. "But we had to get her out, miss. We had no choice."

Ms. Tannenbaum closes her eyes as Edna starts to bawl. Then she puts her arm around Edna's shoulder and guides her to the door. "Let's go see Miss McDaniels," she says, sighing. "Looks like we're going to have to call home."

CHAPTER 33

MAMI IS WAITING FOR ME at the prescription counter. We're picking up Lolo's new medicine before the store
closes for Thanksgiving. It's supposed to be like a new
set of brakes for his memory loss. At least, that's what the
doctor says.

I put the eyebrow pencil on the counter. It's Midnight
Brown, the color Tía Inés said.

"Did you get the card, too?" Mami asks.

I slide it on the counter and try not to make a face. I
picked one with a picture of a rock that has worried eyes.
No hard feelings? Inside it's blank, so I can apologize to
Edna in my own words, the way Mami says I should.

Thankfully, the card is kind of small. If I write in big
letters, I won't have to say much.

"Forgetting something?" Mami holds out her palm. On top of everything, I'm paying for my mistake. Literally. Ten dollars zapped from my bike fund.

"I don't even know what to write," I tell her. "I'm pretty sure she's not speaking to me. Why would she read a note?" I try not to think of Edna's face, all red and rubbery, or how everyone laughed at her.

"We're eating at three," she says as we walk home. "You have plenty of time to figure out what to say by then. Speak from the heart."

"Thump-*thump*. Thump-*thump*. Thump-*thump*," I say.

"Funny," Mami says.

Lolo and the twins are in the yard picking grapefruits while I try to write something.

Papi planted the tree the same year that he and Mami, Lolo, and Tía Inés all chipped in to buy Las Casitas. It's a big tree now, and while it's never been great for climbing, when it blooms late in the winter, the white flowers make the whole yard smell pretty. Those flowers become the fruit eventually in the fall. Abuela likes us to leave the fruit on as long as possible, even though some of it is ready in October. It's the secret to their sweetness, she says. Letting things ripen and not rushing them.

Lolo holds the ladder steady against the trunk. All I

can see of Axel are his skinny legs. The rest of him is hidden inside the canopy.

"Twist the stem," Lolo tells him from below. "Turn until you hear it snap."

A grapefruit drops with a thud and rolls near my chair like a dirty softball. I reach into my pocket for my phone and zoom in. I'll add this picture to what I've already taken. Abuela at her sewing machine. Tía Inés rolling her hair. Mami and Papi watching TV.

"When is it my turn?" Tomás asks. He's tiptoeing around the trunk, creeping up on lizards as best he can. He pulls on Lolo's pants. "When?"

"When I tell you it's time, compadre," he says.

I watch them for a while. It's a good day for Lolo, at least. Maybe the medicine will work. Maybe we'll have Lolo the way he's supposed to be for a long time.

I turn back to the card in my lap, but it's hard to concentrate. The whole yard smells of orange and garlic, and my stomach keeps growling. We don't eat turkey and stuffing on Thanksgiving like most people around here. Not even pumpkin pie.

Instead, we always start Thanksgiving with a cut grapefruit, sugar sprinkled over it the way Lolo likes. Abuela bakes four chickens and boils a big pot of white rice. Tía makes her famous coconut cookies. Mami insists on a salad, of course. Then, like most people, we say "gracias, Señor" and eat until our pants nearly pop.

"What matters is not the menu," Mami is fond of saying. "It's that we spend the day feeling grateful."

"Although not for ruthless colonizers," Roli likes to add. He's been nursing a well-researched grudge against Thanksgiving for years.

Hmpf. Right now, I'm not feeling very grateful at all—for anything. When we get back to school on Monday, I'm supposed to report directly to Miss McDaniels for a meeting with our headmaster. That's simple code for "I'm in trouble." Hannah says she saw Mrs. Santos come to pick Edna up after our disaster in social studies, and it didn't go well. Hannah tried to apologize and explain what happened, but Mrs. Santos was even more upset than Edna.

"I don't get it! Anyone can see that we didn't do it on purpose," Hannah grumbled.

Can you sue people for ruining your eyebrows? I guess I'll find out soon enough.

I look at the card in my lap again. I read in one of Papi's business etiquette books that you should never write an e-mail or a letter when you're mad because you're likely to shoot your mouth off and say something you'll regret. Such as:

DEAR EDNA,
YOU BASICALLY GOT WHAT YOU
DESERVED FOR WRECKING MY COSTUME
AND I'M GLAD. OFFENSE INTENDED.
FROM MERCI

But the weird thing is that I can't write that. Even though Edna can be awful, I know I made a mistake. I didn't have as much fun watching her get laughed at as I would have thought, either. She did agree to help us, and watching Michael and the other kids make fun of her felt all wrong.

So, I decide to stick to the facts, which Roli says never fail anybody. I write her a letter that feels true.

Dear Edna,

I'm sorry we messed up. It really was an accident. I was trying to rescue you because life stuck inside a plaster mask wouldn't be fun. I hope your eyebrows grow back fast. The average kid's hair grows in at about 0.14 mm each day, so in a few weeks you should look like new. Until then, use this.

Merci

I seal the makeup pencil in the envelope when I'm done.

Then I walk over to the tree, where Tomás has dug a hole out of boredom and is kicking at the loose grapefruits like they're soccer balls.

"We have to eat those, you know," I say.

He pulls on Lolo's pant leg again. "Is it my turn?" he whines.

I'm afraid Lolo will get impatient. I should probably make myself useful. "Hey," I tell Tomás. "I have an idea. Come with me."

Tomás isn't the most trusting kid, especially when he's not with Axel, but he follows me to the carport. Lolo's bike is there, right next to mine.

I grab my bike and lift him onto the handlebars. He's heavier than I remember, and he's lost a front tooth, which I can't believe I haven't noticed. Abuela saved Roli's and my first teeth in an old cough-drop tin. I wonder if Axel's is there, too, or if she's been too busy to notice. Or maybe it's just been me who hasn't been paying attention.

"Hang on tight, OK?"

"Vroom!" he says.

I start pedaling.

We start a big, slow loop of Las Casitas, going by each of our houses. Papi and Roli are setting up the patio table and hosing off the chairs. Mami is standing by the kitchen window, chopping lettuce and talking with her brothers on the phone. I wave at Tía and Abuela, who are listening to the radio as they cook in the kitchen. The smell of our holiday dinner reaches to every corner of our yard as we go.

"Don't let that boy fall," Abuela warns me. Or is it Lolo she's talking to? I can't tell, I'm moving so fast.

"Faster! Faster!" Tomás shouts as we zoom along.

I pump my legs hard and lean into the turns as he squeals. Round and round we go until my legs hurt and my shirt is soaked in sweat. White seat stuffing flies in all directions, and for once I just don't care.

How many rides did Lolo give us over the years? I can't count them all. But now it's me who's pedaling, and Tomás trusts me at every swerve. He's laughing so loud that we barely hear it when, at last, Lolo whistles to let us know it's Tomás's turn to climb.

I let him off and straddle my bike. Breathless, I snap a picture as he runs back to Lolo and our tree.

CHAPTER 34

GOING TO SEE THE HEADMASTER at Seaward Academy is scary. So I'm surprised when I get to school to find not only Edna—wearing sunglasses—waiting on the bench but also Hannah and Lena sitting there, too. I told them about having to see Dr. Newman when they texted me over the weekend to see if I'd gotten in trouble.

"What are you doing here?" I say.

Lena stands up. "I know you said not to come, but since we were on the mummy committee together, we wanted to help explain what happened."

"Again," Hannah says, pointedly.

She takes a step closer to Lena. Then they both turn to Edna.

"We're so sorry, Edna," Lena says. "All of us."

Edna ignores her.

"Please, Edna, be reasonable," Hannah says. "What else can we do except apologize?"

Miss McDaniels comes through the door just then. She looks at Lena and Hannah and frowns.

"Hurry, or you'll be late to class, ladies." Then she holds open the door that leads to the back offices. "Edna? Merci? Follow me."

Lena gives me a worried look.

"Thanks for coming," I whisper before I go. "There's no sense in all three of us taking a hit. I'll tell you what happens later."

Edna and I follow Miss McDaniels past the stinky flowers and along all the back offices until we finally reach a big wooden door. She opens it.

Inside is the longest and shiniest table I've ever seen. Dr. Newman sits in a padded chair at the far end. He's wearing a red bow tie and is checking his phone. To my surprise, Ms. Tannenbaum is waiting for us, too. The sight of her sends a wash of relief over me.

"Good morning, girls," she says as we take a seat on either side of the table.

"Hello," Edna says, pushing up her sunglasses.

"Hi."

I took special care to look nice today, which was Roli's advice. "Defendants should look their best," he said. So I washed my face with his soap three times and put on a fresh headband.

I try to sit up tall, but it's hard in these rolling chairs, so I grab the edge of the tabletop to steady myself. The walls are made of dark paneling, and of course there are portraits of our former heads of school and the current board of directors, complete with Dr. Santos on the end. There are framed posters of our school advertising campaigns, too. Every kid in them looks shiny, like Sunshine Buddies on steroids. Roli was the model one year. They stood him near test tubes in the lab with the text: SEAWARD PINES: MORE THAN 50 YEARS OF EXCELLENCE IN INDEPENDENT EDUCATION.

Miss McDaniels clears her throat, and Dr. Newman clicks off his phone.

"Ah. You're here. Well, I hope you ladies had a restful few days with your families over Thanksgiving?" he says. Dr. Newman is known for being pleasant, especially to people who give money to our school for things like athletic fields and greenhouses.

"Yes, sir," Edna says. "We were in Sanibel."

"Ah. Lovely." Then he looks at me and smiles. "How about you, Miss Suárez? Lots of turkey and stuffing?"

My mouth is too dry to explain, so I just nod.

"So, I understand we had a bit of a mishap recently," he says.

Edna shifts in her seat. "Yes, sir. Merci cut off my eyebrows. On purpose." She lifts her sunglasses to prove it.

It's even worse than I remember.

"Is this true, Miss Suárez?" Dr. Newman says, turning to me. "Did you willfully cut off a classmate's eyebrows? That seems like an odd thing to do."

I wonder about this question. "Well, I did cut them off on purpose, but only because she was stuck inside a plaster mask. It was the only way to get her out."

"I see. And you didn't think you should ask your teacher for help?"

My face burns. Another hard one. I can't say for sure if we would have asked Ms. Tannenbaum what to do. She likes us to think for ourselves. But I don't want to say that she wasn't in the room; she'll get in trouble.

Before I can think of what to say, though, Ms. Tannenbaum comes to my rescue.

"Actually, Dr. Newman, that wouldn't have been possible. The girls were working on our Great Tomb Project, which I hope you'll come tour in a couple of weeks. I had stepped out of the room to return some equipment," she says. "It's my fault they were unsupervised. It was foolish of me."

Dr. Newman frowns and clears his throat. "We should discuss that later."

"Yes, sir."

He turns to Edna and steeples his fingers. "I spoke to your parents, and they are, of course, upset. But I wonder why you feel that this was done maliciously, Miss Santos." He pauses to let that sink in. "Do you know what that word means?"

Edna gives him a cold look. "Language arts is my best subject," she says, which is true. She looks over at me. "Merci does mean stuff like that sometimes," she continues. "She hit a new student with a baseball not too long ago and really hurt him."

Miss McDaniels nods when Dr. Newman glances at her to check.

My eye starts to travel. Edna's words are very prim and matter-of-fact, even though they're deadly.

"The baseball thing was an accident," I say. "I hit Michael Clark by mistake."

Miss McDaniels narrows her eyes at me like a cat. "*And . . .*"

"And, well, because I didn't remember to follow the rules."

I look around the table and suddenly remember what Papi said. Dr. Newman can decide that I'm too much trouble to keep here, especially with my track record. So I pull out my envelope and slide it across the table toward Edna as far as my arms will reach.

"What's this?" Edna asks.

"Something to help your eyebrows," I mutter.

Edna purses her lips, but she doesn't take it. Across the table, Dr. Newman and Miss McDaniels exchange looks.

Miss McDaniels opens one of her folders and starts speaking as she looks through the papers inside. "It's regrettable that two of our most charismatic students have decided that they are incompatible. It seems a shame. But for right now, I think there is another pressing matter for all of us to discuss. Dr. Newman, if you will permit me?"

He nods, and with that, she pulls out a printout of a sign-in sheet and lays it down in front of me. It's dated October 30.

"Is this your electronic signature from the tardy log?" she asks me.

I look down and see my own writing. "Yes, miss. That's the day I came in late. It was my brother's fault, though."

She nods and opens her second folder and hands me a printed pass that says *DUPLICATE* across the bottom. "And can you tell me about this item?"

I read the date and name carefully. "It's a copy of the pass you gave me to class," I say.

"To which class?"

"First hour," I say. "Which is language arts for me."

"And the time on the pass?"

"You wrote 8:12, see? I asked you to add a few minutes so I could drop something off in Ms. Tannenbaum's room."

"That is my precise recollection, too," she says. "In fact, you were carrying a costume brought from home, as I recall. Is this correct?"

"Yes, miss."

"And what happened after you left the office?"

As soon as she asks, I feel as though an ice cube is dripping along my spine. Edna stares straight ahead. I feel completely trapped. I glance at Ms. Tannenbaum, who is looking especially somber now. She gives me a nod.

"Speak freely," she says.

My heart is suddenly thundering. Roli said I shouldn't accuse someone without proof, so I stick to the facts.

"I left the costume in Ms. Tannenbaum's room and went to class," I say.

"And was it there when you returned?"

I blink hard and try not to look at Edna. "Yes, but it was ruined and stuffed in the trash."

"Yes. And you have filed a destruction of personal property report, which I have right here."

Miss McDaniels turns to Edna next and opens a second

folder. "Is this your electronic signature on the tardy log of that same day, Edna?"

Edna stares at the sheet. Her lips are pressed tight.

"I don't hear an answer."

"Yes."

"It is also for October thirtieth. I notice the time is exactly twenty minutes after Merci is documented to have arrived at school."

Edna shrugs. "I didn't see her that morning."

"And my notes here say that you reported having bike trouble on the way to school."

Edna nods. "I did. My chain slipped."

"That's unfortunate." She shows her another duplicate pass. "And is this the duplicate copy of the pass I wrote for *you*?"

Edna nods again.

"It says you were on your way to shop class. Is that correct?"

"Yes."

"I see."

Miss McDaniels picks up the remote control next to her folder and presses play.

The flat screen behind Dr. Newman's head flickers on, and we all turn to look.

It's a still shot of the hallway outside our social studies

classroom—and it's not grainy, like some sort of fuzzy security clip you see on the news that makes you think your neighbor might be a bank robber. This is super clear.

There's no sound, but a timer on the bottom lists the date and time. From high above, I see black-and-white me coming down the hall with my bag. Abuela's mask is sticking out of the top. I knock, then check the door and call inside. Then I let myself in. Two minutes later, I walk out without the costume bag.

Miss McDaniels speeds up the tape a bit. We stop again at the same empty hall. Finally, two people appear in the frame. It's Edna, with Jamie in tow. It looks like they're giggling and talking. They look inside the door window and whisper. Then they go inside. Four minutes later they race out of the room and disappear through the doors that lead outside.

The tape runs for two more minutes, which feels endless to watch. No one else visits the room until Ms. Tannenbaum comes back, balancing a huge stack of books and an apple on top.

The conference room is totally silent when Miss McDaniels stops the footage and puts down the remote.

Edna takes one look at Ms. Tannenbaum, puts her head on the table, and starts to cry.

CHAPTER 35

WHAT A MESS.

Sure, Edna got what she deserved for ruining Michael's costume. I'm not sorry about that; it's fair.

But by lunchtime, everyone was whispering about Edna and Jamie's troubles: a week's worth of detentions and sacked from Sunshine Buddies. People looked happy about it. And then Michael told Chase, who came over and told Rachel in a loud voice, that no, Michael definitely does not like Edna Santos. Not at all. In fact, he said she was mean and ugly.

How does it work that the same kids who followed Edna around all the time really seemed to like seeing her in trouble? How can somebody popular have so many people glad to see her crash? *Maybe like* might be confusing, but *popular* is even weirder. Turns out, it's not the same thing as having friends at all.

Papi is waiting for us in the maintenance parking lot on Friday like I told him to. Lena, Hannah, and I lug our cardboard there after the last bell. We need to finish our sarcophagus. We're running behind, so Ms. Tannenbaum thought it might be best if we work on it at home. We've only got a few more days to finish it.

"You can sit up front, Lena. It has a seatbelt," I say. "And, um, a seat."

I turn and wave at Hannah, who's going to follow behind us in her mother's car. She looks like she's dying of embarrassment. Her mom insists on driving her and meeting our family before Hannah can stay.

I climb into Papi's van and balance myself on the paint bucket as usual.

"Ready to roll?" he says, which is usually a private paint joke when we head off to one project or another.

"Ready," I say, although, really, I'm not so sure.

Yesterday, Lena put all our addresses in her phone to see whose house was most convenient, and *bingo,* Las Casitas came up smack in the middle. At first I argued against it, saying I didn't like working at our place. The truth is that I was worried about Lolo. What if he had a bad day? What if he yelled at Abuela in front of them?

But Lena insisted. "Besides," she said, "nobody has a car long enough to load up all the cardboard. A van is perfect."

"I'll bring the gold paint," Hannah said before I could weasel my way out. "And glitter. And the gemstones."

It was settled.

So here I am, fingers and toes crossed that everything is calm at home.

The van squeaks as Papi makes the turn out of the lot.

"Hey, it sounds like your van is singing!" Lena smiles, but then she rubs her bottom. The pesky spring is poking through again.

"Here. Sit on this." I hand her one of my binders. "It helps."

As soon as we pull in, I look around the yard cautiously. Lolo is in his flower bed with the twins. He turns to wave, but he doesn't walk over, thank goodness. I'm pretty sure he's pulling out the flowers Abuela planted just a few days ago, but I can't worry about that now.

"You say you live in all three of them?" Hannah's mom asks, looking around Las Casitas.

"Sort of. I sleep in this one," I say, pointing, "but the rest is sort of flexible."

Lena bends down to scratch Tuerto's ear. "Meow," she says in greeting, like it's the most normal thing to speak in Cat.

"Are you guys hungry?" I ask.

"Starved," Lena says.

"Same here," says Hannah. She turns to her mom. "So, can I stay?"

I guess we've passed inspection because she gives Hannah a peck on the cheek. "Text me when you're ready to come home," she says.

"Let's try Tía's fridge," I say. "She's got the best stuff."

Tuerto follows us the whole way.

We work all afternoon, until dinnertime. Papi supervised us every once in a while to make sure we didn't saw off our fingers as we shaped the thick cardboard. Then we put on masks and used the sprayers to paint all the pieces gold. We drilled with his power tools and attached the sides with plastic fasteners.

"You have to admit this is a masterpiece." Hannah glues on the last bead. "Look at the sparkle! I want to keep this when the Great Tomb is done."

"It does have bling," I say, which is an understatement. There's barely a square inch of space that isn't decorated. There's a mess at our feet from all the work we did, too.

Tuerto bats leftover beads among the tools and scraps lying around.

We're just starting to clean up when the twins appear.

"What's that?" Tomás and Axel are at my elbow, staring.

"A coffin," Lena says. "For mummies."

"It's still wet," I tell them. But Tomás only sticks out his tongue. I'm about to yell for Papi to come get them when Hannah steps up.

"You want some magic dust?" she asks them. "I have some left over."

They turn to her and stare.

"Hold out your hands like this," she says. Then she taps out what's left of the glitter from her test tube into their dirty palms. "I can only give each of you a tiny bit," she says. "It's very powerful, especially the blue pieces, so be careful."

"That girl's hair is blue," Tomás whispers, eyeing Lena.

"Like berries," Axel adds. "And it looks like sticks."

"Yep. And how do you think I got it this fabulous?" Lena says, running her fingers over her spikes. She bends down to let them touch her head. "Hannah's magic dust."

The twins poke at Lena's hair carefully. They exchange knowing looks and then, without warning, they tear across to the other side of the yard, their cupped hands held high.

"Good thinking. How did you know how to get rid of them so easily?" I ask. "It's always a struggle for me."

Hannah shrugs. "It's in the babysitting manual. Lesson four, I think."

"Magic dust to distract troublemakers?" I say.

"Redirection," she says. "Everybody wins."

Just then, headlights pin us in place. We turn to see Mami pulling her rental car into her spot in the driveway. I notice that Roli is in the passenger seat—again. I shake my head. He hasn't been behind the wheel since the crash. He's too young to drive the rental car, and Mami and Papi haven't found a new car we can afford.

He checks the mailbox, waves at us, and goes inside.

"Wow," Mami says when she gets out. She tiptoes around the tools. "Impressive."

"We have to let it dry for a while before we put it back in Papi's van," I say. "We're just picking up now."

"Preciosa."

Lolo's voice makes us all turn. He's still in his gardening clothes, dirty at the knees, and his hands are sandy. I freeze in my spot, studying his face to get any clue about his mood. "Preciosa," he says to me again. "Abuela says it's almost time to eat."

"I'll be right there, Lolo," I say quickly. "Hannah, can you grab that broom?"

Mami comes close to him and kisses his cheek. "You've been in the garden today, I see?"

He smiles. "I was pulling the weeds. Always weeds." He looks back toward his house, thinking. And it's in that beat of time that I start to get worried. Then he turns to me again. "It's time to eat," he repeats. He holds out his hand to me. "Come on."

"I just have to clean up, Lolo. You go on," I say. "I'll be there in a minute." *Please leave,* I think. *Please.*

But he doesn't move. And neither do Hannah and Lena. I can feel their questions in the air. I look to Mami, asking for help with my eyes, but she doesn't seem to notice.

"Merci, have you introduced your friends?" she asks.

"This is Lena and Hannah," I mumble. "They're about to call their moms to go home."

But Mami checks her watch. "Why don't you girls stay for dinner?" she says. "I'm sure there's enough. Abuela always makes plenty. Merci, can you clean up and help Lolo wash up while I tell Abuela?"

I try not to glare at her. Dinner? With our whole family?

But before I think of what to say, Lena sniffs the air and reaches for her phone. "It does smell good. My stomach has been growling."

329

"Picadillo and rice," Lolo says. "My favorite."

"My mom hates to cook." Hannah digs in her purse for her phone. Lena is already texting on hers.

I turn to Mami as soon as they get their moms, but she's already disappeared back inside, leaving me there with Lolo. I've never been ashamed of my grandfather before. And I don't want him to know how I feel.

My face is hot as I turn to him. Lolo is at the spigot, but he can't seem to find the nozzle on the hose. It's tangled, as usual.

"Hang on." I start to fix it, already imagining the disaster that's coming at dinner. Maybe Hannah and Lena will think he's weird. Maybe they'll laugh at him behind my back. Maybe they'll tell people at school.

"Put your hands out like this so I can get your elbows." Does he hear the little knives in my voice? But I can't help it. I have no patience for him right now. I hate that I'm standing here, washing him as if he were one of the twins.

Hannah appears at my side. "I'm in for chow," she says. "She'll pick me up at eight."

She starts sweeping up the glitter, but I can feel her watching me as I rub the rest of the mud from Lolo's elbows and hands. I'm embarrassed by how he's standing there, letting me clean him, but if Hannah thinks it's strange, she doesn't say so. When I'm done, she just walks over and hands me a paper towel from the roll on the shelf. By then, Lena has joined us, too. She's about to start hammering the lids back on the paint cans when she notices something on Lolo's shoulders.

"Uh-oh. The twins must have gotten to you, sir," she says.

That's when I notice blue glitter in Lolo's hair.

Lolo smiles at Lena and shakes it from his shoulders. "The compadres," he says, his face open and sweet.

Papi comes through our screen door just then. He's freshly showered, and he's carrying a huge salad bowl in his hands. He's got two bottles of water tucked under his arm.

"I need a hand with this, Pops," he says, handing Lolo the bowl.

"It's time to eat, Fico," Lolo says.

Papi barely flinches.

"And I'm starved," he says. "Let's go, Pops." He turns to me and points to the empty shelf in the shed. "You can slide those cans over there," he says. "The turpentine is on the bottom, next to the flashlights, if you need it."

Then he and Lolo walk back to Abuela's patio.

I swallow hard as I start to coil the hose, thinking about how to explain Lolo, or even if I should say anything. They're little things. Maybe my friends won't notice.

I keep my eyes down as I work, but I start thinking about secrets and how the trouble with them is that they become lies.

"Just so you know," I say, "Lolo has Alzheimer's."

It's the first time I have said that word to anyone outside of our family.

Hannah looks up from the dustbin. "What is that, exactly?"

My tongue feels thick as I try to find words to explain. "He isn't thinking very well anymore. It's a kind of disease in the brain that makes you forget." I take a deep breath. "Don't be surprised by him, OK? Sometimes he doesn't act like himself."

Like the real Lolo. Like how he used to be, I want to add but don't.

For a second we're all quiet. All I can hear is the scrape of Hannah's broom and the taps of Lena's rubber hammer as she fastens the lids in place.

"My grandfather was sick for a long time," Lena says at last. "He had cancer." She hauls a container to the shelf. "I miss him."

"Some days I miss Lolo, too," I say, "even though he's still here. Strange, right?"

There's another pause.

"But strange can be OK," Lena says at last.

"It's not boring, anyway," Hannah adds. "I hate boring."

We finish picking up our things in silence until we hear giggling. It's the twins, spying on us from the back of the carport.

"Do you see anyone?" Hannah says loudly.

"Nope," Lena says.

Tomás springs out. "Bah!"

"Hey," I say. "Why did you throw glitter on Lolo? That's not very nice."

Tomás rolls his eyes. "Not Lolo. We put a spell on Lolo's *garden*," he announces.

"It's going to grow flying dragons," Axel says. "You'll see tomorrow." He flaps his wings to show us.

I look across the yard at the bare flower bed. Beyond it, Lolo and Papi are setting the table in the screened porch. "How many dragons did you plant?" I ask.

"Ga-millions, dum-dum," Axel says.

"Well, I'll take pictures when they hatch," I tell them.

We start walking over when suddenly Lena stops. "I have an idea. Let's close our eyes and link arms," she says. "You, too," she tells the twins. "Let's be strange and see if we can run backward to their house."

We make our human chain and close our eyes.

"Ready?" Lena says. "Go!"

We all go stumbling as best we can, each with different strides, pulling each other and bumping along the whole way until we finally fall in a heap near the screen door, laughing.

Abuela comes out, holding a steaming tray of meat for the table.

"You're going to bang your heads and grow lumps that will leave you silly forever," she warns. "Then what?"

Which makes us all laugh harder.

And then, because we notice that Lolo is puzzling over which way to open the folding chairs, Lena, Hannah, and I scramble to our feet to help him with the rest. I tuck my friends close to me at the table when we eat.

CHAPTER 36

THERE'S A REPORTER AND photographer who come to see our Great Tomb Project. They walk all through the chambers, snapping pictures along the way. So far, we've had only one problem. The back wall is wobbly, so Michael Clark and Rachel have to pretend to be royal guards and hold it steady with their backs. Rachel's peepers are sort of stuck on golf-ball size as she stands next to Michael. From the goofy way they're acting, I think something is going on between them. There is no *maybe like* in their eyes at all.

"When are they coming?" Lena asks. "This getup is uncomfortable." She hoists her sheet under her armpits again.

None of our parents have been released from the auditorium yet. They're trapped over in Frackas Hall with Dr. Newman, who's reminding them about the annual giving campaign with his gigantic thermometer of donations.

Mami, Papi, and Abuela are there, and Roli, of course. They even brought the twins because the boys wanted to see Hannah and Lena, too. Tía volunteered to stay behind with Lolo, who didn't feel up to coming out tonight.

I watch the photographer from the corner of my eye. She's clicking her camera and checking her shots as she goes. It must be nice to have equipment like that, and not just your phone. She stops to take close-ups of the hieroglyphs, which Edna, who is lead scribe, explains. I try not to pay attention. Things have been pricklier with Edna since she got in trouble, but I'm trying my best to ignore it and move on. I want to take Papi's advice and not have anyone as an enemy, but it's still hard to be in the same room with her.

Finally, the reporter stops at our mummy and sarcophagus. "The main event," she says, smiling. Lena, Hannah, and I sort of cluster together. "This is quite a creation." She walks around it and lifts her camera. A series of fast clicks sound. "Are you the ones who made this?"

"Yes," Lena says. "The three of us."

"We had help," I add. "Edna Santos was our model." We don't mention the eyebrow disaster, but I point to Edna across the room.

Then we spell our names and answer her questions about how we built it.

"One more shot," the photographer says walking over. She poses us with Edna. "Say toenails," Lena whispers to us. We do, and for once, I'm pretty sure my eye stays put.

"All right, everyone. Take your places," Ms. Tannenbaum says, interrupting. "The parents are arriving for their tours!"

We grab our index cards with our speeches, and we're ready.

Ms. Tannenbaum has snacks and a slide show of all of us working so that people don't get bored waiting in the hall for their turn to tour. I can see the whole thing from where I'm standing. Funny, I don't remember her taking these pictures, but I'm glad she did. Nobody is posing, so we all look like ourselves. There we are, out of our seats, talking, pinning things up. There's even a shot of Lena, Hannah, and me taping plastic bags on Edna.

Roli arrives with the twins, who naturally grab two fistfuls of Goldfish crackers and stuff their cheeks like gerbils while they wait.

The line feels endless, and after a while, we get a little

sick of repeating our talk about mummies. But eventually, the last visitors leave and we're done.

Ms. Tannenbaum closes our classroom door and motions us to gather near her desk.

Rachel and Michael leave the wall, and we all watch it tip over with a *ka-boom,* exactly the way it has been threatening to do all night. We're all sweaty, and most of us have raccoon eyes from our melted eyeliner.

You can tell Ms. Tannenbaum is happy by her big smile. "Hands in," she says, and we all stack our palms in the center. Lena and Hannah huddle right next to me.

"You have a lot to be proud of, third hour. I want you to know that a project like this takes a lot of planning, research, teamwork, and problem-solving. Not everything went smoothly, but you didn't let that stop you."

I glance up at Michael, who's squeezed in next to Rachel. Edna is staring at her shoes.

"So, let's all rest over winter vacation and think about what we learned about ourselves and others this first semester. We all get a fresh start in January."

We raise our hands and cheer loudly.

It's winter break at last.

"Merci!"

We're almost to the van when I hear someone call my name. Abuela, Mami, and Papi stop and turn.

When I look to see who it is, I find Edna waiting for me. She's standing between her parents.

Mami puts her hand on my shoulder. I feel Papi move in a little closer, too. "We'll be right here," Papi says.

"Be careful," Abuela says. "You can't trust people with a score to settle."

Edna and I walk to each other. The eyebrow pencil has worked wonders, but I decide to keep that observation to myself.

She reaches inside her pouch and pulls out an official Seaward Pines Academy envelope. My name is written in her fancy writing on the front.

"Miss McDaniels made you write a note too, huh?" I ask. "How many drafts did it take?"

"Three," she admits.

Up close I can see that Edna looks tired, but I can't tell if it's just that she's weary after all the work tonight, or whether it's more. Being the boss of the universe can't be easy. And having people talk about you stinks.

"I am sorry about the costume. Well, mostly."

"Mostly?" I say.

She motions with her chin at Michael and Rachel, who are walking toward the parking lot, saying good-bye before he goes to Disney the way his mom promised him if he got all As. They don't even notice us gawking. Edna rolls her eyes. "I can't believe I ever liked that dope."

"Michael isn't a dope," I say. "He likes Rachel, that's all. You can't make people like you, Edna," I tell her, shrugging. "I should know."

Edna crosses her arms. "People do like you, Merci," she says. "Stop feeling sorry for yourself. It's not like you like me very much either, you know."

"Well," I say, "*no offense,* but it's hard to like someone who is always saying mean stuff to you. About my eye. My hair. Really, everything."

I'm expecting her to come back at me with one of her zingers, but this time she keeps her mouth shut.

The truth is that I've always wanted Edna to like me, at least a little bit. She's the smartest girl in our class, and she's funny. Plus, she knows how to get things done. But it's the mean part that gets in the way. That makes her like a brownie with vanilla ice cream — and sardines. Those three things don't go well together. Two out of three would be better, for sure.

"Anyway, I don't have time to think about Michael

Clark," she says. "We're taking the boat to the Dominican Republic in the morning for winter break, and I'm still not packed."

Oh boy. More showing off. It takes all I've got not to roll my eyes. "Well, have a good vacation, then." I start to turn away.

"My dad is volunteering in a clinic for people with leprosy," she continues. "My mom and I are going along to help."

I stare at her for a second. "Wow," I blurt out. "You?"

She pushes her shoulders back and gives me a stony look. "Now who's being *mean*?" she says.

OK, so maybe she's right. "Sorry," I say. Still, I wonder how she'll like working with people who are very sick and poor, the way I've seen on some of Roli's shows. Will she walk around feeling so much better than they are? Will she complain about not having a TV? It's easy to complain, of course, even when you've got things pretty good. Look at all I say about watching the twins or helping Lolo.

"That's nice of you to help them," I say.

She looks at me cautiously. "What are *you* doing over break?"

I glance at my parents and Roli, who are pretending not to be watching our every move. Abuela is admiring

341

the palm trees that are strung with white lights for the holiday. Farther off, I see Hannah and Lena playing tag in their togas with the twins.

For once, I'm not tempted to lie to Edna. Today at lunch, we planned our time off. Hannah is going to baby-sit the twins for Tía over break so Abuela doesn't have to do it alone. If it works out, she might even do it in the spring so I can try out for softball. Lena promised to come over with her watercolors so we can paint with Lolo. We're going to work on our business plan for the new volunteer club we want to start now that Sunshine Buddies is over. I thought students could visit the Lourdes Killington Residence for seniors who don't see their families enough. Maybe on Grands Day, they can come as special guests for the younger grades. Anyway, our meeting with Miss McDaniels is the first day we get back from vacation. Seven forty-five sharp.

"Same as usual," I say. "I'm hanging out with my friends and family. Have fun on your trip."

Then, just before I turn to walk away, I add, "I'm *really* sorry about cutting off your eyebrows."

CHAPTER 37

IT'S EXACTLY FOUR DAYS UNTIL Nochebuena, and I don't have much time to finish my presents. Usually, Mami takes me shopping one time and I get everything I need at once.

But this year, there's one present that I'm making, and since it's a little more involved than the macaroni picture frame that we all get from the twins, I need other kinds of supplies — and a ride to the store to get them.

Nobody is home today except Roli and me. Mami and Papi are checking out a used car they saw advertised in the paper. Abuela and Lolo walked the twins over to get paletas. And Tía is on the early shift at the bakery.

I find Roli resting in the hammock behind our house and ask him for a ride.

"Can't you see I'm busy?" His eyes are closed, and his skin smells like coconut.

"Sunbathing? Come on, Roli. It's too far for me to go on my lousy bike." I toss him Tía Inés's spare car keys. "Tía drove to work already, but we can ride our bikes to El Caribe and borrow her car from the parking lot. We'll put it back before she has to come home."

He brushes the keys away with his hand. "No, Merci. Ask Mami to take you when they get back."

"But I don't want her to know what I'm making," I say.

"Crafting a weapon, are you?"

"Funny."

He ignores me.

"Are you scared to drive again?" I say quietly.

There's a long pause. When I don't move, he says, "Please, Merci. Go away."

"I know our crash was scary, but seriously, we can't walk everywhere from now on, you know." I push the hammock with my foot.

He opens his eyes and stares at me for a long time, so I know he's going to play it tough. Then he reaches under his back and tosses me an envelope.

I look down and see that it's from a college in North Carolina, the one he's wanted to go to most of all. Mami lit a candle for it and everything.

"It came in the mail," he says. "I'm in at Chapel Hill, and it comes with enough money."

For a minute, I don't know what to say. It's good news, great news, in fact. But North Carolina is three states north, and it's suddenly impossible to imagine that Roli won't be here in the fall. What's Las Casitas going to be like without him? Who'll be here when Lolo gets really bad?

Now it's my turn to get quiet.

"You'll get the whole room to yourself," he says after a while.

"Yeah, it's about time," I say. "And you'll be with other people who want to learn about face transplants and stuff." My eye starts to drift, so I blink hard to reset it.

"And about brains," he says.

He sits up and I slide in next to him on the hammock.

"When are you going to tell Mami and Papi?"

"Tonight, I guess. When we're all together."

"They'll be really happy." My throat feels tight as I say it.

We don't say anything else for a long time.

"I always thought it would be great to leave . . ." he says finally. He stares at his hands and doesn't finish.

I look at Roli long and hard. He's wanted to go to college since kindergarten, when he used to drag around his plastic doctor kit. That's everything Mami and Papi have ever dreamed for him, too. So I swallow hard and say, "You can still be happy to go, dope. Remember you have to hurry up and invent stuff to help Lolo. You don't want Ahana Patel to beat you to it, do you?"

He shoves me a little and grins. "Text me and tell me what's going on here, OK?" he says. "And I'll come home for the holidays."

I give that some thought, trying to push out of my mind how it will be when he's not across the room every day. I won't have to change in the bathroom, at least, or keep my mess on one side.

"Speaking of which—I still need you to take me to the store," I say. "It's the last thing I need for Nochebuena."

Roli sighs. "You're relentless. What's so important that you can't wait for Mami, Merci?"

I cross my arms. "You have to swear not to tell."

He listens as I explain my whole plan. When I'm done, Roli takes a deep breath and holds his palm out for the keys.

"Let's go," he says. "And leave your helmet with your bike, or else."

CHAPTER 38

IT HAPPENS EVERY YEAR. Las Casitas transforms on Nochebuena. And this year, because of Roli's good news, everyone is especially happy.

Papi and Lolo have strung the patio with red and green lights in the shape of chili peppers.

Mami blasts happy Christmas music—and not the "I'm-dreaming-of-a-white-Christmas" kind. It's merengues and salsas with horns and bongos and singers crooning about la estrellita de Belén. The sound makes Tía wiggle her hips the way she does at the Tango Palace, while she fusses with Abuela about recipes.

I'm trying to keep up with Tomás and Axel, who've spent most of the day making trouble with the vuvuzelas that we usually save for watching Papi at soccer games.

They sneak around the house and yard, trumpeting near people to startle them.

But by sunset, we're all showered and dressed as if we're going to a wedding, even though we're just going to sit in our own backyard. I'm wearing a sundress (with shorts underneath) from last year. When I look in the mirror, I notice it's shorter than I like and a little tight in the chest now. It'll be time to go clothes shopping soon, I guess. Maybe Lena and Hannah can come along to help.

When the doorbell rings, I run to get it, thinking it's the butcher delivering the roast pig wrapped in foil.

But when I open it, I find Simón and a boy next to him, about Roli's age. They're standing side by side in collared shirts, holding a long, heavy box in their arms.

"¡Feliz Navidad, Merci!" Simón tells me. "Are you going to invite us in, or should Vicente and I eat the lechón by ourselves?"

"¡Bienvenidos! ¡Adelante!" Tía says. "Thank you so much for picking up the order for us!" Her eyes look sparkly as she gently moves me aside at the door. She's wearing a slinky dress and her hair is curled just so.

"The smell of lechón was driving us mad," Simón announces as they step inside.

He smiles at Tía in a way that tells me something else might be driving him mad, too.

"Well, I'm glad you could both make it." She turns to the boy and smiles. "So, this is your hermanito?"

Simón smiles and claps him on the back. "Vicente is the youngest of my brothers. And the best present of all for me this year," he says. "He got here last week."

Vicente looks just like Simón except with lighter eyes and longer hair. I can't help staring. If he grew his hair just a tiny bit more and braided it, he could look just like . . . Jake Rodrigo.

Just then, Papi comes to the door to say hello, and in a few seconds, he leads them all back to the kitchen where Mami and Abuela are working.

"Do you think Tía will ever fall in love again?" I whisper to Roli. He's watching old Christmas movies on TV.

"We are not discussing love, Merci."

The whole night is fun. It turns out that Vicente doesn't speak much English, so we talk to each other in Spanish instead. I find out that he's a great soccer player, too. He takes one of the soccer balls lying in the yard and pancakes from one foot to the other. Then he pops the ball up in a steady rhythm pretty much the way I do it. He even starts to teach me how to stall the ball on my shoulder blades and on my forehead, too, like a sea lion doing tricks at the aquarium. Lolo and the twins watch us as we practice. The twins go wild, blowing into their vuvuzelas until the whole yard sounds like it's filled with bees.

After, we all eat snacks and set off firecrackers in the yard, and the twins run around in the dark with the sparklers Simón brought for them.

Finally, at eleven o'clock, it's time to eat dinner. It's late, but I'm too excited to feel tired.

Lolo stands at the head of the table and holds up his plastic glass of red wine. "To the best family," he says, looking around at all of us. Abuela stands next to him and thanks God that we are all here together for another year.

Papi raises a glass to my picture in the newspaper and another toast to Roli's college acceptance, which makes Mami cry. Simón raises a glass, too, to say he's grateful for this country and for a good employer like Papi and most of all for his brother's safe journey here. Tía Inés is about to say something, too, when Tomás pipes up to stop her.

"Can we please eat *now*?"

That cracks us all up.

"You're right," she says. "Dig in!"

As always, everything is delicious. The pork tastes of orange juice and garlic, and the moros have the crunchy bacon bits on top that I love.

Finally, after we eat the turrones and Abuela slices the flan, it's midnight. At last it's time for coffee and presents.

The smell of brewed espresso fills the yard as Abuela and Mami walk around with trays, offering the tiny cups of café. The adults settle in around the porch to watch us kids exchange presents.

The twins get an enormous castle with knights and two dragons, a T-ball set, and matching super-water-balloon launchers from Roli. I can already tell that I'm going to have to carry around a towel to protect myself.

Roli gets the 3-D-printed moon lamp he wanted, a light blue T-shirt that says *UNC,* and gift cards so he can get things for his college room next year.

Simón surprises Vicente with a nice pair of cleats.

"We might finally have a good keeper on our team," Papi says, clapping his hands together.

Then it's my turn. I get school regulation shorts and T-shirts from Mami and Papi, and cool Iguanador socks. The fizzy bath bombs and hair clips are from Tía. Roli gets me a new bike helmet—ha, ha. I'm about to sit down when Papi says, "Oh, wait. There's one more thing."

He goes to the side of the house and rolls out a sparkling new bike. It's not a kid's bike, either, but a twenty-six-inch beach cruiser, deep blue, almost like Lena's hair.

"We kept it at Simón's place," Papi tells me.

I stand there, staring at the perfection and wondering if it's a mirage. My heart races as I check out everything up close. The basket, the water bottle, the clamp for my phone, the headlamp and bell. I snap a picture of it and send it to Lena and Hannah before I remember that they are probably not awake.

"What do you think?" Mami says.

"It's so gorgeous! Thank you!"

Lolo walks over to my bike slowly. He smiles as he runs his fingers along the handlebars. He pulls on the bell to ring it, flicks on the lamp that sends a beam into the yard. Is he thinking about the Sunday rides that we don't take anymore?

"Wait here, Lolo," I say. "I have something for you, too. Well, it's kind of for all of us."

I go to our Christmas tree and come back with a large square package that I didn't mark with a name. Then I sit next to Lolo and Abuela and place it in their laps.

"You can open it for us," I tell Lolo.

He smooths his hand over the surface, unsure, so Abuela starts a corner of it for him. And then, because they can't wait for anything, the twins yell, "We'll help," and start ripping open the paper, too.

Inside is the big scrapbook that Roli and I bought a few days ago. It's leather with black pages inside. I've written *La Familia Suárez* in metallic marker on the cover. Inside are pages filled with pictures that I've been taking of all of us. Tía Inés and me looking grungy. Tomás and Axel picking grapefruit and sword fighting. Roli bent over a book. Lolo's bike in black and white. Abuela's hands threading the bobbin at her sewing machine. Papi and Mami unpacking groceries from the van. And underneath each picture, I've written our names in my neatest handwriting.

"I left lots of pages blank in the back," I tell him, "so we can add more this year. It's to help you remember when it gets hard."

Lolo sits with the book in his lap. "Preciosa," he says quietly. He hasn't said my name now in a few weeks, and I miss hearing it. But I'm positive that he still knows it's me, Merci, and that he likes this book.

Abuela and Lolo turn the pages and show everyone each shot. Then I make them all gather in a group — Simón and Vicente, too — and take a picture of our Nochebuena party, so we can add it to the rest.

Later, after we've put away the food and cleaned up, after everyone has kissed good-bye and made good wishes for the coming year, I lie in my bed wide awake. Usually, when I can't sleep, I talk to Roli until I drift off. But he's already snoring, so I'm on my own.

I tiptoe through the kitchen and I slip out into the backyard barefoot. It's almost two in the morning. The sky is dark and only the stars are out. I know Mami wouldn't want me outside at this hour, and Abuela would say I could get attacked by a stray Florida bobcat. But it will only be a few minutes.

I straddle the seat of my new bike in the driveway. Then I flip on the headlight, and the path ahead of me fills with bugs dodging in the beam. I feel tall in this seat, important. Even though I'm barefoot, I decide to do a slow ride around Las Casitas on my new wheels, just to test it.

There are no squeaks from the pedals, and the chain doesn't skip. It's like I'm gliding on clouds. I switch gears and feel the extra weight kick in right away. I grip my toes, and with each heavy push, I move faster and farther than before, so that soon I've made another two loops around our yard. I stand up and pump my legs, sweat gathering behind my knees. It's hard, but I can do it. I go around and around until my legs are wobbly and my heart thumps and I have no choice but to stop.

This is exactly the bike that I wanted. It's the perfect present.

But there are other things that I wished for even harder than I did for this bike, and I know I won't get them, no matter what. Important things, like wishing that Lolo wasn't sick and that everything could stay the same.

Then again, staying the same means that Tía Inés

might not have the chance to love Simón. It means Roli wouldn't go to college and get even smarter. It means that I wouldn't grow up at all. Staying the same could be just as sad as Lolo changing.

I don't know what is going to happen next year, no one does. But that's OK.

I can handle it, I decide. It's just a harder gear, and I am ready. All I have to do is take a deep breath and ride.

A NOTE FROM THE AUTHOR

My grandparents were an important part of my life as a child. What I remember most of all is that my family always lived close by and that we were involved in one another's lives, which was sometimes quite a pain, from my perspective.

Unfortunately, both my grandfathers died before I could truly remember them well, but my grandmothers enjoyed long lives. My Abuela Fefa, on my father's side, had once been a seamstress, and she sewed clothes for me every year. Abuela Bena, on my mother's side, was my babysitter, my storyteller, and our family's greatest worrier.

In writing this book, I wanted to celebrate grandparents and families that live intergenerationally, the way that we often see in Latino families. But I also wanted to write about change in families. We all change, especially as we grow up, but adults change, too. And, as we all know, not every change is a good one.

In this story, Merci's grandfather, Lolo, is changing due to an illness. He's struggling with the effects of Alzheimer's disease, which attacks the brain. Alzheimer's patients of any age lose enough of their memory that it makes their daily life very difficult. They can forget the people they love and the important events in their own lives. Eventually, they lose their memory of how to speak, walk, eat, and even breathe.

Alzheimer's is difficult and scary for the person who is sick, but it is also very hard for all the people who care for them, especially as the illness advances. If you have a family member who has Alzheimer's, you may feel sad or frustrated, you may be embarrassed by the behavior of the person you love, and you may think that you are the only one facing this challenge. But the truth is that thousands of children all over the world are dealing with the same situation. Here are the facts: Alzheimer's disease is the sixth leading cause of death in the United States. Five million people are living with this disease, and many more are family and friends who are taking care of their loved ones.

Although researchers are working very hard, at the time of this writing, there is no known prevention or cure for Alzheimer's. There are, however, promising new therapies, and many ways for you to help by raising money and awareness. And there are ways to *get* help and support by meeting and talking with other young people who love someone with Alzheimer's disease.

For more information, visit the Alzheimer's Association at www.alz.org.

ACKNOWLEDGMENTS

Books happen in my life as the result of the time, talent, and love of so many people.

I'm most grateful to my editor, Kate Fletcher, for her continued dedication to my work. She offered her keen eye, thoughtful questions, and an abundance of patience as we worked around my particularly tricky schedule this past year. This book—and everything I have ever written for her—is better than I could have ever done alone.

Blessed are the copyeditors for they keep us from making ridiculous mistakes in public. And so, a shout-out to my saviors: Emily Quill, Maggie Deslaurier, K. B. Mello, and Maya Myers, who had to wade through my many struggles with commas, dashes, and those pesky time markers, and Teresa Mlawer, who makes sure my Spanish is always in order.

Every book is also a physical piece of artwork. Thanks to Pam Consolazio for the lovely interior design, and a huge thanks to my friend, Joe Cepeda, who is responsible for the evocative cover. It has been a dream of mine to collaborate with Joe, whose work has graced some of the most iconic books in children's literature. I hope this is the first of many more projects for us.

I'm indebted to Candlewick's entire library, PR, and marketing teams for their enthusiasm in getting *Merci Suárez Changes Gears* out into the world and for all the ways they have supported me over the years as we've worked together. Special high fives to: Karen Lotz, Liz Bicknell, Phoebe Kosman, Jamie Tan, Anne Irza-Leggat, Hilary Van Dusen, Jennifer Roberts, Melanie Cordova, Raquel Stecher — you are quite a team.

Many hugs to my agent, Jen Rofé at the Andrea Brown Agency, who has been a tireless advocate for me from day one when a brand-new author and a brand-new agent decided to take a risk on each other.

My beta readers this time were Lamar Giles and Brendan Kiely. You know (because I've told you over and over) how much I value your opinion. Thank you so much for taking the time to help and for asking all the right questions. How lucky I feel to call both of you friends.

And finally, I want to give endless love and thanks to my family—my children, Cristina, Sandra, and Alex Menéndez, but most especially to my husband, Javier Menéndez, who uses rock-solid love to remove all obstacles and cheer me on. They are the reason I know joy.

M. M.